# THE
# SUBSTANCE
## OF
# FEAR

# THE
# SUBSTANCE
## OF
# FEAR

## A Sheriff Francis Hood Mystery

## RICHARD F. MCGONEGAL

LEVEL
BEST BOOKS

*To my other family for sharing their insights and experience.*

"My 'fear' is my substance, and probably the best part of me."

— Franz Kafka

# Praise for The Substance of Fear

"*The Substance of Fear* by Richard McGonegal combines the intricate plotting of Agatha Christie with the human, small town characters from the Longmire series. A story of justice, search for truth, and redemption. As McGonegal's characters show, redemption is an ongoing process for us all."—Bradley Harper, Edgar-nominated author of *A Knife in the Fog*

"Sheriff Francis Hood is back, digging for the truth in this introspective tale of theft, murder, and deadly small-town secrets."—M. A. Monnin, Agatha Award-nominated author of the Intrepid Traveler Mysteries

"A solid investigative thriller with an everyman hero every reader can relate to and cheer for. Amid zigs and zags, the plot never bogs down, the investigative pace stays steady, and the writing is crisp throughout."—Carmen Amato, author of the Detective Emilia Cruz series

# Chapter One

The blood was the first thing Sheriff Francis Hood noticed when he stepped across the threshold into the store.

He wondered what that said about him. The expansive interior was a cluttered jungle gym of junk, but he focused immediately on the viscous pool of blood, its edges coagulating and nearly reaching the contours of a white electric guitar lying on the hardwood floor.

The sheriff widened his vision, like a camera lens drawing back, and took in the entire interior, illuminated by fluorescent light fixtures hanging from a high ceiling.

"What is this place?" Hood asked his chief deputy, Gus "Wally" Wallendorf, who stood nearby.

"It's a second-hand shop—collectibles, antiques," answered Wally, who was first to arrive at the scene. "There's a sign on the back wall."

Hood lifted his gaze to a placard that read: *One Man's Trash....* Below the shop name was the phrase: *If we don't have it, you don't need it.* Smaller lettering identified Chester A. Groner as the proprietor, followed by the Schweinshaupten, Missouri, address, telephone number, and hours of operation. He noted the scheduled closing time was 5 p.m.

An assortment of clocks displayed on a pegboard wall indicated varying times, so he consulted his watch, which read 7:34 p.m.

"What do we know?" Hood asked.

"Dispatch relayed a 9-1-1 call at, um—" Knowing his boss would want details, Wally retrieved a notepad from the breast pocket of his uniform, flipped pages, and added, "6:06 p.m. I got here at 6:23, just before the ambulance. The front door was closed, but not locked. I opened it, switched on the lights. A guy was lying there." Wally pointed to the hardwood flooring where blood had pooled. "While the EMTs worked on him, I cleared the scene, back storeroom, and upstairs living area. By the time I came back down, they were loading him up."

"So he's alive?" Hood asked, the surprise in his question apparent. Although he had learned people were not as easy to kill as portrayed on TV, he also equated the amount of blood loss with a distinct likelihood of death.

"He was when they wheeled him out," Wally said.

"Did he say anything?"

"No. I don't even know if he was conscious."

"Do we know who he is?" Hood asked.

"What's going on, Sheriff?"

Hood turned to the onlookers who stood outside the storefront. In the chilly October evening, their curious faces were illuminated by downtown streetlights. He was surprised by how many people had gathered in the brief time since he had arrived. "Back up and clear that sidewalk out there," he hollered through the open doorway. "This is a crime scene."

"I'm guessing it's the owner," Wally answered, ignoring the interruption. "I don't know for sure, but some folks out there were saying things like 'Hang in there, Chet' when they loaded him into the ambulance."

Hood's vantage point afforded a clear sightline to the back of the store, where a long display case was located parallel to the back wall. He approached the waist-high cabinet and gazed through the top glass at an array of jewelry, knives, razors, political buttons and memorabilia, toy soldiers, and more. Behind the case, a counter stretching the length of the wall contained glassware, kitchen appliances, an old-fashioned cash register, and a dial telephone. Hood wondered if the register and phone were for business transactions or for sale. Above the counter, paintings, tools, and musical instruments hung from hooks and brackets on the pegboard. Hood studied the two empty pegs and blank area where the guitar presumably had been displayed. Keen detective skills weren't needed to deduce it had been chosen as a weapon of convenience. Against a side wall between the display case and rear counter, a roll-top desk with its top open was littered with documents, blank forms, and a ceramic cup, its handle missing, containing pens and pencils.

Hood walked to the rear counter. "I don't see any blood back here by this old phone," Hood said. "Did the victim have a cell?"

"Sorry. Didn't get a chance to check. EMTs were in a hurry."

"No matter. They'll bag and tag it if it was on him. Who made the 9-1-1 call?"

"Dispatch said the caller didn't give a name."

Hood retrieved a pen and pad from a pocket and jotted a reminder to inquire about the origin and content of the emergency call.

As he did so, Wally asked, "What do you think—robbery gone bad?"

"A robber usually comes prepared, brings a weapon. That guitar suggests somebody grabbed what was available." He pocketed the pad and pen. "Do we know if any cash, or anything else, was taken?"

"Not yet."

"And you said the front door was unlocked?"

"Yes."

"Assault could've occurred before the owner closed for the day and locked up. Assailant was either in a hurry or didn't have a key. That would account for the door being left open."

Wally nodded.

Hood surveyed the room, which spanned the entire width of the building and featured a large front window beside the front door. The interior suggested a hoarder's paradise of merchandise and furnishings piled nearly to the ceiling and jammed onto shelving units separated by narrow aisles. "I better have a look," he said, his tone betraying claustrophobic unease. He navigated among wooden tables of varying shapes and sizes, assorted chairs, lamps, sporting goods, camping gear, books, record albums, knick-knacks, and miscellaneous bric-a-brac.

When he reappeared in the center aisle, he asked, "You cleared the scene, right?"

Wally nodded.

"What's the rest of this place look like?"

"Back room's a jumble. Worse than this. Upstairs isn't bad. Looks like his living quarters. It's messy, but not filled with junk."

Hood lapsed into quiet concentration for several moments. "I think I'm going to call Sandra," he said, referring to Sandra Brondel, a Missouri Highway Patrol crime lab analyst who was both a fellow professional and a friend.

Wally nodded. He had been trained to perform routine crime scene tasks, including lifting fingerprints and bagging evidence, but this scenario presented challenges that called for expert analysis. "I'll put up some crime scene tape," he said.

As he left, Hood scrolled to Sandra's cell phone number and placed the call.

"Hello," Sandra answered.

"This is your sheriff," Hood said.

"I know. I also know it's Friday night."

Hood sensed more curiosity than pique in her tone. "I have a situation."

"A situation," she repeated. "Tell me about it."

Hood described the emergency call, the department's response, and the crime scene. "Wally and I could look for evidence and he could lift prints, but I'd really rather have you do it—if you're available, that is."

"Did you say you're in Schweinshaupten?"

"Yes. Take Highway 50 to Route D and—"

"I'm familiar with Schweinshaupten," she said. "I'll need to contact my supervisor, though."

"Of course."

"And I'm in my sweatpants. I wasn't planning to go out this evening."

"Trust me. You won't look out of place here."

"I know. I'll call if there's a problem. If not, look for me in about twenty minutes."

"Thanks." Hood disconnected, exited the shop, and stood on the sidewalk his chief deputy had secured with yellow tape containing the warning: Crime Scene: Do Not Cross.

# Chapter Two

Outside the store, Hood surveyed the two blocks of facing storefronts that made up downtown Schweinshaupten. Like many Central Missouri towns, the German-Catholic agricultural community had been reduced to survival mode. The stately church, St. Anthony's, anchored the downtown and continued to serve the faithful, but the once-thriving livestock industry, and its jobs, had disappeared.

*One Man's Trash...*, a two-story brick building, stood alone at the corner of Main Street and Werner Road. On its opposite side, an alley—reduced to crumbling asphalt and soil by weather and wear—separated the shop from the remaining storefronts. He estimated as many empty facades, some with brown paper obscuring the windows, as viable businesses, including Kelly's Family Restaurant, Scheperle's Feed and Grain, and a branch of Central Missouri Savings and Loan.

He walked to the alley and focused on the debris-strewn, weed-infested parking area, rarely used except by store owners and their employees. A split-rail fence separated the lot from the rusty tracks of the defunct Missouri-Kansas-Texas Railroad line. Beyond the tracks stood the wooden skeletons of holding pens that once confined countless hogs waiting to be marched onto livestock cars headed for slaughter. Hood experienced a twinge of nostalgia as he appraised the distant outlines of derelict hog barns illuminated by ghostly moonlight.

His musings were interrupted by the sound of Wally slamming the trunk of his cruiser after stowing the crime scene tape. His chief deputy fended off repeated questions from the curious onlookers who had gathered, ducked under the tape, and rejoined his boss.

A caricaturist would delight in exaggerating the contrasts between the two men. Hood, at age forty-seven, remained well-muscled. He was nearly six-feet tall and weighed about 210 pounds. His biceps, forearms, thighs, and calves were thick, his shoulders and chest broad, and his waist trim. His round head was topped with short, sandy-brown hair, and his face was dominated by a natural, almost perpetual, smile.

Wally, about two years younger than his boss, was all angles and sharp lines. He was lanky, sinewy, and stood six feet, four inches. His face was lean, almost gaunt, with narrow eyes, thin lips, and a tangle of unruly brown hair. Wally's uniform seemed to dangle from his skeletal body, whereas Hood's uniform was well-fitted and, typically, worn with military precision.

"Did you get hold of Sandra?" Wally asked.

"She's on her way, but it'll be about twenty minutes," Hood said.

"Want to do a walk-around, check for signs of forced entry?"

"Let's wait for Sandra," He turned his attention to the bystanders. "Were any of these folks here when you arrived?" The sheriff indicated not only the group near Wally's cruiser, but a trio of twenty-somethings standing across the street on the sidewalk in front of Chubb's Tavern.

"Those three came out as soon as I pulled up," Wally said. "These other folks must've come later. I guess they heard the sirens."

Hood was familiar with the threesome, which included local slacker Dennis Vivion, his on-again-off-again girlfriend, Rhonda Snellen, and one of Vivion's toadies, Lucas Forck, who went by the nickname Hunk. "I'll take Vivion and his cronies," Hood said. "See what you can get from those folks," he added, gesturing toward the larger group that had been quizzing Wally.

They separated, and Hood angled across the street.

"Sheriff," Vivion greeted Hood as he approached. "What's going on?"

"There was an incident at *One Man's Trash*.... Did any of you—?"

"What kind of incident?" Rhonda interrupted.

"Assault, maybe a breaking and entering. Did any of you hear or see anything? Somebody coming out of the store, maybe running down the street?"

"We were in the bar," Vivion said. "We heard the sirens and saw lights flashing through the windows, so we came out here."

"Were you three the only ones—?"

"A bunch of us came out, but most went back inside after a few minutes," Vivion interrupted.

Hood rubbed the back of his neck, then retrieved his pad and pen. "Okay. I'm going to need some current contact information."

"What for?" Rhonda protested. "We told you we didn't see anything."

"In case I need to follow up." Hood shrugged. "Or you can each take a breath test, and we'll see who needs to spend a night in jail for public intoxication. Then you can talk to me in the morning."

"Rhonda Snellen, 403 Melody Lane here in town. And I haven't been drinking. I'm waitressing tonight." She glanced at her watch, a delicate device featuring rhinestones and a metal band. "Speaking of which, I'd better get my ass back inside before Chubb pitches a fit."

As she entered the tavern, Hood gathered information from the two men, returned the pad and pen to his pocket, and followed Rhonda.

Inside, Ernie "Chubb" Maasen was spritzing a clear, carbonated something—7-Up, seltzer water?—into a mixed drink as Hood's pupils adjusted to the dimly lit interior. The tavern owner slid the concoction across the bar to a middle-aged woman, who carried it to a booth, where she sat alone. Rhonda was serving a group of middle-aged men and women sitting at two joined tables and watching a college football game on the large television mounted on the wall above the bar. A quartet of young people—two men and two women—were shooting pool in a back room, and an older man sat at the end of the bar, his head resting on his arm.

Chubb had owned and operated the bar for as long as Hood could remember. Despite his nickname, he was lean and sinewy. He once told the sheriff he had acquired his nickname as a child because his doting aunts would beseech each other to "pass that chubby baby over here." When his efforts as a teen and young adult failed to produce change, he not only accepted the ironic nickname, but displayed it prominently outside the establishment he opened.

"Hello, Sheriff," the bartender greeted.

"Chubb," Hood said.

"What's all the commotion across the street? Rhonda said Chet left in an ambulance."

Hood nodded as he approached the bar, closing the gap between them. "They took him to the hospital. You see or hear anything?"

"Just what I could see out the window and what Rhonda told me."

Hood gestured toward the bar patrons. "These folks been here most of the evening?"

"Since the game came on."

"Mind if I talk with them?"

"Might have to wake up old Cliff there," Chubb said, nodding toward the man apparently asleep at the bar.

Hood began making the rounds—taking names and phone numbers, posing questions, and learning nothing. He finished moments before he heard the sound of an approaching vehicle and saw headlights flash through the window blinds. "Thanks, Chubb," he called as he pulled open the door.

# Chapter Three

A marketing representative for a cosmetics company would hire Sandra Brondel on sight. Her facial features and physique suggested the rare combination of wholesome girl-next-door and alluring siren.

Ironically, she was without artifice, personally and professionally. She used minimal makeup and gathered her long, tawny hair into a simple ponytail. The impression she created, however, was simultaneously natural and breathtaking. The shapeless gray sweatshirt and baggy sweatpants she wore failed to hide her poise and elegance. Although Hood knew she recently had celebrated her twenty-eighth birthday, she easily could be mistaken as younger.

As he crossed the street to greet her, he was reminded of what he deemed her most captivating quality—the scientific rigor she applied to every aspect of her life. "Thanks for coming," he said. "Hope I didn't tear you away from anything."

"A good mystery and a lap kitty, but Lady Jane doesn't hold a grudge. She was asleep on the sofa before I was out the door."

Over the years, Hood and Sandra had developed an easy banter, not only as colleagues, but as confidantes who shared their respective challenges and supported each other. Sandra knew, for example, that Hood was a recovering alcoholic who recently had reunited with his wife and daughter after a nearly year-long separation. And Sandra had shared her struggles with obsessive-compulsive disorder, commonly known as OCD, and panic attacks.

Hood waited while she retrieved her evidence collection kit and they walked together to the store as Wally fell in step behind them.

"Wally was first on the scene," the sheriff said, deferring to his deputy, who reported the front door was closed, but not locked, and the interior was dark until he switched on the overhead light.

Sandra placed her kit on the sidewalk and removed a flashlight, camera, and gloves, which she pulled on before examining the front door. "I don't see any signs of forced entry or tampering with the lock," she said. "Let me get some pictures and prints." When she finished, she closed the kit and stood. "Have you done a walk-around?"

"Not yet," Hood replied. "Since you agreed to come out, I didn't want to muck up the scene."

"I appreciate you, Francis. You wouldn't believe how many crime scenes get trashed before I get there." As Hood savored the compliment, Sandra added, "Let's have a look."

Wally volunteered to monitor the front door while Hood followed Sandra, who aimed her flashlight to illuminate their path around the outside of the building. She paused periodically to examine windows and a side door that opened to an alley, where broken asphalt crunched underfoot. When they returned to the front of the store, Sandra braced a shoulder against the door jamb, lifted a foot, and examined the sole of her shoe. "I picked up some grit," she said. She removed two pairs of booties from the kit. "Here," she said, "if you're coming in, put these over your shoes as you cross the threshold."

When Hood informed her that he, Wally, and two EMTs had already been inside, she nodded in acknowledgement, stepped inside, and scanned the interior. Hood knew, from her expression and the track of her vision, she was mentally reconstructing the story told by the blood evidence.

"Someone," Hood said, eager to be helpful, "may have used that phone on the counter to call 9-1-1, so we'll need to get prints." He intentionally used the plural rather than singular pronoun.

"We'll get there, Francis. First things first." She approached the pool of blood. "Somebody left us a soil sample. And that looks like a partial footwear impression."

Hood looked at the soil, flecked with white granules, and the tread of a toe print in the blood. "Could be from the EMTs," he said.

"Could be, but they're usually pretty careful about where they step." She examined the blood and adjacent guitar from various angles before taking photographs and collecting samples and fingerprints.

Hood rarely initiated conversation at a crime scene, fearing it might distract the evidence technician, but Sandra frequently engaged in upbeat chatter as she worked. Tonight, there was none. He continued to observe as the shared silence gradually became noticeable and, eventually, puzzling.

When she seemed satisfied with the initial phase of her analysis, including bagging the guitar and handing it to Wally, she moved behind the display case and dusted the rotary phone for prints. "Is there a bathroom here?" she asked.

"Right there," Wally called from the doorway, pointing to a short corridor, which included a restroom on the right, a staircase to the left, and—directly ahead—entry to a second room filled with merchandise.

"Excuse me." Sandra entered the lavatory. Hood guessed she was examining the room for evidence, but she abruptly closed the door. A few minutes later, she emerged and finished processing the phone. Eventually, she began working her way in an expanding circle, searching beyond the display case and along the customer aisles separating stacks of furniture, décor, and memorabilia.

"Interesting," she announced, breaking the silence as she examined the chrome edging on a rectangular kitchen table with a Formica top. "What's this?"

"Find something?" Hood asked, his curiosity apparent.

"A tuft of fabric," she answered. She used tweezers to remove the fibers from the seam of the edging. "Could be from any customer," she added, "but who knows?"

Hood hoped the victim eventually would provide answers and be able to describe, if not identify, his assailant. But that would have to wait. Right now, as Sandra resumed her silent examination, he sensed some indefinable something was troubling her.

He followed her to the storage room, where they negotiated the maze of narrow aisles that separated groupings of furnishings heaped precariously with accessories. Hood was reminded of a game he and his daughter used to play, where the object was to remove a wooden block from a tall stack without toppling the structure. He was thankful nothing in the storage room attracted Sandra's attention and he released a relieved sigh when they returned to the front room.

"There's living quarters up those stairs," Wally said to them when they reappeared. "Everything looked okay to me, but you may want to check it out."

"Does this place have a basement?" Hood asked.

"None that I could find," Wally answered.

"Okay," Sandra said. She started up the steps.

Hood asked Wally to look for a key to the front door, then followed Sandra to the second floor, which contained a living area, small kitchen, bedroom, and full bath. All were unkempt; floors and various surfaces contained dirty dishes, a greasy pizza box, out-of-date newspapers, and scattered unpopped "old maid" kernels. The conditions, however, suggested a messy, solitary tenant instead of some conflict or confrontation.

Sandra was nothing if not deliberate. She entered each room and paced the interiors as she carefully photographed scenes and examined surfaces—from bed sheets to kitchen counters, table tops to sink basins.

She returned to Hood and said, "I don't see anything to suggest any intruders came upstairs. Do you?"

"No."

They returned to the main level and rejoined Wally, who told his boss, "I didn't find a key. I think I've got a padlock hasp in my shop I can use to secure the door, but I'll need to run home."

"Okay."

"You have time to wait, or should I call dispatch and have them send someone?"

"I'll wait, but I might watch the place from Chubb's window if he's got any coffee that hasn't been sitting on the burner since this morning."

"Sounds like a plan," Wally said.

As Wally left in his cruiser, Sandra stowed her kit in the hatch of her SUV. "You know," Hood said, still curious about her apparent unease. "I haven't said this to a woman in more than two decades, but can I buy you a drink?"

"I probably should be heading back."

"Me too," Hood agreed. "But I told Wally I'd wait, and it'd be nice to have some company."

"Okay," Sandra said.

"That's the spirit."

# Chapter Four

They selected a table for two by a window that afforded a view of the facade of *One Man's Trash...* and the side alley. The only change Hood noticed inside the tavern was Vivion and Hunk were shooting pool, replacing the foursome who now occupied a booth.

Rhonda approached their table. "What can I getcha?"

Hood deferred to Sandra, who said, "Water's fine."

"Got any coffee?" Hood asked.

"Any coffee left?" Rhonda hollered to Chubb, who nodded.

"Is it fresh?"

"You want fresh?" Rhonda began, adopting a crappy Mae West impression, "Why don't you come up and see me sometime?"

Hood wasn't certain if Rhonda's brash, loud manner was her normal self or her barmaid persona. A promoter of women's professional wrestling might envision her as a trash-talking, head-locking, body-slamming competitor. She seemed comfortable creating characters and playing dress-up. Her workplace makeup obviously had been painstakingly prepared and her outfit—which included a low-cut crop top and tight, short skirt—deliberately selected. "I'll just go with the coffee," Hood said.

After Rhonda left, Sandra moved the chrome napkin holder from the center of the table to an edge, then repositioned a glass ashtray. Hood knew Sandra's OCD often took the form of repositioning objects in a trial-and-error approach to find a location that relieved her obsession. Momentarily satisfied, she released the ashtray, scanned the interior, and said, "People are staring at us."

"They're probably wondering why someone as young and attractive as you is sitting with an unappealing, older guy in a sheriff's uniform."

"You're not unappealing or old, Francis. And you seem happier than ever."

"I am. I have been since Linda came back."

"How is your wife? How are you both doing?"

Hood rotated the ashtray on the tabletop. He had pondered the question obsessively since the reunion, but was unsure of how much he understood or how much he was willing to share. "We're good," Hood said. "The separation was tough, but now that we're together again, it's like we're forming a whole new relationship, not just mending a damaged one. I think we both had some healing to do. I know I did. I had to admit my alcoholism drove her away, and I needed help."

"How long have you been sober now?

"Fifteen months. Life is different. I'm different."

"You're a lucky man, Francis."

"I am," Hood agreed, relieved Sandra didn't insist on details. "How about you?"

"Another bad relationship ending in another bad breakup." She shrugged as she pushed the napkin holder back to the center of the table. "Maybe I'm destined to become some crazy cat lady."

Rhonda returned and, as she served their beverages, Sandra said to the sheriff, "Did you know the translation for Schweinshaupten is hog's town?"

"I think I heard that somewhere," Hood said.

"Actually, it's pig's head," Rhonda interjected.

"True," Sandra conceded. "I understand the immigrants who founded this community named it for their hometown in Germany."

"Know why?" the barmaid asked. Without waiting for an answer, she added, "They were hog farmers who came from Germany, and, in their home country, they marketed the whole animal, including the head." Rhonda assessed their reactions. "Gross, I know. Can I get you anything else?"

"I think we're good," Hood said.

"No charge, by the way," Rhonda said. "We don't get many coffee drinkers in the evening, so Chubb was probably gonna dump the pot at closing, anyway."

When Rhonda departed, Hood leaned toward Sandra. "You're researching Schweinshaupten?"

"The guy I was dating was from here. Well, not here, exactly. His house is on Route D, a couple miles outside town. He brought me to the Fall Festival here a few Saturdays ago, and the historical society booth had a pamphlet on the town's history, so I picked one up and read it."

"Interesting," Hood said. He sipped his coffee while Sandra rotated her water glass on its coaster. "What about," he gestured toward her hand, "that?"

"Isn't it obvious?" She exaggerated her movements as she moved the tumbler, ashtray, and napkin holder like chess pieces. "I'm trying, but, if anything, it's getting worse." She clasped her hands in her lap. "Helps with the job, though. I tend to be more deliberate, more intentional. I check and double-check everything I do."

"Any thoughts on our scene across the street?"

"I wouldn't get my hopes up, Francis. Fingerprints, fibers, soil, and the partial footwear impression may be helpful, but only if you can track down the source. We'll see. One of the things I like about this job is whenever a person is in a place, material is transferred. Touch something, and you create a fingerprint. Step in something, you take some with you. Rub your face and you dislodge an eyelash or some skin cells. I've got the easy job finding those things. Your job is trickier, determining where—"

She stopped abruptly as Vivion, pool cue in hand, stepped to the side of their table. "I've seen you before," he said to Sandra.

A mythologist might characterize Vivion as a chimera, a being made up of multiple—not necessarily complementary—parts. Instead of the traditional mixture of lion, goat, and serpent, Vivion was a combination of under-achiever, stud, and stoner. He was tall, fit, and agile, but he preferred smoking pot to activities or athletics. Hood had busted him on more than one occasion on misdemeanor drug charges, but that was before state lawmakers legalized possession of recreational marijuana. Vivion's faded Chambray shirt and boot-cut jeans were splotched with paint and putty, evidence of his full-time job at Beautiful Body and Paint, which also served as his part-time residence whenever Rhonda kicked him out of her house.

Noticing Sandra seemed put off by Vivion's intrusion, Hood said, "You're interrupting."

"We know each other," Vivion reminded her. "You're Eric Rakestraw's girlfriend. We all hung out together at—"

"I remember," Sandra acknowledged. She circled her water glass in the ring of condensation it had created. "It's good to see you again, but you'll have to excuse us. The sheriff and I are discussing something."

Vivion looked at her, then at the sheriff. "Yeah, sure. Another time, maybe."

"Another time," Sandra repeated.

"Yeah," Vivion said, his tone skeptical. "See you around."

Hood noticed Sandra seemed visibly shaken as she watched Vivion return to the pool table. "How do you know that guy?" Hood asked.

"He joined us at the Fall Festival I mentioned. He was a jerk the entire time." She shuddered slightly. "He gives me the creeps."

"Well, don't let him bother you. Every community has at least one resident moron, and he's the odds-on favorite here, although Hunk might give him a run for his money."

"Who's Hunk?"

"See that guy he's shooting pool with?"

Sandra looked into the pool room at the tall, scrawny man standing at parade rest with a pool cue leaning against his right shoulder. His facial features were sharp and largely hidden by tangles of dirty blond hair and a scruffy beard. "That guy?" she asked. "How did he get to be called Hunk?"

"The story I heard is he reminded somebody—some movie buff, I guess— of the scarecrow in the 'The Wizard of Oz.' Apparently, it caught on, and people started calling him Hunk, which was the name of the Kansas farm hand portrayed by Ray Bolger, who doubled as the straw man."

Although they lapsed into a companionable silence, Hood sensed something—something he couldn't identify—was bothering Sandra. "Everything okay?" he asked. "You seem a little, I don't know, preoccupied."

"It's fine."

Hood leaned forward. "You know you can be honest with me. You've helped me with my issues. I just want you to know—"

"I appreciate that, Francis, but this isn't the best time."

"Okay." Hood lifted his hands and opened his palms, indicating surrender.

"And just so you know," Sandra said. "I don't let my personal life interfere with my professional responsibilities. You're going to get the best crime scene analysis I can provide."

Through the window, Hood saw a vehicle's headlights illuminate the street. "I never doubted it," he said.

She followed his gaze through the window. "I think that's Wally."

Hood arose from his seat. "Let's get out of here."

# Chapter Five

Brian Rakestraw couldn't breathe. He tried sucking air into his lungs, but his windpipe felt constricted.

Jessie Surface, who sat beside him on the sofa, put her arms around him and pulled him close. "Relax," she whispered. "Breathe with me." She tilted her head back and counted slowly to four as she inhaled.

He felt her chest expand as her lungs filled to capacity. He tried to emulate her, but his attempt was a staccato intake, marked by fits and starts.

"And exhale," Jessie said, resuming her count as she released the air.

David Wilde—who had flopped in a chair facing them—looked beyond the sofa to where his girlfriend, Michelle Bax, paced relentlessly. "Enough already," David said, his exasperation apparent. "Brian, you need to get it together. You stayed in the car. You didn't see anything."

"We're all in this together," Jessie said. "We're all kind of in shock right now. The first thing we need is to calm down. Then we can talk about what to do next."

The four students, juniors at nearby Monroe College, had returned to the home of Jessie's parents, who were spending the weekend closing up their Lake of the Ozarks condo for the winter. Taking advantage of her parents' absence, Jessie had invited her classmates to their house in an upper-middle-class neighborhood in St. Gotthard, the county seat for Huhman County. In Jessie's mind, the interior decor reflected her mother's attempt to appear more affluent than they were. Jessie referred to the family room decor, where the students had gathered, as *early funeral parlor*, although never when her mother was within earshot. After several rounds of drinking games,

Jessie had suggested a road trip to Schweinshaupten, which had ended unlike any of them had imagined.

"You said your uncle wasn't going to be at his store," David said.

"He was supposed to be with my parents at the lake," Jessie explained. "I don't know what happened."

"Well, obviously he didn't go," David said.

"And blaming is not going to help," she countered. "I was as surprised as you were. We called 9-1-1. I'm guessing the ambulance got there quickly. He'll be fine."

"I wouldn't be so sure," David said. "There was a lot of blood."

"Head wounds do that," Jessie said. A serious student and avid equestrian, her riding instructor characterized her as "spirited," which defined her approach to life. Nowhere was this more evident than in the show ring, where she was as tenacious as the three-year-old filly she rode. Although Jessie was lithe, watching her—her chestnut ponytail streaming from her riding helmet—coax the powerful equine to jump obstacles was like witnessing a battle of wills.

"We should tell the police we were there," Michelle said. She stopped pacing.

"We talked about this on the ride home," David said. "We agreed it wasn't a good idea."

"I didn't agree," Michelle said. "We should have stayed, at least until the ambulance got there."

"We were drunk, Michelle," Jessie said. "If we'd stuck around, we'd all be in jail right now."

"I can't go to prison," Brian said, his voice weak and frightened.

"What if your uncle saw us?" Michelle asked. "What if he opened his eyes, even for a split second?"

"He was out," David said. "No doubt about that."

"What if somebody saw your car?" Michelle asked Jessie, obviously unsatisfied by assurances.

"It was dark in the alley," Jessie answered. "Brian stayed in the car. If he didn't see anybody, then nobody saw us. We've got nothing to worry about as long as we stick together."

"This is crazy," Michelle said. She glared at Jessie. "You said everything would be fine. You had your parents' key to the store. You said no one would—"

"Sometimes things go to shit, Michelle. I'm not happy about this either."

"What's done is done," David shouted, ending the bickering. "Jessie's right. I say we sit tight. Jessie's uncle will recover, and it'll be like nothing ever happened. End of story."

"You hope." Michelle's tone was laced with sarcasm.

"The main thing," Jessie said, "is we need to stick together." She noticed Brian's breathing had become more measured, so she disengaged and added, "We need to promise to keep this to ourselves."

Michelle stared at Brian. "He can't promise. He's drunk. I'd be surprised if he remembers anything about tonight, least of all a promise he made."

"Don't worry about Brian," Jessie said. "I'll talk to him. I just need to know you guys are in."

"I'm in," David said.

Michelle stared at him, then at Jessie. "I won't be the one who blabs. Don't worry about me."

"Good," Jessie said. "My parents should be getting notified soon. When they do, they'll call me, and I'll know more about how Uncle Chet is doing."

A heavy, palpable silence ensued until David said, "I'm gonna get a beer. Anybody want one?"

"Get me one," Brian said.

"You're smashed already," David said.

"I'll come with you," Jessie volunteered.

"I'm going outside to smoke a joint," Michelle announced. She went to the front door as David and Jessie walked through the kitchen and into a two-car garage where her parents kept a refrigerator stocked with beer, soft drinks, and bottled water.

Jessie removed two beer bottles, handed one to David, and said, "I'm worried about Michelle. I'm not sure she's entirely on board."

"She'll be okay. I'm more worried about Brian right now."

"Why's that?"

"What if he doesn't believe we found your uncle unconscious? What if he thinks we surprised him, and one of us whacked him on the head? What if he decides to cut his losses and tells the cops we were there?"

"Don't worry about Brian. I'll deal with him."

"You sound pretty sure of yourself." David eyed her quizzically as he twisted and removed the bottle cap. "What do you see in him, anyway?"

"That's really none of your business."

"You know what I think?"

"No, David. Why don't you tell me what you think? I'm dying to know." She uncapped the beer and took a swig.

David released a plosive breath. "I just don't know why you hang out with that guy. That's all."

She brushed past him and he followed her to the family room, where Michelle remained missing, and Brian appeared to be passed out in a corner of the sofa.

Before Jessie or David sat, the ringtone to her cell phone sounded.

"Hello," she answered, silently mouthing the words "my father" to David. She listened, then feigned surprise by saying, "But I thought he was meeting you at the lake this weekend." She resumed listening, interspersing questions—"The hospital?" "Is he okay?" "Should I meet you there?"

When she disconnected, she said to David, "They took him to Huhman County Hospital. He's alive, but he's going right into surgery. I told my parents I'd meet them there."

As she spoke, Brian leaned his head over the sofa arm, retched, and vomited on the hardwood floor.

"Great," Jessie said. "Another fucking mess to clean up."

* * *

Hood made inquiries at the hospital and learned Chester Groner was undergoing surgery, and his family members had gathered in the waiting area near the operating suite.

Familiar with the hospital layout, he walked briskly to his destination, paused in the corridor outside the waiting room, and peered through a window. Clustered in a corner was a lone group of people—a middle-aged couple and a young woman, presumably their daughter. The man sat upright at the end of a row of seats and rhythmically tapped his left foot, the woman beside him was bent forward, wiping the corner of her eye with a tissue, and the daughter had pulled her feet under her and was staring at a cell phone screen.

Hood entered and approached them. "I'm your sheriff, Francis Hood," he said.

The man stood. "Are you in charge of finding whoever attacked my brother-in-law?"

"Yes. I'm sorry to meet under these circumstances."

"I can't believe—" the man began, then stopped. "Where are my manners? I'm Adam Surface." He offered his hand, and Hood shook it. "And this," he said, turning to his partner, "is my wife, Irene. She's Chet's sister."

"Thank you for coming, Sheriff," Irene said.

"And," Adam added, gesturing toward the person beside his wife, "that's our daughter Jessie."

Jessie glanced at Hood and offered a perfunctory "Hi."

"Hi," he acknowledged.

"Did they tell you anything about his condition?" Adam asked.

"No," Hood said. "Only that he's in surgery."

"That's all we know, too."

"Our department will be supervising the investigation," Hood explained as he retrieved his pen and notepad from his pocket. "Schweinshaupten is a fourth-class city, but it doesn't have its own law enforcement, so it contracts with us."

"Of course," Adam said.

"Can I get your contact information?" Hood asked. After recording the information, he added, "What can you tell me about Chester? Any immediate family?"

"He goes by Chet," Adam corrected.

"We're his only family," Irene added. "Chet was never married. He was, well, he just didn't, that's all."

"What happened?" Adam asked Hood. "All we know is that he was assaulted. Did someone break in? Did somebody try to rob him?"

"We're piecing that together," Hood said, defaulting to the vague language he used when discussing an investigation. "There's no evidence of forced entry, but there obviously was a confrontation. We'll know a lot more after we've had a chance to talk to him."

"This should never have happened. He was supposed to come—" Irene blurted before being overcome by uncontrollable sobs.

Adam sat beside his wife and put an arm around her shoulder.

Hood remained silent until Irene collected herself, then asked Adam, "What does she mean?"

"We were at our lake condo," Adam said. "Chet was supposed to join us, get in a last weekend of fishing, and help us close it up for winter. He called at the last minute, said he couldn't get away."

"When did he call?" Hood asked. "What, exactly, did he say?"

"I didn't talk to him," Adam said. "He called Irene on her cell."

Hood looked to Irene, who stammered, "This afternoon. All he said—"

"What time?" Hood interrupted. "Could you check your phone?"

She did, and reported Chet's call was received at 4:37, which Hood noted. "Go on."

"He said something had come up, and he wouldn't be able to make it." Losing her struggle to maintain her composure, she cried out, "Who would do something like this?"

"That's what we intend to find out," Hood said. "Do you know if he has any enemies?"

"Not that I'm aware of," Irene answered.

"He pretty much keeps to himself," Adam added. "He isn't what you'd call 'warm and fuzzy' or anything like that."

"What about valuables?" Hood asked.

"It's mostly just junk," Adam said. "Like the sign says: *One Man's Trash ...*"

"Sometimes, junk dealers happen upon rare or historic items that turn out to be worth a lot of money."

"If he did," Adam said, "he didn't tell me." He turned to his wife, "Honey?"
She shook her head.

Hood glanced at Jessie, who remained occupied with her phone.

"Anything else you can tell me?" the sheriff asked.

"I don't think so," Adam answered. "We're just waiting to hear something."

"Do you mind if I wait with you?" Hood asked.

"No," Adam said.

Beside Jessie was a chair piled with their coats, followed by empty seats.
As Hood sat in the chair beside the coats, he noticed Jessie's phone screen
darken.

She glanced at him, and they exchanged awkward smiles before she opened
a new app, which appeared to be some sort of video game.

"Are you a student?" Hood asked her.

"Uh-huh." Her fingers deftly tapped the small screen.

"I have a daughter who goes to R-1 High School."

"I'm a college student," Jessie said.

Hood heard the implication—the two young women couldn't possibly
have anything in common; they were worlds apart. He sat silently with the
family until the silence became uncomfortable, then excused himself and
paced a segment of the hallway where he couldn't be seen from the waiting
room.

Patience was not among Hood's strengths. He counted his steps, looked
repeatedly at the clock, and was debating whether to leave when a man
wearing surgical scrubs emerged from the operating room and crossed the
corridor. Hood rushed back to the waiting room as the family members
stood in unison, and the surgeon introduced himself as Dr. Williams. "The
patient is stable and resting comfortably," the doctor said. "That's the good
news. But he's suffered a severe blow to the head. What we don't know
at this time is whether he's suffered any short-term or long-term loss of
cognitive ability. The scans indicate a cranial injury but, until he awakens
from the anesthesia, we can't know if he has neurological complications."

"I don't understand," Irene said. "Are you saying he's got, like, brain damage?"

"It's simply too soon to tell," Dr. Williams replied. "Right now, rest is the best medicine for the patient, and patience is the best medicine for the rest of us."

Hood guessed from the doctor's delivery that he had used the phrase frequently.

Irene collapsed in her seat.

"We have your contact information so we can update you immediately on any changes," Dr. Williams said.

"We'll be right here," Irene said.

Hood detected the exhaustion in her tone.

"If you'll excuse me," the doctor said. He returned to the surgical suite.

Hood produced a card and handed it to Adam. "If you think of anything else, you can reach me at this number."

As Adam pocketed the card, Jessie asked, "Is it okay if I go? I've got a riding lesson early tomorrow."

"Of course, dear," her mother said. "I'm sure they've got him sedated, so we probably won't hear anything. You go ahead."

"Okay," Jessie said. She reached for a blue wool car coat, triggering Hood's recollection of the fibers Sandra had found at the store.

"Here," Hood said. "Let me help you with that."

"Thanks."

Hood performed a cursory examination as he held the coat so she could slip her arms in the sleeves but saw no obvious tears or flaws.

"Okay," Jessie said. "Gotta go. Call me if there's any news."

# Chapter Six

"Good morning." Hood's greeting was as cheerful as his morning mood.

"Morning," Linda responded. She assessed the blue flame under the cast iron skillet, the ingredients on the counter, and the spatula in her husband's hand. "What's cooking?"

"Breakfast sandwich. Want one?"

"English muffin?"

"Yes."

"Vermont cheddar?"

"Of course."

"Sounds great." She took her favorite mug from a cabinet, filled it with coffee, and sat at the counter. The mug—a birthday gift from their daughter, Elizabeth—identified her as *World's Greatest Mom*. She tested the temperature with a cautious sip and asked, "What time did you get in last night?"

"Before ten, but you were already asleep."

"Couldn't keep my eyes open. Elizabeth up yet?"

"On Saturday morning? Are you kidding?"

How'd everything go last night?" Linda asked, curious after he responded to the Friday night incident.

Hood shrugged as he spread the butter melting in the skillet. "Assault at that junk shop in Schweinshaupten. Ambulance already had transported the victim when I got there. Crime scene's a puzzle. I called Sandra."

"How is she?"

Her question came as no surprise. Linda routinely inquired about mutual acquaintances and—perhaps as a result of her experience as a nurse—listened attentively and expressed genuine concern about their welfare. Hood popped muffins into the toaster as he mulled how to answer. He would be honest, but—because Sandra had confided in him about her history of failed relationships and challenges with OCD—he intended to respect her privacy. "She's Sandra," he said, as if that was a sufficient answer. "And, so you know, we had coffee—well, I had coffee, she had water—at Chubb's last night."

Linda sipped from her cup but said nothing as she watched her husband crack two eggs into the pan and break the yolks.

Hood contemplated what he had said. During his active alcoholism, his actions had been based on rationalization, justification, and denial. His program of recovery emphasized honesty, and he had embraced the slogan—*examine your motives.*

Why, he wondered, had he felt compelled to tell his wife about sitting in a small-town tavern with an attractive, younger woman? Did he feel guilty? Did he fear Linda might hear about it from another source? Was he trying to elicit some response from his wife? If so, what? *Don't overthink it,* Matthew, his sponsor in recovery, frequently advised. Hood knew Matthew's counsel was accurate and applicable, but—like many aspects of his program— knowing it and practicing it were two different things. He flipped the eggs, added cheese, and plated the muffins.

"Want to eat on the patio?" Linda asked.

Hood heard no trace of suspicion or pique in her tone. "Sure."

"I'll wipe down the table." She grabbed a kitchen towel while he assembled the sandwiches. Together, they finished preparations efficiently, unfolding chairs, carrying out the food, and activating the fountain on the decorative pond centered in the herb garden. Their daughter, as an adolescent, had insisted upon stocking the pond with a dozen goldfish. The fish had survived three winters while Elizabeth, now age 15, had acquired other interests. Although Hood had adopted the twice-daily task of feeding them, he didn't mind.

He recalled the time when he found fault, assigned blame, and harbored resentments if people didn't meet his expectations or conform to his standards. Practicing recovery principles—acceptance, tolerance, open-mindedness—had eased his former frustrations.

While Linda blessed the meal, Hood reflected on his transformation. He was grateful for his recovery, for the reunification of his family, and simply for being surrounded in the present moment by the constant, yet ever-changing, sound of cascading water.

*　*　*

The clatter of dishes aroused Brian from fitful sleep. He opened his eyes to orient himself and realized he was in the bedroom of Jessie's off-campus apartment. The digital clock on her nightstand read 7:24. He stumbled to the bathroom, slowed by the heaviness of a massive hangover. He splashed water on his face and stared at his reflection in the mirror.

He didn't like anything he saw. Never had. He was no Charles Atlas, a comparison that had persisted since grade school, when he first saw a *Superman* comic book advertisement promising a "he-man" body. His friend, Albert Gordon, had a sizable collection, including vintage comics inherited from his father. In the ensuing years, Brian had forgotten the stories and illustrations, but he vividly remembered the inside back cover depicting the bodybuilder touting his instructional program. Although the free coupon accompanying the ad had long expired, Brian was motivated to improve his physique—a failed effort he had repeated countless times before frustration forced him to give up. He allowed himself a lingering look at his image, muttered "pathetic," and returned to the bedroom, where he had left his clothes strewn on the carpet.

Brian buttoned the long-sleeved, flannel shirt and pulled on the faded jeans, both a size too large—hand-me-downs from his older brother. He adjusted the baggy outfit as he walked to the kitchen.

"Good morning, bright eyes," Jessie greeted. Showered and dressed, she was seated at her dinette table, which held two disposable cups of coffee and an open box of pastries.

"How long have you been up?"

"Since about 5:30. I've got a riding lesson, and then I'm heading to the hospital."

"Hospital? What's going on?"

"Do you remember anything about last night?"

"I remember we played some drinking games at your parents' house, and I got pretty trashed, and at some point, we all piled into your car and went somewhere." He lifted his coffee and sipped.

"That's all?"

"I think I woke up at some point, and I was alone in the passenger seat, and the car was parked in some alley. That's pretty much it."

"Do you remember throwing up at my parents' house after we got back?"

Brian shook his head. "Sorry."

"David and Michelle helped me get you into my car so I could bring you here before I went to the hospital last night."

"Who's in the hospital?"

"My Uncle Chet. We went to his store. I had a key. We found him on the floor, unconscious, so we called 9-1-1 and got the hell out of there."

"You left him?"

"He was bleeding. He'd been assaulted. We weren't going to stick around and answer questions about something we didn't do."

"Why did we go there in the first place?"

"I wanted you guys to see the store." Brian's expression indicated he was baffled and unsatisfied by her explanation, so she added, "Look, I'm not proud of it, but we'd all been drinking. I was driving and probably couldn't pass a breath test."

"But still?"

"Still what? It was a spur-of-the-moment thing, so don't judge me. And you were no help. You were passed out. Again."

"I'm trying, okay? I've started going to those meetings like you asked, but then you and I get together with friends, and we start partying like last night, and you know once I start, I can't stop."

"I just don't want you to end up like your parents."

"Me neither, but you can't have it both ways. I can't be your drinking buddy and your sober boyfriend."

"No more drinking together then. Okay? Your drinking has become a problem, and I think you know that."

"Yeah, but knowing it and quitting are two different things," Brian said. "You know I've got anxiety problems. Drinking helps me mellow out."

"I know your anxiety can be off the charts, and I know the drinking helps, but now it's become its own problem. When you drink, you're non-functional—like a zombie. It's like you've substituted one problem for another."

They stared at each other silently until Jessie added, "I don't know how much longer I can do this."

Brian closed his eyes and contorted his lips into a grimace, and Jessie knew from experience he was on the verge of tears. "I don't know if I can quit on my own," he said.

"What about getting a—what do they call it—sponsor? I've got a cousin in recovery, and he's all about having a sponsor. Is there anybody at the meeting—?"

"There's this one guy. His name's Francis. I only know his first name. We don't use last names."

"Would you ask him? Would you do that? For me?"

"Okay."

# Chapter Seven

The arrangement of Sandra's workplace reminded Hood of his wife's kitchen. Although Monday's workday hours had ended, the crime lab remained illuminated by bright lighting no shadow would dare to darken and its gleaming surfaces had been scoured to eliminate any germ, stain, or smudge.

However, the lab's state-of-the-art instruments—spectrometers, chromatographs, x-ray fluorescence analyzers—appeared far more sophisticated and expensive than the microwave, coffee maker, and toaster oven he used routinely.

Hood considered the differences. His home appliances were time-saving conveniences. Sandra's sophisticated equipment was designed to find potentially life-altering evidence.

"Remember, Francis," Sandra warned. "No touching."

Hood clasped his hands in mock obedience. "Any results yet?" he asked.

"I did some work over the weekend. I hope you appreciate that," she chided playfully, as she retrieved a single sheet of paper. "Here's a copy of the footwear impression. It's a partial, only the toe, but if you find the footwear, I'd sure like to analyze them. The wear and tear on the heels and soles can be distinguishing, almost like a signature. Also, I put the soil from the shop floor under a polarizing light microscope. I found traces of corn starch, salt grains, calcium phosphate, and calcium carbonate."

"What's that mean?"

"I don't know. I'm going to drive back later and get some comparison samples from the alley and around the shop."

"Anything else?"

"The fibers I collected are pure wool, navy blue," she added, triggering Hood's recollection of Jessie's coat. "Did you trace the 9-1-1 call?"

"It came from that rotary phone in the shop, and it was a man's voice," Hood answered. "Chester had his cell phone and his keys on him when they transported him to the hospital. The only call he made on his cell yesterday was to his sister, which she told me about—"

A sound from around a corner startled them. They turned and saw Howard DeWesplore, the fingerprint specialist, exit a nearby cubicle.

"Howard," Sandra said, "I thought you were gone for the day." She plucked a ballpoint pen left on a desktop and returned it to the drawer designated for writing implements.

"Just finishing up," he answered. He turned to Hood. "Sheriff."

"The sheriff's here about a crime scene we worked," she said, as if an explanation was necessary.

"Of course," Howard replied. "Need anything before I go?"

"No," Sandra answered. "We're good."

Silence ensued as they watched DeWesplore push through the double glass doors to the hallway. As soon as he disappeared beyond their sightline, Hood asked, "What about the fingerprints and blood?"

"As you might have guessed, Howard did the prints, and Victoria took care of the blood work. She said all the samples—on the floor, guitar, everywhere—came from the victim. Many of the—"

"So the guitar was used as a weapon?"

"Have a look." She led him to a counter where the guitar was positioned. "This is a Fender Stratocaster. It's written on the headstock. It was made in 1993. The neck is maple, and the body color is Olympic White. It weighs a little over seven pounds. We found traces of skin and blood there." She pointed to the lower contour of the guitar's body.

Hood placed his right palm against his cheek. "I'm guessing the assailant held the guitar by the neck and whacked the victim on the head?"

"That's likely."

"What about fingerprints? Any on the guitar's neck?"

"Yes. And on the guitar body and on every other surface where Howard lifted prints. He ran dozens of them—fingers, palms, partials, smeared. That's no surprise. Customers are in the store handling merchandise all the time. And your victim, the owner, was hardly a neat freak. There's no telling the last time he used a dust rag or glass cleaner. The problem, Francis, is not a lack of evidence. It's an overabundance."

"Any way to tell which prints, if any, came from the assailant? I mean, if he held the neck and swung it like a baseball bat, wouldn't the prints be upside down?"

"It's possible. I'll ask Howard to check, but handing it to a customer also could—" The ringing of a telephone at a nearby workstation interrupted her. "Hold on." She walked several paces to a desk and lifted the receiver.

Hood stepped away as a courtesy, but his interest was piqued by her whispered question, "How did you get this number?" He tuned in immediately, like a canine reacting to a dog whistle. "Don't call me here. Don't call me ever." Her voice was adamant, but Hood also detected a trace of fear. She appeared to resist her impulse to slam the receiver into its cradle. "That was, um—"

Sensing her discomfort, Hood said, "Not my business."

"Thanks. Where were we?"

"You were saying how there was too much evidence, how—" Hood stopped, aware that Sandra's facial features had become contorted. "Are you okay?"

She held up a hand, signaling she needed a moment, then turned and abruptly left the room through the double doors.

Hood watched her cross the hall and enter the women's restroom. He didn't know what to do. He had received instruction about how to respond to a variety of scenarios, but nothing in his job training or life experience seemed helpful. Should he remain in the lab, follow her to the hallway, knock on the restroom door? Before he could decide, Sandra emerged into the hall and returned to the lab.

"Sorry. I just needed a minute," she said, her tone relaxed.

"You're sure you're okay?" Hood remained perplexed by her rapid rebound.

"Yes."

"Was it a panic attack?"

"Not exactly."

"Has it happened before?"

She looked around the lab, as if seeking a new topic, then said, "I'd rather not talk about it right now."

Hood took the hint. He glanced at the wall clock and said, "Well, I'd better get going. Call me if you need anything."

\* \* \*

Hood descended the stairs to the St. Cecilia Catholic Church basement, a gymnasium that also hosted a range of sacred and secular activities, including basketball and volleyball games, preschool classes, wedding receptions, group meetings, and, on occasion, local election balloting.

Twice each week, it was the venue for Recovery Rules, an evening gathering hosted by Hood's sponsor, Matthew. Most of the participants were alcoholics like Hood, but people suffering from any addiction—drugs, gambling, eating disorders—were welcome.

Although Hood was nearing fifteen months of recovery, Matthew's meeting was the only one he attended. As sheriff, he remained careful about protecting his anonymity. He never wore his uniform to the session and, like the other participants, identified himself only by his first name. Matthew emphasized anonymity and closed each meeting with the reminder, "Who you see here, what you hear here, let it stay here when you leave here." Hood wasn't certain if anyone recognized him from newspaper photographs, periodic campaign ads, or public events, but, if so, no one revealed it to him or, he hoped, to anyone outside the meeting.

Hood exchanged greetings with his peers seated in folding chairs around a rectangular arrangement of tables, then chose a seat beside Brian, a young man who had attended about a half-dozen meetings.

A casting director might select Brian for the role of a nerdy weakling in a television sitcom. The oversized sweatshirt and loose trousers he wore failed to disguise his slight frame, slender wrists, and spindly limbs. His sharp facial features were framed by long, straight hair and accentuated by retro-style eyeglasses.

Matthew approached from the kitchen, set two coffee carafes on the table, and opened the meeting with the Serenity Prayer. "God," the group recited in tattered union, "grant me the serenity to accept the things I cannot change, the courage to change the things I can, and the wisdom to know the difference."

Afterward, as was customary, Matthew asked if anyone had something to report or was facing a challenge. When no one spoke, he said, "I thought tonight we could talk about fear. For me, fear is a double-edged sword. Alcohol helped me deal with—or, at least, numb myself to—my fears and anxieties, but eventually, the drinking took on a life of its own, and I was afraid of living life without it. Who wants to start?"

"Angie, alcoholic."

Hood joined the chorus of greetings for the forty-something, single mother of two teenage children. He realized that although he had known some of the members for months, he knew their backgrounds based only on what they had shared at meetings.

"I was full of fear. I think that's one of the reasons I drank. When I came in here, people told me if I have faith in a higher power, I won't have fear." She sipped coffee from her disposable cup. "Well, I still have fear, so either that's bullshit, or my faith is pretty shaky. I think the last one is true. I've tried, but if I'm being honest, I don't understand God, I don't trust God, and I don't have faith in God. I guess I still have a ways to go. Pass to Mac."

"Hello everyone, my name's Mac, and I'm an alcoholic."

Mac, like Matthew, was a regular at Recovery Rules. Neither had missed a meeting during the time Hood had attended. And, although Mac never mentioned his time in recovery, his knowledge and experience suggested decades of sobriety.

"For me," Mac said, "I believe fear is a basic human emotion. It's a factory-installed survival mechanism, and no amount of faith will entirely eliminate it. Nor should it. But there's a vast difference between practical fear and paralyzing fear. Practical fear reminds me not to put my hand on a red-hot burner. Paralyzing fear tells me not to go in the kitchen because there's a stove in there. My alcoholism led to paralysis. I didn't go places. I distanced myself from family and friends. Eventually, I became alone and miserable. What got me here was complete and utter defeat. That's all I've got."

The sharing continued around the table to Hood, who introduced himself and waited until the greetings subsided. "I was full of fear when I first came through the door," he said. "Part of me was afraid I couldn't get sober and I would live the rest of my life drunk in the evenings and hungover in the mornings. And the other part of me was afraid of how I would live life, if did get sober. Even when I realized surrender was my only option, I resisted because it was contrary to everything I'd been taught. When I was growing up, everything I heard was 'be a man,' 'pull yourself up by your bootstraps,' 'don't be a crybaby.'

"What I've come to believe—as a result of this program—is surrender is the most courageous thing I've ever done. It certainly is the hardest thing I've done. Today, I know surrender has given me a strength and serenity I could never have imagined. I'll pass to Brian."

"Thank you all for being so open," Brian said. "I think I'll just continue to listen."

After the meeting, Hood was headed to the stairs when he heard Brian call his name.

"Can I talk to you for a minute?" Brian asked.

"Sure."

Brian scanned the gymnasium, where people were folding and stacking chairs. "I was hoping it could be private."

Hood looked to an enclosed room with a large rectangular window and a door marked *Nursery*. "Grab a chair and follow me," he said.

The metal chairs they unfolded in the nursery were the only adult-size furnishings in the room. Surrounding them were smaller plastic seats, tables, and blocks in primary colors. Hood acknowledged the incongruity of two adults preparing to discuss addiction in a room accessorized with objects and toys in red, blue, and yellow. The nursery did, however, provide a quiet space.

Brian gazed at the linoleum. "I wanted to tell you I appreciate what you said tonight—about being frightened, I mean."

"I just shared what it was like for me."

"Me, too," Brian said. "I'm scared. I'm scared this won't work, and I'm scared it will. What you said makes me feel like I'm not alone."

"You're not alone. When I came in here, I thought I was unique. I looked for ways I was different from the others because I didn't want to be an alcoholic. But the more I listened, the more I understood what I had in common with the people here, and the more I felt like I belonged."

"I don't feel like I belong anywhere."

"Give it a chance," Hood said. "Recovery is a process. It doesn't happen overnight."

"That's what Matthew said when I talked to him before the meeting. My girlfriend thinks I should get a sponsor and he thought that was a good idea."

"I agree."

"I was wondering," Brian said, "if you'd be willing to do it—be my sponsor, I mean?"

Hood knew this day would come. He knew sponsorship was a time-honored component of the program of recovery. As a regular meeting attendee with more than a year of sobriety, he knew he would be asked eventually, and he both anticipated and dreaded the possibility. He looked at Brian and saw a measure of hope, albeit faint, in the young man's expression. "Yes," Hood answered.

Brian lifted his gaze from the floor. "Thank you, Francis. I really appreciate this."

Hood knew humility was a fundamental aspect of recovery, but he couldn't help feeling validated, empowered even. He would need to talk with Matthew about pridefulness. "So you know," he said, "I've never sponsored anyone before, so I should probably ask you a few questions."

"Ask away. I've got time."

Hood looked through the window and saw Matthew remained busy cleaning in the kitchen. "Okay," he said to Brian, "how and when did your drinking start? When did you first notice it was out of control? That sort of thing."

"I've dealt with social anxiety for as long as I can remember. I'm not what you'd call a 'guys' guy.'" Brian knew he was unlike his older brother, Eric, or even his friend, David, who were comfortable flaunting their physiques, strutting naked in locker rooms, and snapping towels at the asses of other men. "But the first time I drank, it lowered my inhibitions. I could be around other people without feeling like the odd man out. And if we all got drunk, I wasn't afraid of doing something stupid because we were all doing stupid stuff."

"So drinking helped you fit in," Hood said, more an observation than a question.

"Yeah," Brian answered.

"I'm guessing at some point your drinking became more of a problem than a solution. When did that start?"

"I don't know, exactly. I'd always have a few drinks before I went out—to prime the pump, so to speak—so I was pretty well lit by the time I got to a party or whatever. Then I'd just try to keep the buzz going, but I always went over the line and passed out or blacked out. That's when things started getting bad."

Hood nodded in shared understanding.

"Five years ago," Brian continued, "my parents were killed in a head-on collision. My father was driving drunk. It was his fault, but blood tests showed my mother was also way over the legal limit. They were both drunks, so it was only a matter of time." Brian focused on an orange and yellow molded plastic, foot-propelled kiddie car with its nose resting against some large blocks. "Thank God they hit some trees instead of another car."

Hood heard the angst in Brian's tone, but decided it was too early in their relationship to pursue it. Instead, he said, "That must have been difficult."

Brian shrugged. "It happened. My brother and I accepted it. That's a lot of what this recovery program is about, isn't it? Acceptance."

"Yes."

"So that's what we did. We moved on. I was a junior in high school when the accident happened. My brother is six years older than me—I was a bonus baby—so he did what needed to be done. He had a job, and we inherited my parents' house, which was paid off. He got authorization from the court—guardianship or whatever it was—and now we live in the house."

"Is your brother a drinker?" Hood asked.

"Not like me. I mean, he can get pretty smashed at parties, but he doesn't drink much otherwise—certainly not every day. Why?"

"It's helpful for me to know a little about your circumstances—whether there's drinking going on at your house, whether your brother supports your desire to quit, that sort of thing."

"My girlfriend sure wants me to quit," Brian said. "I think she's ready to dump me if I don't."

"I get that," Hood said. "My wife and daughter moved out for nearly a year, which was a wake-up call for me. I had tried to quit drinking for them, but—after we separated—I realized they hadn't left me, I had driven them away. And that's when I realized I had to do this for myself."

"So you're saying I need to get sober for me, not to satisfy her."

"If you're anything like me, I think you will come to that realization on your own."

"So what do I do?"

"Give recovery a chance. If you stick with it, things will get better."

"Sounds simple enough."

Hood smiled. "I've heard people say recovery is simple, but not easy."

"I don't expect it to be easy," Brian said.

"Then you're already off to a good start."

* * *

Linda waited for her husband to get settled, which included removing his shoes, collapsing into his recliner, and elevating the footrest.

"Where's Elizabeth?" he asked.

"She's still at the dance studio. They added an extra hour after class to rehearse for the recital."

Hood nodded. "Want me to pick her up?"

"That would be great. Do you mind?"

"Not at all. Between school, homework, dance class, and hanging out with her friends, it seems like I never see her anymore." Hood recalled a time when his drinking trumped volunteering to drive. He wouldn't volunteer and, if he had, Linda wouldn't allow it. Her intent was to protect their daughter, but a consequence was enabling her husband to drink with abandon. An added consequence came when he realized he could use impairment to avoid interaction.

Linda lowered the newspaper and folded it in her lap. "How was your meeting?"

"I got a big surprise tonight. Someone asked me to be his sponsor in recovery."

"That's wonderful." She assessed her husband's concerned expression and added, "Isn't it?"

"I'm not sure I'm ready."

"Have you talked with Matthew about it?"

"I should. I mean, I will, but I already said yes. This kid—I say kid, but he's probably in his early twenties—looked so lost. When he asked, I just blurted out 'yes.'"

"Well, I'm sure you'll do fine."

Hood sometimes thought Linda had more confidence in him than he had in himself. He knew his alcoholic behavior had caused their separation. Linda and their daughter had moved in with Linda's younger sister and husband, Sarah and Otto Kampeter. After several months as house guests, they rented an apartment. Since returning home about four months ago, Linda had been a steadfast supporter of her husband's recovery. "I appreciate your faith in me," he said.

"And I appreciate your commitment to staying sober."

Hood pondered her phrase—*commitment to staying sober*. Although Linda had warned him she could not stay and watch his descent into alcoholic, slow-motion suicide, he had failed to stay sober. The separation became his turning point—his recognition that he had experienced the first of many consequences that would accrue if he continued on the path of addiction.

His initial impulse had been to use whatever manipulation or guile was required to get her back, but Matthew discouraged him. "You need to heal yourself," his sponsor had said, "and give your wife and daughter time to heal. You cannot control the outcome, Francis, but if you stick with a program of recovery, you create the opportunity for your family to reunite."

Hood looked at Linda, allowing his gaze to linger long enough for her to ask, "What?"

"Nothing." He reconsidered his response. "No, that's not true. I'm feeling really grateful right now."

"For?" Linda elongated the monosyllable.

"For you. For Elizabeth. For us getting back together. I wasn't certain it would ever happen. When I started in recovery, I met some other guys like me—separated, divorced. I even heard someone say more marriages break up not while, but after, the alcoholic gets sober. We have a slogan—*There but for the grace of God go I.*"

Linda smiled. "You'd better get going if you plan to pick up our daughter on time."

\* \* \*

Elizabeth was among other girls—mostly adolescents and teens clad in tights and loose sweatshirts—standing outside In Step Dance Academy.

When Hood stopped, she pulled open the passenger door, tossed her backpack containing her dance shoes and other accessories into the rear seat, and got in.

He remained mesmerized by the transformation she had undergone during the separation. Linda had left with a gangly adolescent and returned with an engaging young woman. Elizabeth had developed a sprightly quality, evident in her nimble movements—on and off the dance floor—lively look and animated expressions.

"Seat belt," Hood reminded. He listened for the click as she fastened it before he pulled away from the curb.

"Guess what?" she asked, almost immediately.

"What?"

"We're doing a father-daughter dance at our recital next month."

Hood heard excitement, and a hint of amusement, in her tone. "What's that?"

"Our instructor saw one at another recital and decided she wanted to try it this year. It's where the girls in the class and their dads perform a dance routine together."

"At the recital?"

"Yep. In front of everybody. Miss Heather said it cracked people up."

Hood had no desire to dance onstage in front of an audience and no intention of "cracking people up" by displaying his incompetence. "We'll see."

\* \* \*

Brian entered the front door of the two-story farmhouse he and his brother had inherited. The structure, more than a half-century old, was located on Route D, about a mile outside Schweinshaupten.

"Eric," he shouted to let his brother know he was home, before continuing to the parlor and collapsing in one of a matching pair of overstuffed armchairs. Hearing no reply, he took his cell phone from his pocket—switched it from silent mode, the setting requested to avoid disruptions during meetings—and saw he had missed a text message from Eric. It read, *Weird shit happening. If you don't hear from me tomorrow, call the authorities.* He noted the message was sent nearly ninety minutes ago.

He stood and listened. He was able to sense a difference between silence—no one is making noise—and the profound stillness that signifies no one is present. Although he was convinced he was alone he again called his brother's name. No answer. A cursory search of the house, including looking out a kitchen window and noting Eric's truck was not in the driveway, confirmed his suspicions.

He phoned his brother and left a voicemail, then followed with a text and another unanswered call. He reread Eric's message. He knew something had been troubling his brother recently but assumed it was a result of his recent breakup. Questions collided in Brian's mind. Was something else weighing on his brother? Was the text part of some plan Eric had devised? What was intended by the deadline to contact authorities?

Brian tried to calm himself. He needed to talk to his brother. He called again. No answer. He set his phone on an end table and gazed at the varying shapes, sizes, and colors of the bottles atop the liquor cart. The appealing alignment seized his attention.

# Chapter Eight

Hood steered his cruiser into the circular drive of the Surface residence, an impressive two-story brick, colonial-style home in Fair Meadows, a newer subdivision on the eastern fringe of St. Gotthard.

The cruiser's digital dashboard clock indicated he was early. As he exited the vehicle, Irene—who apparently had heard him arrive—appeared from a corner of the house and approached. She carried a hand rake and plastic bucket, and Hood deduced she was taking advantage of the unseasonably warm October afternoon to clear fallen leaves from around the foundation plantings.

"Hello, Sheriff," she called. "We've been expecting you. Adam's inside. Follow me."

She left the implements on the brick porch and led him to an expansive family room, where Adam was seated in a recliner, reading a newspaper. He folded the paper, stood, and greeted the sheriff. After drinks were offered and everyone was settled, Irene said, almost apologetically, "Jessie isn't here. She has her own apartment. I can call her if you want, but she's usually at class, a riding lesson, or with her boyfriend."

"Not necessary," Hood said. "Anything new on Chet's condition?"

"No change," Adam replied. "He hasn't regained consciousness."

"They've got him hooked up to all sorts of tubes and wires," Irene added. "It's heart-breaking."

Hood nodded sympathetically. "I wanted to learn more about Chet and to ask if you'd be willing to go with me to his shop after we've cleared it as a crime scene. I'm trying to determine if anything was taken. When we spoke at the hospital, I got the impression you were familiar with the inventory."

"Adam more than me," Irene said. "Bless his heart, he went out there about once a week to help my brother and keep him company."

"Are you thinking it was a burglary gone bad?" Adam asked. "Because I've been thinking about it. If a burglar knew Chet was supposed to be with us, maybe the person broke in, figuring the store would be empty, but Chet surprised him."

"At this stage, I'm just trying to gather facts." Hood didn't mention the door had been unlocked, and nothing suggested a break-in. Although he also indulged in postulating theories, experience had taught him to gather facts to ascertain such fundamentals as means, motive, and opportunity.

"I'm willing to go with you and have a look," Adam said, "but I'd be going from memory. I don't think Chet kept any kind of inventory."

"My brother isn't much of a record-keeper," Irene added. "He just likes to buy, sell, and trade. It's really more of a hobby than a business."

"The shop isn't his livelihood?" Hood asked.

"He was career Navy," Irene answered. "He lives on his military pension. The shop gives him something to keep him busy."

"How old is he?"

"He's four years older than me," Irene said, "so he was 66 on his last birthday."

"Is he a lifelong resident of Schweinshaupten?"

"No. We were born and raised here in St. Gotthard. He moved there after he retired for what he called 'some peace and quiet.'"

Hood twisted his mouth into a frown. The use of the guitar as a weapon suggested a personal motive—perhaps an ongoing feud sparked the assault. "What about enemies?" Hood asked, revisiting a question he had posed at the hospital. "Did he mention any dissatisfied customers who might hold a grudge?"

"He never mentioned anything to me," Irene said, "but I suppose it's possible. I mean, small-town people can be small-minded."

Hood decided to change tack and explore a possible robbery. "We didn't see a safe at the store. Do you know of any hidey-holes—false floorboards, wall panels, that sort of thing—where he may have stashed money or other valuables?"

Adam and Irene shook their heads.

"Okay." Hood hoped his expression didn't reveal his disappointment. With nothing to bolster his theories, he would need to re-evaluate motive. "I'll be in touch when we can arrange a visit to the store."

* * *

By mid-morning, Hood returned to his office, which was small in comparison to those of other county department heads and not nearly as opulent. His wooden desk—disproportionately large for the space—swivel desk chair and three captain's chairs for visitors were all prison industries' products. The oak surfaces had been smoothed, scarred, and stained from years of use. Despite its basement location, his office featured a window. From a seated posture, his view was tree limbs and sky, but, when standing, the view spanned the courthouse lawn, a single oak tree, and the parking lot beyond.

He appreciated his window, both as a source of light and as a connection to the outdoors. He recalled his downward spiral of alcoholism, a self-imposed descent into darkness, isolation, and confinement. He had insisted his demands be met and—if they weren't—the result was envy, jealousy, and resentment. When desperation drove him to try recovery, his sponsor introduced him to the concept of *enough*. "I don't have everything I want," Matthew had said. "But I have everything I need. I have enough."

Sunlight from the window warmed Hood, as he watched a family of squirrels scamper playfully through the grass and around the oak tree where they had made their nest. Eventually, they turned to the task of burying acorns in preparation for the coming winter.

Hood took that as his cue to return to his desk chair and review the overnight reports, which included a brawl at The Sportsmen's Bar and Grille, a domestic disturbance at an apartment on Shepherd Road, and a theft of tools and building materials from a J&R Builders' trailer at a construction site on Route C. The theft marked the second recent construction site theft. He jotted a note to confer with Wally, who had filed the report, lifted his empty coffee cup, and headed for the coffee maker located on a counter near the dispatcher's station.

As he refilled his cup, he turned to his veteran dispatcher, Maggie O'Brien. "Need a warmer?"

"Of course."

While he poured, he indulged in a grateful, almost whimsical, reflection. Maggie had been the night shift dispatcher when Hood joined the department as a rookie deputy. After 24 years working together—the last decade with Hood as her boss—he conceded she knew him as well as anyone. At age sixty-two, Maggie was nearing retirement age but not interested. Hood was relieved, because he considered her irreplaceable. She was capable, dependable, and her institutional knowledge was unsurpassed. In addition to her duties, she served as de-facto counselor, mentor, and matriarch for the department.

When Hood returned the coffee pot to the burner, he noticed Howard DeWesplore at the window separating the department from the foyer. "Could you buzz Howard in?" Hood asked Maggie.

The fingerprint analyst entered. As the door closed automatically, he said, "Sorry, Francis, I don't have an appointment, but I was hoping I could catch you for a few minutes."

"Sure. Coffee?"

"Thanks. Black is fine."

Hood filled a disposable cup, handed it to Howard, and led the way to the office. His guest sat in one of the three chairs facing the desk, and Hood occupied a similar chair at the end of the row, leaving a vacant seat between them. When a conversation was not official business, the sheriff intentionally avoided the intimidation suggested by his massive oak desk and high-backed chair.

"Everything going okay at the lab?" Hood inquired, curious about the nature of the surprise visit.

"Yes," Howard answered. "Well, yes and no."

Silence gathered. Hood had learned silence could be an effective prompt, so he reached for the coffee he had left cooling on his desk and sipped. "This is probably none of my business," Howard added, "but I saw you at the lab with Sandra the other day, and I was wondering if you noticed anything—I don't know—odd or unusual about her."

Hood set his cup on the desk. Some indefinable something about Sandra's demeanor had puzzled him, too. "What do you mean, exactly?"

"She's gotten a few phone calls lately, and I've noticed that, afterward, she's visibly upset. Sometimes, she rushes to the ladies' room."

"Do you know who the caller is?"

"No. Not really," Howard answered. "I'm guessing it's her ex-boyfriend, but I don't know that for sure."

"Ex-boyfriend?" Hood asked.

"Name's Eric—Eric Rakestraw. They were going out for a while. He would often wait in the hallway—you could see him through the glass doors—until she finished her shift. Based on what she said, he was a recruit at the Patrol Academy at the time. But I guess things went sour because I haven't seen him lately."

Hood recalled the name. Dennis Vivion had referred to Sandra as "Eric Rakestraw's girlfriend" when he approached their table at Chubb's bar. "How long were they dating?" Hood asked.

Howard shrugged. "About two months."

"When did you notice he stopped showing up at the lab?"

"I don't know. Maybe a week ago."

"And when did you start noticing the phone calls and Sandra's behavior?"

"That's the thing. It pretty much started right after he stopped showing up."

"Do you suspect he's harassing her?"

"I'm just concerned. We've been working together for a while now. She's a good person."

"She is," Hood agreed.

"I didn't know if she said anything to you. I don't feel comfortable asking her about it. I mean, we work together, plus we're both single."

Hood sipped coffee as he contemplated how to respond. "She mentioned something about a bad breakup but didn't offer any details. Of course, I can see how it might be a sore subject. She and I are working on a case together, so I'll keep my eyes and ears open."

"Thanks, Sheriff. I care about her." Howard stood, then added, "I mean, I care about all of my co-workers."

"Of course." Hood arose, and the two men shook hands.

"I almost forgot," Howard said. "I did find upside-down fingerprints on the guitar neck—three sets, in fact—but none are in our database."

After Howard left, Hood made a note about the fingerprints and added it to the file.

* * *

Hood sat in a booth at Millie's Diner and awaited Matthew's arrival.

A familiar waitress, Nadine, approached and asked if he wanted coffee.

"Sure. I'm waiting for somebody," he added, as if sitting alone in a booth constituted a crime.

Nadine scanned the sparse crowd, filled his cup, and promised to return.

The sheriff removed his cell phone from a pocket and scanned his messages. When he looked up, Matthew was sliding onto the seat across the table.

"Thanks for coming," Hood said.

"Of course."

"I hate to bother you with something that's probably trivial."

"If it's on your mind, it's important to you. What's up?"

"I've been asked to sponsor somebody in recovery."

"Congratulations," Matthew said.

"But I'm not sure if I'm ready," Hood said.

"Why not?"

Hood had adjusted to Matthew's habit of answering a question with a question. At first, he was piqued by the practice, but he had come to understand it was Matthew's way of leading questioners to solve problems on their own. "For one thing, I've only been in the program about fifteen months. There are plenty of guys who have more recovery time."

"All of us are somewhere on the continuum of recovery. There's no minimum requirement. It's the quality, not quantity, of recovery that matters."

"Do you think I'm ready?"

"I don't think that's the issue. Would you like to do it?"

Hood lifted his coffee cup but didn't sip. "I already said yes. It was a spur-of-the-moment thing. Now I'm having second thoughts."

"When I have second thoughts," Matthew said, "they're based on fear."

Hood pondered while he sipped coffee. "I guess I'm afraid I won't be good enough, that he could find somebody better."

"There's always somebody better. That doesn't mean you're not competent and capable."

"So you think I should do it?"

"Only you can answer that. The first time I was asked to sponsor someone, I wanted reassurance, so I asked my sponsor, much like you're doing now. He reminded me sponsorship wasn't about me, and it certainly wasn't about inflating my ego. He advised me to do some prayer, meditation, and self-analysis, then act according to what my heart, mind, and intuition suggested."

"But what if I'm lousy at it?"

"Sponsorship isn't brain surgery. My job as a sponsor is to share what helps keep me sober."

"What if he gets drunk?"

"I have to remind myself I can't get anybody else drunk, and I can't make them sober. I don't have that kind of power, and serving as a sponsor doesn't give me that power. I can't take credit if a sponsee stays sober, and I can't blame myself if a sponsee gets drunk."

Hood recalled his conversation with Brian and sharing the recovery slogan—*simple, but not easy*. Matthew had made sponsorship sound simple, but Hood suspected it might be far from easy.

# Chapter Nine

Brian sat in a corner chair—upholstered, according to Jessie, in burnt sienna—amid the earth tones that dominated the living area of her apartment. He fixated on a wall hanging made of braided ropes and twines of various thicknesses and colors, including shades of cream, taupe, bronze, and beige.

He hated the item—he refused to call it an artwork—hung above the sofa and displayed as a focal point of the room. He recalled the day Jessie had invited Michelle and him to see her new purchase. He recalled making some banal comment—perhaps "interesting"—but withheld his true sentiments until afterward, when he and Michelle were alone.

"What did you think of it?" he had asked Michelle.

"She's obviously very proud of it."

"That's not what I asked. I don't get it. It's not like her at all. I don't think it reflects her tastes, her personality, anything."

"It's her apartment," Michelle had protested.

"It's horrid."

Now—sitting in the room with Jessie, Michelle, and David—a new thought intruded. His recovery program had suggested self-analysis as a way to see from other people's perspectives. What, he asked himself, if Jessie was attracted to the wall hanging because she considered it an expression of *not Jessie?* And what if his dislike of the item was rooted in his fear that he also was a symbol of *not Jessie?* He always had been insecure about being Jessie's boyfriend. He felt he didn't measure up, didn't deserve her. He never had understood, or become comfortable with, the reasons why she had agreed to date him.

His musings were interrupted when Jessie stepped into the archway from the kitchen and said, "Thanks for coming."

"Sure," Michelle said. She was clad in a mocha sweater, which complemented the ocher sofa. David, who was perched on a kitchen chair he dragged into the living area, wore a red Kansas City Chiefs sweatshirt that clashed with the decor. "I could use a beer. Got any beer, Jessie?" he asked.

"In the fridge."

He stood. "Anyone else?" he asked as he squeezed past Jessie.

"No, thanks," Jessie answered.

"I'll take one," Michelle said.

"None for me," Brian said.

Jessie waited until the bottles were distributed, and David was seated. "I wanted to let you all know that my Uncle Chet is in some kind of coma, so he hasn't been able to tell anyone what happened."

"I'm still not sure what, exactly, did happen," Brian said.

"Like I told you," Jessie answered. "We were drinking at my parents' house. I took their keys to my uncle's store because I wanted you to see it. We let ourselves in after hours, and we found him lying on the floor, bleeding from his head, so we called 9-1-1 and took off."

"I don't feel good about leaving him there," Michelle said.

"None of us feels good about it," Jessie said. "He's my uncle, for heaven's sake. But he'd been assaulted. We'd have to explain why we were there. We'd all be suspects. We had to leave. We had no choice."

"We could have chosen to stay," Michelle said.

"Whoa," David said, exasperated. "We've already agreed we're all in this together, and we aren't calling the authorities."

"Who's we?" Brian asked. "I didn't agree to anything."

"You were so out of it you were either drunk or asleep," David said. "So, yeah, the three of us decided. I don't see what we're arguing about. What's done is done. We can't call the cops now. How would that look?"

"That's why I wanted us to get together," Jessie said. "It's important that we stick together. Right, David?"

"Absolutely."

Jessie shifted her focus to Michelle.

"I don't feel good about this, but, like I said the other night, I'll keep my mouth shut."

"Brian?" Jessie said, her tone expectant.

Brian looked at his shoes. "I didn't even go in," he muttered.

"Now you're starting to piss me off," David said, his anger rising. "Don't sit there and sulk like a baby. And if you're thinking about calling the cops and cutting some kind of deal, think again. There's no place for rats in—"

Brian lifted his head and stared at David. "I'm not a rat," he protested.

"I hope not," David said, "but you get knee-walking drunk every night, and when you're like that, there's no telling what you'll do."

"We're working on that," Jessie said. "He's been going to meetings."

"But nothing's changed," David said. He guzzled the remainder of his beer. "Having a drunk for a friend is getting old. I can't count on you for anything."

Brian again lowered his head, cowering like a whipped puppy. "I don't know why bad shit always happens to me."

"This isn't just about you," Jessie countered. "This happened to all of us, and now we all need to stick together." She looked at each of her friends, focusing last on Brian. "I need you to promise me, Brian, you're with us on this."

Brian hesitated momentarily, then nodded.

"Say it," David insisted.

"I promise."

* * *

"Hold up."

David's shout was overpowered by the drone of the leaf blower, operated by a Monroe College maintenance worker clearing the brick walkways linking campus buildings. David trotted ahead, bypassing the worker, and caught up with Jessie. He tapped her on the shoulder.

When she stopped and faced him, he said, "We need to talk." His black fleece jacket was unzipped, and the Chiefs logo on his red tee-shirt remained visible.

"We talked this morning. Besides, I have a class."

"This won't take long. I'm worried about Brian."

"And I'm worried about Michelle."

"Don't be," David said. "I've got it under control."

"That's why I'm worried," Jessie said. "Michelle's not an 'it.' She's a person with a mind of her own. You might think she's under your control, but she's not."

"You don't think so, huh," David said, his tone defensive. "But I'll bet you think you've got Brian wrapped around your little finger."

"No, but I think he'll listen to reason, and I think he'll eventually agree the best thing is to say nothing."

"Well, that's what I meant. Michelle will listen to reason."

"Fine," Jessie said. "I've got to go. I have a class."

She began walking, and David matched her step for step. "You know," he said, "maybe we should talk some more. Lunch, maybe, after your class. You're pretty sharp, the way you pick up on things."

"I'm meeting Brian for lunch."

"Yeah, well, I can't for the life of me figure out how you two got together. He's—"

"Stop, David." She put a finger to his lips. "Don't say any more." She turned, trotted up the concrete steps, and disappeared inside the building.

# Chapter Ten

Hood approached the coffee maker at the same time Maggie arose from her seat to assist a visitor standing at the glass partition designed to serve walk-in traffic.

As Hood filled his cup, he recalled a time—not long ago—when the sheriff's department was not separated from the public by locked doors and bulletproof glass.

"Francis?"

Hood turned to the familiar voice and saw Brian at the window.

"You two know each other?" Maggie asked.

"Yes," both men said, almost simultaneously.

"Go ahead and buzz him in, Maggie," Hood said.

Once inside, an obviously puzzled Brian studied Hood's uniform. "You're the sheriff?"

Hood nodded. "Let's talk in my office." He led the way and, this time, he sat at his desk, which displayed a bronze nameplate, a gift from Maggie, that read: *I'm Your Sheriff, Francis Hood*. Although intended as a gag gift to mock Hood's customary way of introducing himself, he cherished the item.

"I had no idea you were the sheriff," Brian said.

"At the meetings, I'm just another alcoholic. Matthew and I are the only ones who know what I do—maybe a few others if they've seen pictures of me in uniform." When Brian remained in what seemed like stunned silence, Hood added, "If you want to reconsider having me as a sponsor, I understand."

"No," Brian said. "It just caught me off guard."

"What can I do for you?" Hood asked.

"My brother's missing. The one I told you about."

"I remember."

"He sent me a text the other night—the night I asked you to be my sponsor." Brian retrieved his phone, recovered the text message, and showed it to Hood. "He didn't come home that night or all day yesterday. His truck's gone, too. I've called and texted him a bunch of times, but no response."

Hood tapped his keyboard and called up a missing-person form on the monitor. As he keyed in the time, date, and content of the phone message, Brian asked, "How long do we have to wait before we file a missing person report? Is it like forty-eight hours or something?"

"Only on television or in movies," Hood replied. "We're going to do that right now, so I need to ask you some questions."

"Okay."

"First, I need your contact information. Full name?"

"Brian Anthony Rakestraw."

The surname flashed in Hood's memory. Although Rakestraw was not an unfamiliar name in Huhman County, Hood had heard it twice recently. Both Dennis Vivion and Howard DeWesplore had identified Sandra's exboyfriend as a Rakestraw. The sheriff turned from the computer and faced Brian. "What's your brother's name?"

"Eric. Our address—"

"Hold on." Hood puzzled over the Rakestraw connection and what it meant. He returned his fingers to the keyboard, asked a series of questions, and entered the information.

Brian reported he and his brother lived in their deceased parents' house on Route D. Although Schweinshaupten was the mailing address, the residence was about a mile outside the town's boundary.

Hood also keyed in Eric's age, 29; marital status, single; physical description, tall, athletic build, brown hair, and eyes. He entered a description of Eric's truck—a white 2018 Ford F-150 pickup—and requested a recent photo of Eric, which Brian forwarded to Hood's cell.

Although Eric currently was unemployed, Brian said, "My brother always wanted to be a cop—I'm sorry, police officer—and he worked for the St. Gotthard PD for a while, but it didn't work out. He tried the Highway Patrol Academy to become a trooper, but that didn't work out either."

"What can you tell me about the people he associates with?" Hood asked, intentionally adding, "Does he have a girlfriend?"

"When he was at the academy, he was seeing a girl named Sandra. I met her a couple times. She seemed like a real nice person."

"Last name?"

"I never knew it. I think she also worked for the patrol, but she wasn't, like, a trooper or anything."

Hood leaned back in his chair. The link between Sandra and Eric, coupled with Sandra's unusual behavior, elevated his concern. "What about other friends, people he spent time with?"

"He mostly hung out with some guys from Schweinshaupten. For a while, he was hosting keg parties at our house, but he stopped when people started getting trashed and tearing up the place."

"Do you remember any names?"

"One guy they called Hunk, which I thought was funny, because he was like the skinniest person I've ever seen. And there was this laid-back dude who went by a girl's name, Vivian."

"It's a last name," Hood interjected. "Vivion with an 'o.'"

"There were others, but they were all older than me, so I kept my distance. I'd wait until everybody got really blotto, and then I'd start hitting the keg. That's how this whole drinking thing got out of control."

Hood waited a beat after Brian finished, then asked, "Anything else?"

"No. So what's next?"

"First, I'll print you a copy of this report so you can verify the information. Then I'll file it with some agencies that go by acronyms. Plus, you've given me some names of people I can talk to who might have more information."

"Sounds like a lot of trouble. I hate to put you through all that if he's just on some kind of a bender."

"Do you think that's the case?" Hood asked.

"I don't know," Brian said. "That text has me thinking something's wrong."

\* \* \*

Hood suspected trying to locate a person he'd never met would be like chasing a ghost. He'd done what was required by filing the report with the Missouri Uniform Law Enforcement System (MULES) and the National Crime Information Center (NCIC). He'd called Eric's number—no answer— and printed a copy of his photo. But he knew nothing about Eric Rakestraw or what made him tick.

Although he was eager to talk with Sandra about her relationship with Eric, he decided to wait until her workday ended. In the meantime, he called Ron Buschjost, a longtime acquaintance and a shift commander at the St. Gotthard Police Department.

"I've got a missing person," Hood told Ron. "My information is he used to work for your department, but I've never met the guy. I know you can't discuss specific personnel, but I'd appreciate anything you can tell me."

"You have time to stop by?" Ron asked.

"Sure. When?"

"I've got time now."

"I'm on my way."

When Hood arrived, Ron met him in the lobby. As he escorted the sheriff to his office, the two men exchanged pleasantries and updates about their families. Inside the small, windowless room, Hood felt immediate discomfort, not caused by claustrophobia, but by clutter. The surroundings reminded him of *One Man's Trash...*, with precarious stacks of paper, reports, and books substituting for furniture, equipment, and memorabilia.

Ron scooped a parcel of documents from the lone visitor's chair. "Have a seat," he invited.

As Hood eased onto the chair, Ron climbed over a cardboard box to get behind his desk and said, "Sorry about the mess. We're out of space here, so— in my spare time—I'm trying to convert these personnel files from paper to electronic before they store 'em in some warehouse somewhere." He chuffed an abbreviated laugh. "Spare time. What a joke. It's been like this for nearly a year."

"I hear you." Hood's acknowledgement was a courtesy. He couldn't live like this for a week, let alone a year.

"What's the name of your missing person?" Ron asked.

"I'm aware of confidentiality protocols," Hood said, apologetically. "I know—"

"His name, Francis?"

"Eric Rakestraw."

Ron's expression indicated he was familiar with the former officer. He folded his hands on the desktop. "You and I both know specifics can come back to bite you in the ass, so I'm going to speak in generalities. This is just me and you talking police work. Okay?"

"Absolutely."

"I like to think police work is built on partnerships, teamwork. There's this stereotype about cops on the take, bad apples. That may be true in the big cities—I don't know, I've never worked in one—but I haven't found that here. There's just not enough graft and corruption to make it worthwhile."

Hood nodded.

"The problem I find," Ron continued, "is not crooked cops, it's cops who aren't team players. Partnerships are part of the job. Partners need to be comfortable with each other; they have to trust each other to make split-second, sometimes life-or-death, decisions. There's no room for error, and there's no place for someone who's selfish or independent. Once you get that reputation, you become a pariah no one wants to work with, let alone partner with you."

Again, Hood nodded.

"Some applicants fit the mold," Ron added. "They're team players. Others, not so much. They get into law enforcement for all the wrong reasons."

Hood knew the type. He had worked with people who craved authority and hoped a badge and gun would give them stature.

"I get the picture," Hood said. The picture was troubling, but at least it was becoming clearer.

* * *

"The fucking sheriff?" Jessie said.

"Keep your voice down," Brian pleaded. "I didn't know he was the sheriff when I asked him." The two were seated side by side on a wooden picnic bench in Huhman County Park. They were alone except for walkers and joggers—solitary or in groups of two or more—interspersed along the trail circling the lake. "Besides," he added, defensively, "you were the one who asked me to get a sponsor."

"I didn't tell you to ask the sheriff! You know he's investigating the attack on my uncle. He was quizzing my parents at the hospital and my mom told me he also came by the house."

"I didn't know," Brian said, his tone defensive. "The recovery program is based on anonymity. We only use first names at the meeting. Everybody just called him Francis. He wasn't in uniform or anything."

"So, how did you find out he's the sheriff?"

"My brother's missing. I went to the sheriff's department to file a report and there he was in uniform."

"Eric's missing?"

"Yes."

"Why didn't you tell me?"

"I'm telling you now. I didn't want you to worry."

"Are you doing okay?" Jessie asked, her tone softening.

Brian's gaze wandered to two elderly ladies who maintained a brisk pace as they circled the lake. "Do you mean, have I been drinking?"

"Have you?"

"Not a lot. Sometimes I get so keyed up, I need something to take the edge off."

"How long has Eric been missing?"

"A couple days."

"Look at me," Jessie said. She waited until her distracted boyfriend focused on her. "You know he's probably on one of those three- or four-day binges. He's probably passed out on someone's sofa."

"I know," Brian conceded, wounded by the reminder of the struggles he and his brother had inherited.

"I mean, it's not like he hasn't done it before."

"I know," Brian repeated, "but this time, he sent me a text. It was almost like he expected something bad might happen."

"What'd it say?"

Brian retrieved his phone and scrolled through his messages. "Here it is. *Weird shit happening. If you don't hear from me tomorrow, call the authorities.*"

"Do you know what weird shit he was referring to?"

"No idea."

They lapsed into silence and—when it became awkward—both turned their attention to walkers and joggers circumnavigating the lake at varying paces.

"I'm curious," Jessie said, finally. "If anonymity's such a big deal, why did you tell me the sheriff is in recovery?"

"I wrestled with that. I did. But the program's also based on honesty. I didn't want to keep a secret from you. I don't know if there's a difference between anonymity and secrets, but I need to be honest with you."

"Thanks." Jessie leaned and kissed him on the cheek. "I appreciate that."

"And I thought if I shared this secret with you, you might trust me enough to tell me what really happened."

"What do you mean?"

"Did you guys really find your uncle unconscious?"

"I don't believe this," Jessie said. She arose from the bench. "You think one of us attacked him, don't you? You think we made up some story—" She stopped in mid-sentence. "David was right."

"David? What did he say?"

"Forget it." She turned, and Brian reached for her sleeve, but she yanked her arm free and briskly walked away.

"No, wait," he hollered as he jumped up from the bench. "Jessie," he called. His gut told him to chase after her, but he knew this was not the time.

# Chapter Eleven

Hood parked his cruiser, walked to the front door of Sandra's townhouse, and rang the bell. He had called ahead to arrange the visit but hadn't disclosed the reason.

She opened the door, greeted him, and stepped aside, allowing him to enter under the watchful yellow eyes of Lady Jane. With the exception of white toes on her front paws, the cat was entirely gray—a nod to her namesake, Lady Jane Grey. "Is this about the case?" Sandra asked.

"Not exactly."

"You sound serious. Let's go to the kitchen. It's the brightest room." She led him through a spartan living area into a kitchen dominated by white cabinets, chrome appliances, and aqua accents. "Something to drink?" she asked, motioning him to an oval table centered in the room.

"No thanks." They sat at the table facing each other. Lady Jane curled herself on the cushion of a chair perpendicular to them. "I don't know how to bring this up, but you and I are friends, and I think we can be honest with each other."

"What's going on, Francis?"

"Do you know a man named Eric Rakestraw?"

She made a disgusted, plosive sound.

"Is that a yes?"

"He's an ex—I don't even know if boyfriend's the right word. We went out a few times, but it didn't work out."

"Is this the bad breakup you mentioned the other night at Chubb's?"

Sandra nodded.

"How did you meet?"

"I typically bring my lunch to work and eat on one of the benches in that grove between the crime lab and the headquarters building. He walked by one day, introduced himself as a Patrol Academy recruit, and asked if he could share my bench."

"When was this?"

"A couple months ago. I'm going to say late July or early August. It was during that dry spell."

Hood nodded acknowledgement.

"I like to eat lunch alone, but I was finished, so I said okay. We talked a little—he seemed like a nice guy—and he showed up again the next day and the day after that. That's when he asked me out."

"You said the breakup was bad. I know this is personal stuff, but can you tell—"

"What's this all about, Francis?"

"Eric Rakestraw is missing."

"Since when?"

"Since two days ago. His brother reported it yesterday."

"Brian?"

"You know Brian?"

"We've met. Nice kid. Is Eric missing, or is he just, you know—" She shrugged. "Eric doesn't have a job. He's not accountable to anyone. Adults don't have to check in; they can go anywhere they want."

"I know," Hood said, "but Brian's concerned. He got a strange text from Eric. Something about contacting the authorities if you don't hear from me."

"That does sound strange," Sandra agreed.

"That's why I'm here. When you two were dating, was Eric involved in anything—did he say or do anything—that seemed unusual?"

"No, but I didn't know him that well."

"What can you tell me about him?"

"Not a lot. I dated him because, when we met, he seemed gentle, sensitive even. On our first date, we went to a movie, and it was fine. Then he took me to a concert, and afterward we went to his house, which is the house he inherited after his parents died. That's when I started getting a bad vibe. He became progressively more demanding. And it happened quickly. Let's just say I'm attracted to tenderness, and he started getting rougher than I like." She stopped, seemingly lost in reflection as she reached to pet Lady Jane.

"Was that when you ended the relationship?"

"No." She folded her hands in her lap. "Eric asked me to go with him to the Schweinshaupten Fall Festival last month. They have music, kids' games, and they serve really good barbecued pork steaks and pulled pork sandwiches. It's a daytime family event, and it's well-attended, so I felt okay about it. We were enjoying ourselves, but then some of Eric's Schweinshaupten friends met up with us, and they all got really drunk and started acting obnoxious."

"Do you remember the names of any of these friends?"

"One was Dennis, the guy who came to our table at Chubb's the night of the assault."

"Dennis Vivion," Hood said.

"Yes. Another guy they called Hunk, which I thought was weird because he was skin and bones. Some others would come and go, but all I remember is they mostly used crude nicknames—like shit-face or ass-wipe—to refer to each other. Thankfully, I had my own vehicle, so I left." Sandra inhaled and released a long breath. "Eric called the next day, but I told him it wasn't working out, and I wasn't interested in seeing him again."

"How'd he take it?"

"At first, he was all apologies. He said he was sorry he drank too much and acted like he did, and it wouldn't happen again. He pleaded, pretty much begged, for me to keep seeing him. I said 'no way,' and he got really angry. He said some pretty ugly things."

"Was that the last time you talked to him?"

"No. He called the crime lab phone the day you were there. I didn't know it was Eric until I answered."

"I remember that phone call," Hood said. "You seemed upset."

"I don't know the criminal definition of stalking, but—" She stopped mid-sentence and gradually pushed herself back against the chair. "You said Eric's missing. Am I a suspect?"

"No," Hood said, realizing he'd waited a beat too long to be convincing. "It's just that I've noticed you've been acting differently."

"Has it been that obvious?"

"Maybe it's more obvious to me because of what you've told me."

"The OCD?" Sandra asked.

Hood nodded.

"It's gotten worse. And there's something else I struggle with that's kicked in again."

Hood folded his hands, elbows on the table, and rested his chin on his fingers.

"Ever heard of somatic OCD?" Sandra asked.

"No. Is that some form of what you've got?"

"It is," she affirmed. "You know I've said how my obsessive behavior can be a blessing and a curse in my job?"

Hood nodded.

"Well, somatic OCD is a curse—period. It's a neurological condition that involves obsessive thoughts or compulsive actions about automatic bodily functions, such as breathing, heartbeats, swallowing, blinking, etc. People can get so obsessed with a routine activity, sometimes they can't do it at all."

"How can that be? You have to breathe. Your heart has to beat."

"That's the thing," Sandra said. "Most people don't think about those things. They just happen. But with somatic OCD, the brain fixates on what should be an automatic, unconscious function and disrupts the process. And the disruption triggers fears and anxieties and panic attacks, and everything goes haywire."

"And you have this?"

"I have a form of it. For me, it's swallowing. When I start thinking about eating or drinking, I can't stop worrying about swallowing, and I become fixated on whether I can do it. Sometimes, I can't even swallow my own saliva."

Hood's memory flashed to the untouched glass of water in front of her at Chubb's and, with it, the realization he had never seen her eat or drink anything. "What do you do when that happens?"

"I spit it out. That's why, sometimes, I excuse myself and go to the ladies' room. Some days, I can only swallow under certain conditions. I've become accustomed to having lunch on the bench outside the crime lab because I can swallow sometimes if I'm alone and I'm not seated at a table."

"Sounds horrible," Hood said.

"That's not the worst of it. It affects my entire life. That's why I don't go out for coffee, go to bars, go out to eat. I know people think I'm antisocial or something, but that's not true. What's true is it's embarrassing being stuck with a mouthful of something you can't swallow. I was seeing a counselor who has some experience treating this kind of thing, but she's in St. Louis, so it's about a five-hour round trip. Once I started to improve, I stopped going. I guess I need to rethink that."

Hood's mind conjured a mental comparison of alcoholics he had met who had quit drinking, assumed they were fine, stopped working a program of recovery, and got drunk. "So," he asked, "it's a neurological condition, not a physical one?"

"Exactly. There's no corrective surgical or medical procedure, and the only drugs that would help would leave me too catatonic to function. The only effective therapy is ERP, exposure, and response prevention."

Hood leaned back in his chair. "I had no idea you were dealing with this."

"Most people don't," Sandra said. "It's not something I talk about. I've become accustomed to masking it and acting as if nothing's wrong."

"Well, I'm glad you shared it with me."

"I felt I had to. Stress and anxiety make everything worse, and I've suffered some setbacks lately. And hearing about Eric being missing doesn't help."

"I'm sorry," Hood said.

"Don't be sorry. It's part of your job. I understand."

* * *

Hood traveled eastbound on Highway 50 and, although he attempted to focus on the upcoming meeting with Adam and Irene Surface, Sandra's disclosure dominated his thoughts. How, he wondered, could she live with such a debilitating condition? If she constantly worried about whether she could swallow, how could she concentrate on anything else?

He occasionally experienced obsessive thoughts, but nothing like what she described. His had occurred primarily when he was younger. He recalled walking home from school and having a thought that if he didn't pick up a piece of litter—a candy bar wrapper or scrap of paper—something bad would happen. Sometimes, he would pass it by and walk a block or so before his obsession compelled him to go back and pick it up. He remembered the debate that went on in his head. Logic argued no connection existed between picking up trash and suffering consequences, but an intrusive voice cautioned: Why risk what you can easily avoid?

The obsession created its own problems. The walk to or from school took about twice as long, and he arrived at his destination with pockets full of trash. He recalled the first occasion when he had intentionally defied the obsession. He waited for something bad to happen, but it never did. So he tried it repeatedly, each time without consequence. He wondered now if he had adopted some unconscious, practical version of what Sandra called ERP, exposure and response prevention.

But, he contemplated, what if he hadn't? What if those obsessive thoughts had remained into adulthood? How would his life—his family, his career, his recovery—be different if obsessive thoughts and compulsive behaviors dictated his day-to-day existence?

As he turned onto Route D, he attempted to transform his thoughts into a simple appreciation of the colorful foliage lining both sides of the roadway. Although he was no horticulturalist, much of his youth had been spent with his father, fishing farm ponds and hiking trails. And he had learned, seemingly through osmosis, to identify the oak, maple, hickory, and other varieties of trees, as well as the reds, oranges, and yellows they produced before surrendering to winter. The wildflowers, he noticed, also were changing their hues, displaying arrays of gold, purple, olive, and auburn.

The natural palette was left behind as a white sign with black letters welcomed him to the blocks of brick buildings and concrete sidewalks of downtown Schweinshaupten. Hood steered his cruiser to the curb in front of *One Man's Trash...*, where Adam and Irene Surface were standing out front. Irene seemed to shiver in the sunny, but chilly, October afternoon.

Hood exited his vehicle. "Sorry," he said. "Have you been waiting long?"

"We just got here," Irene said.

As Hood opened the padlock Wally had installed, Irene said, "Jessie didn't come. I assume she's at the riding stable or out somewhere with Brian."

The name seized Hood's attention. "Brian?" he asked.

"Her boyfriend," Irene clarified. "Brian Rakestraw. Do you know him?"

"I know a Brian Rakestraw," Hood said, "but you can't throw a rock in Huhman County without hitting a Rakestraw."

"You got that right," Adam agreed.

"Is he also a student at Monroe College?" Hood asked.

"Yes," Irene answered as they crossed the threshold. She and Adam stopped just inside the doorway, as if neither knew what to do next. "I wish I had some idea of what we were looking for," Irene said.

"It's not so much what's here as what's missing," Hood said. "Concentrate on what seems out of place, what's been moved, what isn't here."

"Where do we start?" Irene asked.

"Doesn't matter," Hood replied. "But stay together, and don't be afraid to mention anything that seems unusual or out of place. I'll be with you to make notes, and we'll go through room by room, this floor, and upstairs."

The inspection began. Hood was pleased that Adam and Irene moved slowly and deliberately, scrutinizing the interior and the merchandise on display. He was disappointed that they said little, and nothing they mentioned seemed helpful to the investigation. They had nearly finished their inspection of the second floor when Adam's cell phone sounded.

He answered, listened, then said, "We'll be right there."

"What?" Irene asked.

"It's the hospital," Adam answered. They want us to come right away."

"Is everything all right?" Irene asked, her anxiety apparent.

"I don't know," Adam replied. "Are we done here, Sheriff?"

"Yes," Hood said. "I'll follow you."

\* \* \*

Dr. Williams intercepted the trio at the second-floor nurses' station and invited them into a windowless, rectangular enclosure.

The room was designed to comfort, from its wallpaper—green tendrils and blue trumpet flowers set against an off-white background—to its soft furnishings in muted colors. Hood didn't see a sharp edge anywhere.

"Have a seat, please," the doctor invited.

Irene selected a love seat, which seemed to cushion and embrace her body. Adam remained standing, his expression stoic. Hood perched on the edge of a chair.

"I'm sorry to have to tell you this," Dr. Williams said solemnly, "but Mr. Groner has passed away earlier this morning."

Irene released a pained moan, followed by arrhythmic sobs she attempted to squelch.

Adam grimaced.

Hood respectfully withheld the questions that tumbled in his mind.

"I knew it," Irene blurted. "I'm sorry." She waved a hand in front of her face as if to disperse her tears. "I thought I'd prepared myself for this, but—" Leaving the sentence incomplete, she added, "Did he suffer?"

"No," the doctor replied. "He never regained consciousness."

"So there were no final words?" Irene asked, voicing a question that was on Hood's mind.

"No," Dr. Williams answered. "He died peacefully."

"I guess we can find some solace in that," Adam said, his tone soothing.

Hood, however, found no solace in the development—his assault investigation had become a murder case.

# Chapter Twelve

"My uncle died," Jessie said.

Her classmates—Brian, David, and Michelle—again had gathered in her apartment, at her request.

"I'm so sorry," Brian said. Seated beside her on the sofa, he took her hand and held it.

"Did he ever come to?" David asked. "Did he tell anyone what happened?"

"No," Jessie answered.

"That's a relief," David responded.

"David," Michelle said. "What a horrible thing to say."

"What? I didn't mean it that way. I'm just saying what we're all thinking."

"I just don't know about you sometimes," Michelle said.

"It's okay," Jessie said, trying to smooth the discord.

"Is there anything we can do, Jessie?" Michelle asked.

"I don't think so, but thanks," Jessie said. "My parents will be making the arrangements, but I'll keep you posted."

"Just let us know," Michelle said.

The exchange between the two women triggered Brian's curiosity. He had sensed, on multiple occasions, some special bond among women he never had experienced or witnessed among men. Was it a shared trust, compassion, understanding, or something else? He never had experienced that type of connection with other men, and he wondered if he was missing out. Eric, David, and other men he knew seemed so at ease in male company, trading barbs, banter, even insults. He knew he was uncomfortable in those situations; what he didn't know was why.

His musing continued as the conversation switched to everyday issues—overly demanding professors, other students' immature behavior, problems with parents—before the gathering broke up. After David and Michelle left the apartment, Jessie stopped Brian as he put on his coat. "We need to go back to Uncle Chet's store," she said.

"Why?"

"I need to get something."

"What?"

"Uncle Chet left something for me."

"What?" Brian repeated.

"Some money. He had a stash he was saving for me. He showed me where he kept it. He said I could have some or all of it any time I wanted. That's one reason why I took you guys there the other night. I needed some money. But after we found him, I knew we had to get out of there."

"We can't go back to a crime scene," Brian said. "What if someone sees us this time?"

"It'll only take a few minutes."

"Can't it wait until everything's over—the funeral and all? At some point, your parents will start closing things up and auctioning what's left. There will be plenty of time—"

"I can't take that chance. The money's in a hidden compartment in an old desk. What if somebody who knows about that sort of stuff—the auctioneer or an antique dealer—finds it? What if my folks sell the desk to somebody?"

"Jessie." Brian pronounced the syllables as a plea.

"Please."

Even as he framed additional arguments opposing the idea, he knew he would give in to her.

* * *

Twenty-One Curves was a rite of passage for teen drivers at Huhman County High School and a bane of the sheriff's department.

Officially, Rock Hill Road, the winding, seven-mile stretch of two-lane blacktop connected Route B and Old Cedar Creek Road. Its length was bordered on one side by a drainage ditch parallel to a rock cutaway and, on the other, by a ravine channeling shallow water.

The unwritten rules were simple: Any driver who could negotiate the length of the road in record time earned bragging rights, including spray-painting their initials and time on the rocky outcropping.

For the sheriff's department, most emergency calls from Twenty-One Curves required not only a deputy's cruiser, but also an ambulance and wrecker.

Brian steered his frail, weather-beaten Toyota Corolla onto Rock Hill Road not to challenge the record, but because it was the most direct route to his destination. Aware of the yellow "Falling Rocks" sign on his right, he intentionally maintained the speed limit.

When the nondescript pickup truck closed on his rear bumper and loomed largely in his rearview mirror, he silently cursed his bad luck. He was miffed. Why, he asked himself, did everyone seem to be in such a goddamned hurry these days? He feared his leisurely drive would become a nerve-wracking nail-biter. And, he knew from experience, no turnoffs were available to allow a motorist to pass on the winding road.

He glanced again in his rearview mirror and guessed the truck was within a few feet of his rear bumper, too close to see its license plate and, by his estimation, too close to avoid a collision if he braked. The truck was painted a rust color that Brian associated with primer, but something about the pickup seemed oddly familiar. He accelerated slightly to signal his willingness to accommodate the obviously impatient truck driver. And that was when he felt the tap on his bumper. "What the hell," he said aloud. He felt another bumper tap, this one more jarring. When he glanced in the mirror, the truck pulled from behind him into the lane for oncoming traffic.

Brian panicked. His senses heightened, and his heart rate quickened as adrenaline coursed through his body. What, he asked himself, was wrong with this guy? Was he crazy? Was this some bizarre form of unprovoked road rage?

Brian slowed along a short straightaway and waved the driver to pass.

Instead of passing, the driver steered into Brian's front fender, forcing his Corolla off the asphalt and into the drainage ditch, where his grillwork careened into an embedded boulder. The impact propelled Brian forward. His seat belt prevented him from hitting the dash, but the pain in his ribcage was immediate.

He focused on the truck, which had stopped and was idling on the roadway about twenty yards ahead. He felt paralyzed as he tried simultaneously to assess the danger and make sense of the situation. The truck had no license plate and no tailgate, but the body style reminded him of his brother's truck, which—like his brother—was missing. Brian looked into the cab, but the features of the lone driver were concealed by a dark ski mask. As he watched, the truck slowly began to back up toward him.

Brian jammed the gear shift into reverse and stomped on the accelerator. His car seemed almost to jump backward onto the roadway and across the asphalt. Brian pressed the brake as he felt a rear tire slip over the precipice to the ravine. The truck continued backing toward him as he pressed the gas pedal. He heard his left tire spin wildly while the right spewed mud and rock in an attempt to gain purchase. His car didn't budge, and he realized he had no time to abandon the vehicle. He braced himself and watched helplessly as the truck gained momentum, slammed into his front bumper, and pushed him over the precipice.

Unadulterated fear gripped him as his Toyota somersaulted once in an agonizing fit of moaning metal and landed on its wheels.

* * *

When his cell phone sounded, Hood glanced at the display and noted the caller was his chief deputy. "Hood," he answered.

"It's Wally. I'm at the scene of a wreck on Twenty-One Curves. EMTs are loading Brian Rakestraw into an ambulance. He asked me to call you."

"What happened?"

"Don't know yet. From the looks of things, either he ran off the road, or someone ran him off. Looks like his car overturned as it went over the embankment and landed on its wheels in the creek."

"Is he okay?"

"He's talking to the EMTs, so that's a good sign. They'll be transporting him to the hospital if you want to meet them there."

"I'll head there now."

"Okay. I'll work the scene. Keep me posted."

"Will do," Hood said.

When Hood arrived at the hospital, he learned Brian had arrived at the ER and was being treated. He asked an attendant to keep him updated about Brian's condition, then shuffled to the sparsely occupied waiting room.

He collapsed into a chair that appeared comfortable but wasn't. A fundamental of his recovery program—which he tried to apply to all aspects of his life—was action. Lately, however, he seemed mired in inactivity. He had made little progress on the assault of Chester Groner. Similarly, he was no closer to solving a missing person case reported by his first sponsee, Brian, who was now being treated for injuries after what was either an accident or an altercation. Whenever Hood became frustrated and angry—like he was now—Matthew advised him to do a self-assessment. He knew he was wallowing in self-pity, but he was unable to lift himself.

"Sheriff."

The voice startled him from his reverie. Hood looked into the eyes of the nurse who stood in front of him.

He stood. "How is he?"

"Very fortunate. He suffered some minor lacerations and some bruises, largely to the shoulder and ribcage, where the seat belt did its job. I'm told the vehicle flipped over."

"That's my understanding," Hood said.

"He'll be sore for a while, but otherwise, he seems okay. You can talk to him if you'd like."

"Thanks."

She escorted the sheriff to Brian's ER bed, then pulled the curtain as she left.

"I heard you had an accident," Hood said.

"It wasn't an accident. I was run off the road."

"Do you know who it was?"

"It was an older pickup, painted with what looked like rust-colored primer. It had no rear license plate or tailgate, but the style reminded me of my brother's Ford truck."

"What model and year was that?"

"A 2018 F-150, but my brother's is white."

"Could you see the driver?"

"Had a ski mask on. Couldn't see his face."

"Alone?"

"As far as I could tell."

"I'm going to put out a description of the truck," Hood said. "Did you see the wheel covers, notice any dents, other distinguishing features?"

"No."

"Be right back," Hood stepped outside the curtain, relayed the truck description and instructions to dispatch, then returned to Brian's beside. "Last question. Do you think this was a road rage thing, or do you feel like you were deliberately targeted?"

"I didn't do anything to provoke this. And I have no idea who might want—" he began, then stopped abruptly in mid-sentence. "I was on my way to see you."

"Me? Why?"

"I got another text from my brother. I wanted you to see it." Brian attempted to shift position, prompting a painful wince. "My phone's on that table. Press 'Messages.'"

Hood accessed the text, which read: *Tell the authorities to search Sandra's SUV.* The message was sent about two hours ago from Eric Rakestraw's number.

Hood contemplated momentarily, then asked, "Does this make any sense to you?"

Brian shook his head.

# Chapter Thirteen

At the sound of the doorbell, Sandra peeked through the window, saw Hood and Wally, and opened her front door. "Hello," she said. Unable to read the sheriff's dour expression, she added, "Something wrong?"

"I have a warrant to search your SUV," Hood said. He reached out to hand her the document he held.

"My SUV?" she asked as she accepted the document.

"Yes." Hood had known in advance he would detest this chore and decided the only way to do it was by the book. "Is it in the garage?"

"You don't need a warrant, Francis. You could have just asked."

Hood shrugged.

"May I ask what you're looking for?"

"We're acting," Wally interjected, "on information we received."

"From?" Sandra asked.

Hood sensed, from the tone of her voice, her initial curiosity was morphing into irritation.

"A source," Wally said. "May we inspect it?"

She stepped outside, walked to the garage door, and keyed in her access code. When the door lifted, Hood and Wally entered while Sandra folded her arms across her chest and leaned against the garage doorframe. As the two officers carefully examined the SUV's immaculate interior, Sandra quipped, "You know, this is usually my job."

Hood said nothing while he continued to search the floorboards and under the seats. Wally offered a sheepish smile as he moved to the rear of the vehicle and opened the hatch. The search continued in silence until Wally lifted the hinged lid of the spare tire well. "Francis," he called.

Hood came beside him, took a pen from his uniform pocket, and speared, from the metal hub of the spare tire, a silver ring with a green gemstone. He lifted it to eye level, the stone glinting in the brighter light. Hood noticed a hint of red—dried blood, possibly? —in the setting.

"Looks like a man's ring," Wally remarked, as Sandra stepped forward for a closer look.

"Recognize this?" Hood asked her.

"Eric wore a ring like that. Could be his."

"Could be or is?"

"That's an oval peridot in what's called a cabochon setting," Sandra said. "Peridot is the birthstone for August, which is Eric's birthday month. It's either his or a near duplicate. We could run some tests."

"Sandra," Hood cautioned, "you and I both know you can't be—"

"I meant the lab, not me personally."

Hood already had decided to use an independent lab. He abandoned the topic and asked, "Do you have an explanation for why it's here?"

"No."

"Because, if he changed a tire for you, he could have taken it off —"

"No," she repeated.

"Do you recall any times when you left the vehicle unlocked? Does anyone else know the key code—"

"I need—" she managed as she gasped for breath. Sweat began to break out on her forehead, even as tremors shook her shoulders and arms. "I, I need to—excuse me," she stammered as she hurried to the interior door to the kitchen and disappeared inside.

Hood followed, but Sandra was nowhere to be seen.

* * *

Hood preferred not to summon employees to his office. The practice struck him as arrogant and disrespectful.

He arose from his desk chair, walked the few steps to Wally's adjacent office, and stood in the open doorframe. "Got a minute?" he asked, his customary question when requesting a conversation.

"Sure," Wally said, looking up from his computer screen. "My place or yours?"

"Here's fine."

Wally motioned his boss to one of the visitors' chairs, and Hood sat. "What's up?"

"Two things, actually," Hood said. "I noticed you've been working those thefts from construction sites."

"Uh huh," Wally said. "There's been three. Lester worked the first one, but I caught the last two."

"Any notable similarities? You think we've got a theft ring working the area?"

"Hard to tell. I talked to Lester about it but we didn't come to any conclusions. The first one was a Custom Home Improvement trailer out on—hold on." He tapped his keyboard as he watched the computer monitor. "On Shepherd Hills Road on the west side. The second was from some homes in a new subdivision being built by Loethen Construction. That was on Old Highway 50."

"Where?" Hood asked, aware the old highway extended for miles.

"Pretty much central. Near the intersection with Kempker Boulevard."

"Okay."

"And then the most recent was the theft from J&R Builders' site on Route C."

"Which is east," Hood said. "So the locations are all over the county."

"Exactly, but the thefts are similar—power tools, building supplies, expensive stuff. Of course, that's what you're going to get when you rip off construction sites. I put out the word to warn builders and alert pawn shops if any of the tools show up, but, so far, zilch."

"Okay, keep me posted," Hood said. "The other thing is I got the analysis of the ring found in the spare tire compartment of Sandra's SUV. The ring had a partial print and traces of dried blood between the stone and the—what did Sandra call it?"

"Cabochon setting."

"Yeah. The print and the blood both belong to Eric Rakestraw."

Wally grimaced in disbelief.

"I know," Hood agreed. "I can't believe it, either. I keep looking for other explanations. I thought I'd run some ideas by you for a second opinion."

"Sure."

"First," Hood said, "what if Eric planted the ring? He didn't take the break-up well, and Sandra said he was practically stalking her."

"Sounds plausible."

"Except I know Sandra well enough to know she's diligent about locking her house and her vehicle."

"Could he have gotten her car key or a spare key from the house?" Wally asked. "Maybe he copied her car key while they were dating. This Eric guy sounds a little strange to me. Sometimes, those guys plan ahead for any eventuality."

"Possible," said Hood. "I don't know much about the guy. The profile I'm getting makes him sound like the take-charge type who likes to get his way, but there're a lot of blanks to fill in. But if it wasn't him, another possibility is somebody else planted the ring to frame Sandra for Eric's disappearance."

"Who?"

Hood shrugged. "Whoever sent Brian the text that led to us searching her SUV. It could be somebody who's not even on our radar. Somebody who, for some reason, wants to make life miserable for Sandra."

"Sandra's one of the nicest people I know," Wally said.

"She's also intelligent, attractive, and single, which could make a target. Remember that 'Peeping Tom' case that started when the guy fixated on a girl who handed him his fast-food order from a takeout window? Sometimes random people become an object of obsession—they get stalked or watched— and don't even know it."

"So, maybe somebody with a resentment or some random creeper."

"I know it's weak," Hood conceded. "The other possibility—the one I hate to admit—is Sandra attacked Eric, hid the ring in the spare tire compartment, and hadn't gotten around to disposing of it before we found it."

"She didn't seem nervous or concerned about the search. As I recall, she said we didn't need the warrant. She sure freaked when we found the ring, though."

"She did," Hood affirmed, unsure whether her reaction was sparked by guilt, surprise, or some manifestation of her neurological disorder.

"I'm sorry," Wally said. "I can't believe Sandra is capable of hurting someone."

"I agree, but I'm keeping my mind open," Hood said. "Stranger things have happened."

# Chapter Fourteen

Hood noticed Brian wince in pain as he lowered himself into one of the folding chairs they had carried into the basement nursery at St. Cecilia's church, where they had arranged to visit one-on-one before the weekly meeting began.

"You okay?" the sheriff asked.

"Still sore," Brian answered, "and I'm still trying to figure out what's going on."

"Let's talk about that," Hood said. "I need to be straight with you. In my capacity as sheriff, I'm not sure it's appropriate for me to remain as your sponsor."

"You mean because my brother disappeared?"

"That's part of it. His disappearance is an ongoing investigation; you've received texts with relevant information, and now you've also been targeted in a hit-and-run."

"I can't help any of that," Brian said. "I'm just telling you what's been happening."

"I understand," Hood said. He retrieved from his pocket a man's ring sealed in a transparent plastic bag. "Can you identify this?"

Brian examined the piece of jewelry in the bag. "It's Eric's."

"You're sure?"

"Absolutely," Brian answered as he examined the gemstone. There's a flaw, a brownish spot, at the top right of the stone. I can see it even through the plastic. Where'd you get this?"

"I can't say."

"I don't get it." Brian hung his head. "I thought recovery was all about honesty, but honesty doesn't seem to be working because now you're saying you can't tell me where you got my brother's ring and you're telling me you can't be my sponsor anymore."

"It's not that simple," Hood said. "And, as long as we're talking about honesty, your name also came up in another case I'm investigating."

Brian looked up, his facial features pinched in a quizzical expression.

"I learned you're dating Jessie Surface, the niece of Chester Groner, who died after he was assaulted during a break-in at his store."

"I've never even met the guy. Yes, I'm dating Jessie, but it seems like all this shit is happening around me, and I'm the one being punished."

"I understand. But it seems like my roles as sheriff and sponsor are overlapping, and I'm not comfortable with that. Are you?"

Brian leaned back in his chair. "I didn't know you were the sheriff when I asked you to be my sponsor. All I know is drinking is ruining my life. It's killing me. I need to get sober, and I know I need help. You seem to have your shit together, so, yeah, I'm okay with that."

Hood rubbed the back of his neck. He didn't want to disappoint Brian, but the truth was he didn't want to disappoint himself. Although his recovery program warned about selfishness, sponsorship had boosted his ego, and he wasn't ready to let it go. "Okay," he said. "We'll keep things as they are for now, but if things get complicated—"

"What's that phrase I'm always hearing? *Keep it simple.* Let's just keep it simple, okay?"

\* \* \*

Hood parked his cruiser in the gravel lot among a group of grimy pickup trucks and a red Mustang accessorized with a rear spoiler and chrome mag wheels. A fine sprinkling of road dust covered its otherwise immaculate exterior. He guessed the car belonged to Jessie.

He exited and surveyed the rural expanse, which included a long stable, corrals, and seemingly endless pastures bordered by white fences. As he approached the stable, he encountered a man wearing coveralls and pushing a wheelbarrow containing a bale of hay. "I'm looking for Jessie Surface," Hood said.

"In the ring." The man had stopped but didn't lower the wheelbarrow.

Hood looked around helplessly.

"Behind the stable," the man added, gesturing with his chin.

Hood turned the corner and walked to a fenced area, where Jessie sat astride a muscular chestnut horse and guided it along a circuit that included jumps of varying heights. He noticed she was wearing a sweater and an insulated vest, not her navy blue coat.

As she navigated a turn, she acknowledged him with a slight nod but continued her session.

Hood braced his foot on the bottom rail of the fence and watched. He had learned from experience that patience was useful in his profession. Coaxing and prompting weren't always necessary; sometimes, simply being present produced results.

After two additional circuits, Jessie reined the horse to a stop on the opposite side of the fence. "Sheriff," she said, towering above him. "What brings you here?"

"I was hoping I could ask you a few questions," he said.

"Sure." She dismounted. "Duchess needs to cool down. Come and walk with us."

Hood walked to the gate, lifted the latch, and entered the ring. The filly eyed him cautiously as he approached. "She's beautiful," he said. "Is she yours?"

"I wish," Jessie said. "Owning a horse is a luxury I can't afford, but Duchess and I have been together for a while now." She stroked the filly's snout. "Haven't we girl?"

They began walking, with Jessie loosely holding the reins.

"I understand you're dating Brian Rakestraw," Hood said. He didn't know if Jessie was aware he was her boyfriend's recovery sponsor, but decided not to mention it unless she brought it up.

"That's not a question," she said, "but, yes, I am."

"Did Brian tell you his older brother, Eric, is missing?"

"Yes."

Experience had taught Hood some interview subjects volunteered volumes of information while others, like Jessie, were concise. He decided to abandon yes-or-no questions, which were producing terse answers.

"How would you characterize Brian's relationship with his brother?"

"Are you investigating Eric as a missing person?"

"Yes."

"I honestly don't know Eric very well, and all I know about their relationship is what Brian has told me."

"Which is?"

"I'm really not comfortable talking about this," Jessie said. "Have you asked Brian?"

"Yes." Hood realized she was now posing the questions and he was answering in curt monosyllables.

"What did he say?"

"I don't mean to be difficult, but I can't discuss an active investigation."

"Okay," Jessie said. "My session's about over. I need to put this girl in her stall." She led the horse to the gate.

"Before you get away," Hood said. "I want you to know I'm sorry about your loss."

"Thank you."

"Are you doing okay?" he asked.

"Uncle Chet was my only uncle. I'm going to miss him, but I guess I'm doing as well as can be expected."

"Good," he said. "I know your parents were at their lake condo the night your uncle was assaulted, but I've been meaning to ask where you were that night."

Hood caught a defensive tic in her expression and wouldn't have been surprised if she asked if she were a suspect, but she didn't. Instead, she answered, "At my parents' house."

"Alone?"

"No. I was with Brian and another couple."

Hood took out a notebook and asked the identity of the other couple. He wrote the names and contact information she provided for David Wilde and Michelle Bax, closed the notebook, and pocketed it. "I guess that's all for now."

\* \* \*

When Hood entered his kitchen, Linda was stirring the simmering contents of a Dutch oven on the stovetop.

"Smells great," he said, inhaling deeply.

"Beef stew," she said. "It's the recipe you like, the one with gnocchi."

"I'll wash up."

"Good, because this is ready."

Hood washed and dried his hands in the main level half-bath, then returned to the kitchen, where Linda already had filled their bowls and was seated at the table, which was set for two.

"Where's Elizabeth?"

"Upstairs in her room. She says she's not hungry and has a ton of homework." Linda said grace, and Hood lifted a spoonful to his lips, savoring the aroma and flavor. "What are you smiling about?" Linda asked.

"I've been feeling very grateful lately," Hood answered.

"About what?"

"I had a conversation with someone, and it's caused me to rethink gratitude."

"Can you tell me?"

"I guess. I found out someone I know—someone we both know—has a debilitating neurological condition I never knew about. It's called somatic OCD. It's a kind of obsessive-compulsive disorder that affects automatic body functions like breathing, swallowing, even heart rate—things most people never think about."

"Sounds horrible."

"It is. The person who told me about it obsesses over swallowing. She said it controls every aspect of her life, like not going out for lunch or dinner or excusing herself from company because she can't even swallow her own saliva."

Linda winced but made no remark.

"I always thought," Hood continued, "gratitude was for what you have, but now I'm feeling grateful for what I don't have."

"But you do have a debilitating condition, Francis," Linda reminded. "You're an alcoholic."

"You're right," Hood said. "I guess what I'm saying is as long as I don't drink, I don't suffer the consequences."

"But it requires effort," Linda responded. "You go to meetings, you have a sponsor, you work to change your attitudes and behaviors."

"I guess it's similar. It's just that she has this thing that—" He shook his head, his helplessness apparent. "I don't know."

"I've noticed you've become much more empathetic since you started your recovery program, Francis. I was in the nurses' lounge the other day, and I was reading an article about meeting people where they are."

Hood lowered his spoon to the table, picked up his napkin, and listened.

"It's like imagining yourself in someone else's shoes, but it's more than that. Instead of bringing your priorities to the conversation, you listen and try to gauge where the other person is coming from. Are they grieving, heartbroken, lonely? It helps you tune in to their needs, not your own."

"I wish I could help her in some way, but I have no idea how to go about it."

"Listening goes a long way," Linda said. "Sometimes when I say what's on my mind, I don't expect anyone—or even want them—to fix it, I just need to share it."

"One of the people at the meeting often says, 'A burden shared is halved, and a joy shared is doubled.'"

"Exactly," Linda replied. "From what you've told me, that's what your meetings are all about. You're not there to fix each other. You share what worked for you and what didn't, and, in the process, you help each other."

Hood smiled. Although he believed people who didn't suffer from an addiction had a difficult time understanding it, Linda seemed an exception.

Was her compassion, he wondered, shaped by her training as a nurse, her faith, or some other combination of factors? "You're right," he said. "I'm not a doctor, I'm not a counselor, but I can be a friend."

"I just want you to be careful."

"How so?"

"I know how invested you can get in situations—and people—and I know how devastating it can be for you when things don't work out the way you want."

"Are you referring to my alcoholism?"

"I'm just repeating what you told me after you did that self-analysis about why you drank."

"Failure has always been hard for me. I'm better now that I've been in recovery for a while. I realize I can't solve everything."

As he cleared bowls and silverware from the table, he said, "By the way, I may have to pull an evening shift tomorrow."

Linda, who was stooping to load the dishwasher, looked at him. "But that's the first rehearsal for the father-daughter dance."

He rinsed a bowl and extended it toward her. "I know, but the work schedule's kind of a mess right now."

She straightened. "Francis, the rehearsals have been on the calendar since the date was set."

"It's just—" He shrugged, aware of her disappointment. The bowl remained in his outstretched hand, like a ceramic pariah. "Things change."

"What's going on?"

Her question hit him like a jab in the chest. He couldn't respond. He couldn't be honest. He knew—regardless of how much he rehearsed and practiced, in spite of his daughter's apparent delight at the prospect of dancing with her dad—he feared he would make a fool of himself. "Do you think Elizabeth would be upset if I didn't do the dance?"

Linda eyed him curiously but, thankfully, didn't probe deeper. All she said was, "You'll have to ask her." She took the bowl. "Go ahead. I'll finish cleaning up."

He climbed the stairs, feeling the sting of dismissal and the recognition he had deserved it. The door to his daughter's room was open. Elizabeth was seated at her desk and working at her computer. He knocked on the jamb, and she turned. "Hello, Daddy."

"Hi. What're you working on?"

"It's a project for English class. We're doing sonnets. What's up?"

"Can I talk to you for a minute?"

"Sure." She turned away from the computer.

Hood sat on the foot of her bed. He picked up Goo Goo—the stuffed animal he had won for her at the county fair when she was four—and twirled the green dinosaur in his hands. "I see you still keep Goo Goo nearby."

"Of course. He's good luck. I brought him with me when you and Mom were separated."

Hood laid Goo Goo on the bed. "What do you think of the idea of this father-daughter dance?"

"When Miss Heather first announced it, I thought it was kinda lame. But then some of us talked about it after class, and we decided it could be fun."

"Because I don't want you to feel like you have to do it—if you don't want to, I mean."

"No. I'm good. You're looking forward to it, too? Right?"

"Of course," he lied.

# Chapter Fifteen

Sandra's alarm jolted her from fitful sleep.

The annoying sound also triggered activity from Lady Jane.

Although Sandra could hit the snooze button, she knew it would be only a matter of time before the cat began pawing her face.

Sandra sat up and tested the floor temperature with her bare feet. Her head felt thick. She recalled dreaming but couldn't recall the content.

Lady Jane insisted the first order of daily business was being fed, so Sandra walked to the kitchen with the cat meowing repeatedly as she weaved between her owner's steps. While the feline ate, Sandra adjourned to the bathroom to brush her teeth and shower. As she dried herself, Lady Jane returned to the bedroom to watch her owner style her hair, apply makeup, and dress for the workday.

For breakfast, Sandra routinely had a bowl of cereal while watching the local news and weather forecast. Not until she opened her front door to retrieve the newspaper, did she notice a letter-sized, white envelope partially tucked under the mat. As she carried the items to her kitchen, she noticed the envelope was blank. She set the morning edition aside and shook the envelope, producing a scratching sound. Using a letter opener, she slit the seal and peered inside. No letter or note was present. She upended the envelope above the countertop and gently shook it. A fingernail—not a clipping, an entire fingernail—fell to the surface.

Lady Jane watched curiously as Sandra picked up her phone and called the sheriff.

\* \* \*

Hood and Sandra looked at the fingernail, resting on a stainless steel tabletop in the crime lab. Positioned beside it was the blank envelope.

"You found the envelope on your doorstep this morning?" Hood asked for the second time.

"Yes."

"And you brought the envelope inside and opened it?"

"Yes," she repeated, a hint of frustration in her tone. "But I had no idea what it contained. I called you as soon as I saw what it was."

The door opened, and Howard—who had been called by Hood and informed of the situation—joined them at the table and studied the object. "Any idea who it belongs to?" the fingerprint analyst asked.

Sandra and Hood looked at each other. "I'd rather not speculate," Hood said. Sandra remained silent.

"I do fingerprints, not fingernails," Howard deadpanned. "I don't think it will tell us much unless we do DNA analysis and there's a match in the system. Is it worth it?"

Hood had contemplated again using the independent laboratory but decided against it. "I'd like to know more. How long will DNA testing take?"

"I can find out," Howard replied. "I'll let you know."

"Thanks," Hood said.

He walked to the door, and Sandra followed. "Do you have time for a cup of coffee?" she asked.

Hood's initial impulse was to decline, but he reconsidered. Sandra's expression suggested the question was more a plea than an invitation. And she was visibly distressed. "Okay."

She led him from the lab, onto a down elevator, and along a hallway to the break room, where she filled a disposable cup from a coffee urn and handed it to him. As they sat at a small table in the nearly vacant room, Hood noted she had not poured coffee for herself.

"Are you thinking what I'm thinking?" she asked.

Hood blew across the surface of the steaming liquid, reminding himself to glean, not give, information. "What are you thinking?"

"My first thought is it's one of Eric's fingernails."

"Why?"

"I don't know," Sandra answered. "First, you found that ring that looks like the one Eric wore."

"It's Eric's," Hood said. "His brother confirmed it."

"And I remembered I did leave my SUV unlocked one time—the day I went back to Schweinshaupten to take soil samples from the alley next to *One Man's Trash* ..."

"When was that?"

"After you and I had that conversation about the composition of the soil sample, I scraped from the floor of the shop. Remember, I said I was going to get samples from the alley for comparison, so I went back that afternoon. Now that I think about it, I may not have locked my car, but it was only out of my sight for five or ten minutes."

Hood attempted to remain expressionless, but his brows lifted slightly, indicating skepticism. Although he wanted to believe, to trust, her explanation, it sounded almost too convenient.

"But, then, you found Eric's ring in my vehicle," she continued, "and now someone leaves a fingernail on my doorstep. It's like someone's trying to send a message. But who's the someone, and what's the message?"

Hood heard frustration in her tone. "Has there been anything, other than the ring and today's surprise, that's been unusual or different lately?"

"Not—" She stopped, obviously reconsidering.

"You were about to say something," Hood prompted when she failed to continue.

"It's nothing. It's silly, really."

Hood had learned, from experience, that the seemingly silly is sometimes valuable. "Okay, but tell me anyway."

"Howard asked me to lunch the other day. He's so sweet, so shy. I almost didn't have the heart to tell him no. But, you know, I have the OCD thing, so I made up some excuse. I hope it didn't sound too lame."

"Has he asked you before?"

"No. I mean, a couple times I think he was working up to it, but that was the first time he asked."

Hood decided to back off. Sandra had suggested the scenario of an infatuated co-worker being involved in the disappearance of a rival suitor. Hood knew he was getting ahead of himself, considering motives before the fingernail had been identified. He reminded himself of a popular recovery maxim—*First Things First*. He decided it was time to practice that precept.

# Chapter Sixteen

T he sheriff dipped his fingertip in the holy water font and made the sign of the cross as he stepped into the sanctuary of St. Anthony's Catholic Church.

He signed the guest book and joined the line of mourners waiting to pay their respects. As he waited, he lifted his gaze to the white columns and the network of gold and white arches supporting the ceiling of the Gothic-Romanesque church. St. Anthony's had anchored Schweinshaupten since the celebration of its first Mass in 1851. Hood recalled reading, as a child, how these early churches were designed to infuse the congregation with God's lofty majesty. Images painted on the walls and etched in stained glass depicted Jesus instructing his disciples. Hood was recalling a lesson from his catechism when he arrived at the casket. He silently recited the Lord's Prayer, then offered condolences to Adam, Irene, and Jessie Surface, the only family members present for Chester Groner's funeral.

As Hood turned into the aisle, he saw Brian, who rose from his seat in the second pew and greeted the sheriff.

"Any news about my brother?" Brian asked.

Hood hesitated. Not only had he decided not to inform Brian about the fingernail until it was identified, but he believed a funeral service was not the proper place for an update. "No," he answered.

Brian returned to his seat while Hood walked toward the rear of the sanctuary and attempted to make himself comfortable in the unforgiving wooden pew. He waited impatiently until Father Wieberg approached the altar, his presence reducing the bustle and chatter to reverential solemnity.

The clergyman delivered a humorless eulogy—more formulaic than personal. At one point, Hood had to ask himself if the priest's remarks mildly chastised the deceased for his lack of attendance and financial support.

After the service, Hood fell in line with the mourners who followed Chester's casket from the church and watched it being loaded into a white hearse parked at the curb. Across the street, Dennis Vivion and Hunk stood on the sidewalk.

Hood watched as Vivion approached Jessie while she stood beside the driver's door of her car parked in a line of vehicles at the curb. Vivion appeared to whisper in Jessie's ear—a comment Hood was unable to overhear—and her expression registered confusion. As she pulled open the door and Brian got in the passenger seat, Vivion retreated across the street.

Hood shifted his gaze to a college-age couple engaged in an animated conversation that appeared to escalate into an argument, which continued as they climbed into the last car in the funeral procession and loudly slammed shut their respective doors.

\* \* \*

"You've got an overactive imagination, Michelle." David started the ignition. "I don't know where you come up with this stuff."

"I didn't imagine anything," Michelle said. "I saw it with my own eyes. You were flirting with Jessie—again. And at her uncle's funeral, no less."

"I was trying to lift her spirits. That's all."

"Don't think I haven't noticed, David. And don't think Brian hasn't, either. I don't get it. I mean, he's your best friend."

"He's not my *best* friend." David slapped his palms on the steering wheel. "Are they ever going to move this fucking funeral procession?"

"If you want to break up with me, that's one thing. But making a play for Jessie while we're still going out is messed up. It's embarrassing for everybody, but mostly for you."

"Now you're starting to piss me off," David said.

"Is this some ego thing with you? See how many notches you can—"

"Enough!"

His shout was both surprising and frightening. Michelle sat silently, momentarily stunned. "I think I'm going to skip the cemetery. I'll find another way home." She opened her passenger door as the hearse pulled from the curb, and the other cars began to move.

"No. Don't," David pleaded. "I'm sorry. We can work this out."

"I need some time." Michelle stepped out of the car and onto the sidewalk.

"Fuck" was the last word she heard David say as she closed the car door and he pulled from the curb.

\* \* \*

"What'd he want?" Brian asked as Jessie followed the hearse and limousine containing her parents.

"Who?" Jessie said.

"That guy who came up and said something to you just now."

"I never saw him before."

"His name's Dennis Vivion."

"You know him?"

"He and my brother hung out sometimes. Eric used to have parties at our house, and sometimes Vivion and some of his loser friends would show up. What'd he say?"

"What do you know about him?"

"Not a lot. My brother said Vivion's kind of squirrelly."

"What does that mean?"

"I think he meant unpredictable."

"Great," Jessie muttered, her sarcasm apparent.

"So what did he say?"

"He said he saw my car parked in the alley next to Uncle Chet's store the night of the assault."

"Shit. That's all we need."

"You think this is going to be a problem?"

Brian didn't answer. He couldn't. Problems were crowding him. He didn't need another.

# Chapter Seventeen

Hood was enthralled by the sublime interplay of the rising and falling notes being played by a string quartet. He admired musicianship, perhaps because one of his regrets was he never learned to play an instrument. How fulfilling it must be, he thought, to be able to entice an emotional response from listeners through rhythm, melody, and tempo.

The fault was his. After his maternal grandmother passed away, his parents inherited her upright piano and moved it into a corner of their dining room. He was not interested. When, at around age fifteen, he became enamored with rock music and the electric guitar, his mother had arranged for and taken him to lessons. What he learned was he possessed little natural talent. He gave up on the instrument when he earned his driver's permit, purchased his first car, and began dating.

Now, inside Mitchell Hall, the music building on the Monroe College campus, he traced the source of sound emanating from wooden double doors. He had learned that music major Michelle Bax would be attending a class that ended at 11:15 a.m. His intention was to learn if Michelle would corroborate what Jessie had said. In the aftermath of Chester Groner's funeral, he also was interested in Michelle's version of her argument with the young man he assumed was her boyfriend, David Wilde.

He entered the rehearsal hall—a large room featuring stadium seating that descended to the stage—surveyed the student audience and sat in the back row. As the string quartet finished the composition, Hood focused on the cellist.

When the final note faded, a man arose from his front-row seat. "Bravo," he shouted as he applauded. "You see, class, that's how it's done. The music must dance. Music is much more than sound. Sound is just noise. Music is—" he paused to dramatize his point, "life."

As if on cue, a buzzer sounded, triggering a cacophony as the students stood and gathered books, bags, and instruments. Hood stepped into the aisle and pushed against the tide of students moving toward the exit. When he reached the stage, he approached the cellist, who was stooping to encase her instrument.

"Michelle Bax?" he asked.

She looked up and noticed his uniform. "Yes," she said, a shaky monosyllable.

"I'm your sheriff, Francis Hood."

She stared quizzically.

"I'd like to talk with you."

"Me? Why?"

Hood didn't need detective skills to see she was frightened and nervous. "I have some questions. It will only take a few minutes."

"Did I do something wrong?"

"No." Hood looked around. For the most part, the room had cleared, and the few students who remained were busy packing and paying no attention to their quiet conversation. "I saw you yesterday at the funeral for Chester Groner."

"I'm a friend of Jessie's—Jessie Surface. Chester was her uncle."

"So I understand. I'm told you were with Jessie at her parents' house the night Mr. Groner was assaulted."

"Did Jessie tell you that?"

Hood typically didn't reveal his sources of information, but he decided to make an exception. "She did."

"Then, yes. I was."

"Who else was present?"

"Our boyfriends."

"That would be Brian Rakestraw, her boyfriend, and—" Hood removed a notebook from his pocket, flipped pages, and added, "your boyfriend, David Wilde."

"Yes."

"What did you do that night?"

"What did Jessie say?" Michelle repeated.

"I appreciate your loyalty to your friend, but I've already talked to Jessie, and she is not the topic of our conversation." Hood intentionally adopted a more authoritative tone. "I'd like to know what you recall."

"Just talked, mostly." She shrugged. "Had a few beers."

"Did you go anywhere?"

"What did—?" she began, then stopped. "I don't think so."

"You don't remember?"

"I was drinking. I may have been a little tipsy. But," she added, an afterthought, "I didn't drive anywhere."

"Did someone else? Did you take a trip that night?"

"A trip where?"

"Miss Bax," Hood said, trying to rein in his frustration. "I'm asking you—not someone else—some very basic questions about what you did that night. I would appreciate some cooperation."

"I'm trying." Michelle was visibly flustered. "I guess I had too much to drink, because it's all hazy to me."

Hood said nothing, hoping the protracted silence might induce Michelle to disclose whatever she was withholding. When it didn't, he said, "The assault on Jessie's uncle is now a homicide investigation, so if you know anything about what happened, it's in your best interest to tell me."

Michelle stood. "I have another class." She hefted her cello case. "I have to go."

"One more question," Hood said. "Before the funeral procession left the church, I saw you arguing with a young man. Was that David, your boyfriend?"

"I'm not so sure about that anymore."

Hood's expression revealed confusion.

"This is personal stuff," Michelle added. "I don't see why you're asking—"

"I understand," Hood said. "I saw you get in his car but, before the procession pulled away, I also saw you get out."

"I decided not to go to the cemetery. I needed to get back to the dorm, so I hitched a ride with another classmate who attended the service." She scanned the empty music room. "I've really got to go."

Hood had learned little, but detaining Michelle seemed pointless. He thanked her for her time and stepped aside.

\* \* \*

Back in his office, Hood reacted to the ringing of his desk phone. He pressed the lighted button and answered, "Yes, Maggie."

"Howard DeWesplore from the crime lab is on the line. I'll transfer him."

When the connection was made, Howard said, without preamble, "The fingernail Sandra brought in belongs to Eric Rakestraw. Eric provided a DNA sample when he became a patrol recruit."

Hood didn't bother asking if the analyst was certain. Instead, he said, "Have you told Sandra?"

"No. You were my first call, but I can tell from her body language she's itching to know."

"I'll do it." Hood wanted to gauge her reaction to the news. "Tell her I'll be by in, say, a half-hour."

"Sure."

\* \* \*

Gunmetal-colored clouds threatened rain as Hood crossed the crime lab parking lot. In the lobby, he announced himself and waited while Sandra was notified. When she appeared, they exchanged pleasantries while she signed him in, handed him a visitor ID, and escorted him to her office.

As soon as they were seated, Hood said, "The fingernail belongs to Eric."

"I'm not surprised."

"How angry was he about the breakup?"

"He was disappointed. I know that."

"Disappointed enough to tear out his own fingernail?"

She winced. "I don't know."

"Do you think he's trying to frame you for his disappearance?"

"I can't explain why his ring was in my car, and his fingernail appeared on my doorstep. All I did was break up with the guy. What did Howard say about the envelope? Any prints?"

"None."

Sandra exhaled a long sigh. "I guess I'm a suspect, then."

"Unless someone's trying to frame you for Eric's disappearance. Any ideas?"

"No. Do you want me to come in and give a formal statement?"

Hood pondered the question for several beats before responding. "I think I need to do some more digging first."

* * *

"What are we going to do?" Brian asked.

Jessie straightened the pad she had draped over the back of the filly. Duchess was tethered to the door of her stall while Jessie prepared for her riding lesson. "About what?"

"That Vivion guy. He told you he saw your car outside your uncle's store."

"So?"

"I don't know," Brian answered. "What if he tells somebody?"

"Who?" She added a blanket and meticulously smoothed the wrinkles.

Brian shrugged. "The sheriff, maybe?"

"Vivion doesn't strike me as the kind of guy who would help the sheriff." Jessie lifted the saddle onto the filly's back. "You're the one who's met him before. What do you think?"

"Maybe he'll try to blackmail us or something."

"I haven't heard from him. Have you?"

"No. Maybe he wants us to sweat about it before—"

"That's a lot of maybes, Brian." She cinched the straps, walked around

Duchess, and pulled at the saddle to be certain it was fastened securely. "Maybe we shouldn't be making a lot of assumptions and get all worked up about it. Maybe we'll never hear from him."

"I can't help but get worked up. There's something weird about that guy."

Jessie reached for the bridle. She fit the bit into the horse's mouth as she worked the leather headpiece into place. "Then we wait until he shows his hand." She turned to Brian and pulled him closer. "I know this is hard for you. I know you want to know what's going on, but he's probably doing the same thing, wondering what we're thinking. Let's let him come to us."

Brian exhaled a long breath.

"Trust me on this," Jessie said. "Sometimes, the best thing to do is nothing."

\* \* \*

"What about shoes?" Hood asked. He stood among the other six fathers and daughters who formed a line on the hardwood floor and faced a wall-length mirror.

"Wear whatever's comfortable, fathers," the dance instructor advised. "We're not doing tap or ballet, only some rudimentary steps. I'm not expecting Mikhail Baryshnikov or Gregory Hines. Just have fun with it."

Hood frowned.

"Okay, girls," Miss Heather announced. "We're going to start with a pair of basic jazz squares with hands on hips." The daughters formed a line of their own and executed the choreography. Hood was impressed; their movements were synchronized and graceful.

"Okay, dads, your turn."

Although the movement, a variation on the box step, seemed simple enough, Hood nearly stumbled in his first attempt. Lined up beside Warren Reinkemeyer—father of his daughter's best friend, Claire—Hood tried to watch and mirror the man's movements, but immediately realized he had chosen a poor example. Although Warren's broad smile indicated he was having fun, his movements were as awkward and clumsy as the sheriff's.

As the rehearsal continued, Hood berated himself for each misstep. By the time they began practicing a third step, a ball change, Hood realized the rudimentary dance moves were more challenging and complicated than he expected. He would ask Elizabeth to chart the routine so he could practice in his free time, when he was alone.

If he was going to do this thing, he was determined to do it well.

# Chapter Eighteen

A real estate professional might describe the Rakestraw house as a fixer-upper with historic charm and immense possibilities.

Brian answered the sheriff's knock, and Hood stepped inside. He surveyed the neglect—scuffed hardwood floors, faded drapes, and peeling paint on doors and window frames. But the swirled plaster ceilings, crown molding, and antique hardware offered a vision of what comprehensive renovation could awaken.

"Have a seat," Brian invited, motioning the sheriff to one of two wingback chairs, their brocade shiny and frayed, in the expansive living room. "I know what you're thinking. Why do my brother and I stay in this old, rundown house?" They sat in the matching chairs facing each other. "I guess it's a nostalgia thing, plus it's paid off, but I've got to admit this place seems a lot creepier since Eric disappeared."

"That's why I'm here," Hood said. "I need to inform you we've come into possession of a fingernail that has been identified as Eric's."

"You mean, like a clipping?"

"No. The entire nail?"

"Wouldn't that hurt?"

"Yes," Hood repeated. "Can you think of any circumstances that would cause your brother—"

"He would never do that." Brian's tone was defensive. "First his ring, now his nail. What the hell is going on?"

"That's what I'm trying to find out."

"What do you mean by 'came into possession?'"

"It was delivered to the residence of one of the crime lab analysts," Hood answered, without hesitation. "She found it on her front stoop."

"Was it the woman he was dating— Sandra something?"

"I'm not going to identify—"

"What do you know about her? Could she be some kind of psycho bitch who—"

"I've known her for years," Hood interrupted. "I'm not ruling anybody out, but I don't think she's involved."

"But you don't know. So why would somebody tear off my brother's nail and deliver it to her? Why would somebody do that?"

"I thought you might have some ideas."

Brian shook his head, clearly distracted by the puzzling scenarios in his mind. "I don't."

"When you first reported your brother was missing, you mentioned some parties—?"

"My brother liked the spotlight. He liked playing to a crowd. Not me. Whenever Eric had people over, my social anxiety would go through the roof. I'd stay in my room, except when I'd sneak downstairs to tap the keg."

"You mentioned the social anxiety when we first talked."

"It can get pretty bad." Brian leaned forward in his chair. "Can I tell you something in confidence?"

"Everything we discuss is confidential."

"Because I've never told this to anyone, not Jessie, not my brother. I think they suspect something, but they don't actually know."

The gravity in Brian's tone was obvious to Hood. His concern was not whether he could keep the secret—he knew he could—but whether he was willing to carry the weight of it. "I need to caution you, Brian. If this involves a crime, I advise you to consult an attorney."

"No. It's nothing like that," Brian said. "It's something I deal with. It's embarrassing. You have an addiction, so you know what it's like when you can't control something, and it screws up your life."

Hood nodded.

"Ever heard of shy bladder syndrome?"

"Yes," Hood said. "We had an inmate in the county jail who couldn't use the toilet in his cell. He asked to talk with someone from the county health department, and the nurse advised us to have the jailer escort him to a private restroom when he needed to go."

"I can't use public restrooms. Even if they're empty, I worry someone will come in, and I get tense."

Hood thought of Sandra's inability to swallow and how it altered her choices and lifestyle. "Did you see somebody, you know, like a counselor?"

"I was always too embarrassed to tell anybody. Besides, my parents didn't have the money for something like that. They'd say it's all in your head, which it is."

"So what did you do?"

"Mostly, I stopped going places. If I couldn't avoid going, I'd dehydrate myself. I'd eat bread or rolls and not drink anything. Then I discovered alcohol, which is ironic because when I was drunk, I went more often, but I didn't care. Alcohol solved the problem."

"Self-medication," Hood said.

"Exactly," Brian said. "And it worked. It still works, except now the drinking has become its own problem." He fixed his gaze on the sheriff. "So I guess I'm screwed either way. If I don't stop drinking, life sucks, but if I do stop drinking, life still sucks, just in a different way."

Hood pondered the paradox. "When I started looking at the reasons I drank, I uncovered some fears and anxieties I didn't even know I had. I figured if I could get rid of the fears and such, I could stop drinking. That didn't work. After talking to my sponsor and some other people in recovery, I realized I had everything backwards. I had to quit drinking first and, when I did, my fears and anxieties diminished. They haven't gone away completely, but they don't rule my life anymore. I'm not paralyzed by fear the way I once was."

"I hear what you're saying," Brian said. "I just don't know if I can do it."

\* \* \*

Hood paused inside the door and observed the activity within Huhman Performance, a local fitness center. The range of motion included lifting weights, pulling cables, performing stretches, jumping rope, running and walking on treadmills, pumping pedals on stationary bicycles, and more. And the participants included men and women, young and old, some wearing loose-fitting, nondescript sweatsuits, others clad in revealing sportswear designed to display taut, flexed muscles.

Hood walked to the counter, attended by a young woman wearing a pink leotard with black polka-dots and a name tag introducing her as Lily. "I'm your sheriff, Francis Hood," he said. "I'd like to speak with David Wilde. I believe he's one of the personal trainers."

"Of course, officer," Lily said in a perky, customer-service tone. She glanced at a clock above the door. "He's with a client now, but he should be free in about five or ten minutes."

"I'll wait."

"We have seating in the juice bar there." Lily pointed to an interior door. "You look very fit, but if you're not a member, you're welcome to look around and consider joining our Huhman Performance family." She smiled broadly, leaned across the counter, and added, as if sharing a secret, "It's a play on words—Huhman County, human performance."

"I get it." He had gotten it when he first saw the sign outdoors.

"We have all types of fitness apparatus, free weights, treadmills, and—" she reached for one of the brochures in a clear plastic rack, "we have a special promotion if you sign up now."

"No, thanks," Hood said. His comment stopped Lily in mid-reach. "I'll wait in the juice bar. Please let David know I'm here."

"Sure," she said. "May I tell him what this is about?"

"I'll do that," Hood said. He entered the juice bar, which was not crowded; patrons sat at fewer than half of the small, round tables within. He had no interest in overpriced juice, so he sat at a table in a quiet corner and indulged in solitary moping. He had made no progress—none—on either the homicide or disappearance case. He was considering which recovery maxim might lift him from his pity party when he sensed a presence hovering near his table.

"Sheriff?" As Hood stood in response, the man added, "I'm David."

"I'm your sheriff, Francis Hood." He extended his hand, and they shook. Hood felt the strength in David's grip and matched it—an effort to neutralize any one-upmanship, real or imagined. "Have a seat," Hood invited.

"What's this about?" David asked as he seated himself.

"I understand you and Michelle were with Jessie Surface and Brian Rakestraw the night Jessie's uncle was assaulted."

"Did Michelle tell you that?"

Hood was miffed his questions again were being answered with questions. "Why do you ask?"

"Because she said you talked to her. I figured I'd be next."

"If you would please answer my question. Were—?"

"Yeah. We were at Jessie's house. Well, her parents' house. The one here in town. Her parents were at their lake condo."

"Anyone else with you?"

"Just the four of us."

"What were you doing?"

David shrugged. "Just hanging out, having a few beers."

"What else?"

"That's it. Jessie got a call from her parents about her uncle being assaulted, so she went to meet her folks at the hospital, and we went home."

"All three of you?"

"Well, Michelle and me. We put Brian in Jessie's car. He was pretty drunk."

"You said Jessie received a call from her parents about her uncle being assaulted."

"That's right."

"Which parent did she speak with?"

"I think it was her father, but I could be wrong."

"But she specifically used the word 'assaulted?' She didn't just say her uncle had been hospitalized?"

An alarm sounded in David's mind. Had he unintentionally revealed something? "What are you getting at?"

"I'm not 'getting at' anything. I'm asking so I can reconstruct what was said."

"I don't remember if she used the word 'assaulted' after the call. Maybe I misspoke. Like I said, we'd been drinking and all."

"Misspoke?" Hood repeated a question.

"Yeah. We found out later that's what happened, so maybe I assumed that was what Jessie was told on the phone." David looked at a wall clock. "Look, I've got to get ready for another client."

Hood sensed the man was withholding something. He also sensed additional questions wouldn't pry it loose. He handed David his card, asked him to call if he remembered or learned anything else, and left.

As he passed the front counter, Lily insisted he "have a nice day."

* * *

Howard DeWesplore's arrival at the sheriff's department was timely. At Hood's invitation, the fingerprint analyst had agreed to stop by after his workday had ended.

"How did Sandra seem today?" Hood asked. He, like Howard, was seated in one of the visitors' chairs, suggesting the visit was a conversation rather than an interrogation.

"She seemed fine," Howard replied. "How did she take it when you told her the fingernail was Eric's?"

"I don't think she was surprised. Were you?"

Howard shrugged. "I stick to analysis. I don't make assumptions."

"You've known Sandra a long time, right?"

"Since she came on board," Howard answered. He squinted his nose as he calculated. "Let's see, that would be about five years now."

"Did you help train her? Do you consider yourself her mentor?"

Howard shrugged. "I helped show her the ropes, but not any more or less than the rest of the staff. We're mostly just co-workers, I guess."

"Have you noticed any changes in her behavior?"

Howard hesitated. "I'm not sure what you mean."

"Has she seemed more anxious lately— edgy, distracted?"

"She was kind of moody when she was dating Eric. Sometimes, she seemed preoccupied, like she had other things on her mind."

"Did that create any problems?"

Howard shrugged. "She still did her job. Her work was thorough and accurate, but I could tell sometimes her mind was someplace else."

"How did you react to that?"

"To be honest, Eric seemed kind of egotistical, full of himself. Sandra's a good person. I thought she could do better." Howard removed a ballpoint pen from his shirt pocket and clicked it open, then closed. "But it's none of my business."

"I know, for me, it can be difficult maintaining professional boundaries. When you're working with somebody on a day-to-day basis, it's hard not to get invested in their personal issues, whether it's sick kids, aging parents, bad boyfriends, whatever."

"I know," Howard said. "I mean, I care about Sandra, and I thought Eric was bad news, but I felt like it wasn't my place to bring it up."

"Did she ever bring it up?"

Howard returned the pen to his pocket, and straightened in the chair. "Why are you asking me this?"

"I'm trying to explore all possibilities."

"Are you thinking one of those possibilities is I had something to do with Eric's disappearance?"

"Did you?" Hood asked.

"No," Howard said. "I'm a lab geek. I'm not the hero who rescues damsels in distress from poor choices."

"Okay," Hood said. "Thanks for your candor."

"Is that all?"

"Yes," Hood said. He stood.

Howard stood also. "I know about Eric's disappearance, the ring, the fingernail, but I don't think Sandra could be involved in any of that. You agree, right?"

"I'd like to think she isn't involved."

"But you're exploring all possibilities?"

Hood nodded.

* * *

"Hey, Michelle," Brian greeted.

Michelle looked up from the book she was studying. "What's up?" She sat on a bench outside Mitchell Hall.

"Killing time between classes."

"Me, too."

"Can I join you?"

"Sure." She shifted her books to make more room on the bench.

Brian sensed Michelle was not her effusive self. He also had seen her vacate David's car before the funeral procession to the cemetery. "How's it going?" he asked as he sat beside her.

"Okay, I guess."

"Just okay?"

She nodded.

"I noticed you arguing with David the other day. Want to talk about it?"

"David can be an ass."

"What did he do this time?"

"He wants what he doesn't have. He's never satisfied. He's like the poster child for 'the grass is always greener ...'"

"What's he wanting now?"

"He wants a new girlfriend. He's ready to trade me in for a newer model."

"Then he's making a big mistake. I think you're great."

"Thanks, but I'm not feeling too good about myself right now."

"You know, it says more about him than it does you. He's the one who needs to change, not you."

Michelle remained silent.

"What're you going to do?"

She shook her head. "Don't know."

A bell sounded, signaling the beginning of the next class.

Brian hefted his books and stood. "Gotta go."

"Brian," Michelle said, before he had taken a step. "Keep your eye on him."

Brian leaned forward and whispered. "I hear you. We've been friends for a long time, and I want to trust him, but in my gut—" He stopped himself in mid-sentence. "Let's just say I hear you."

\* \* \*

"I may have screwed up," David said. He sat with Jessie and Brian at the small table in Jessie's kitchen, finishing the final slices of the sausage and mushroom pizza they had ordered. Jessie's invitation had included Michelle, but she had declined politely, claiming a prior, but unspecified, engagement.

"Screwed up how?" Jessie asked.

"That sheriff came to see me. He asked a bunch of questions. I told him the four of us were together when you got a phone call from your parents about your uncle."

"So did I," Jessie said. "So what?"

"So, I said you were told your uncle was assaulted, and the sheriff jumped all over that word. He asked whether the caller specifically used the word 'assaulted' or just said your uncle had been hospitalized."

"I don't see why—" Jessie stopped herself in mid-sentence as the realization solidified. "Oh, because at that point, my parents probably hadn't been told what happened."

"That's what I'm thinking," David affirmed.

"I can't believe it," Brian said. He faced David, who sat perpendicular to him. "You worry about me ratting us out, and then you blurt out something like that."

"Fuck you, Brian," David shot back. "I explained to the sheriff I didn't remember exactly what was said. It's not like there's a recording of the call or anything. It's no big deal."

"It is a big deal," Brian countered. "You're careless, David. Careless with what you say, what you do, how you treat people. I talked to Michelle."

"Michelle and I are none of your business."

"I thought you said we were all in this together."

David stood. "You better be careful, or you're gonna find yourself in the hospital."

"Big talk," Brian countered. He remained seated.

"Stop," Jessie pleaded. "We can't do this. We are in this together. Sit down, David. Please."

"I'm outta here." David yanked his coat from the back of his chair and left, slamming the door to punctuate his hostility.

# Chapter Nineteen

Sandra sat on the bench outside the crime lab. Although the October day was brisk, but not cold, she wore a white windbreaker to shield herself from an intermittent breeze. She periodically dipped a cracker into a clear, plastic container of tuna salad and nibbled while reading a cozy mystery.

A shadow crossed her page, prompting her to glance at the young man who had approached and now hovered over her. She recognized him immediately. Although his lean, angular body type was unlike his older brother's more muscular frame, they shared similar facial features—notably the eyes and cheekbones.

"Do you remember me?" he asked.

"Of course, Brian."

"I don't mean to bother you. I'm here because my brother is missing."

"I know. The sheriff told me he's investigating."

"He told me Eric's fingernail was received in the mail by a crime lab technician."

Sandra looked at the food beside her but didn't clear a space for him to sit. "I can't discuss the forensics with anyone outside—"

"I understand," Brian interrupted, "but is there anything you can tell me about your relationship that might explain why he's missing?"

Sandra's professional impulse was to end the conversation, but she couldn't. Brian seemed lost. To rebuff him when he seemed so vulnerable would be cruel. "I don't know what your brother may have told you, but we—no, let me rephrase that—I ended our relationship. It wasn't working out."

"So he hasn't been in touch with you at all?"

"Not since I learned he was missing."

Brian lifted his gaze and looked at Sandra. "I know my brother can be a jerk. When he first went missing, I thought maybe he was trying to mess with you somehow. But now, with the fingernail—"

"Mess with me?" She sounded simultaneously confused and indignant.

"I know. It sounds crazy, but that was my first thought. Eric was hurting when you broke up with him and his typical response is to retaliate, lash out. But now I think it must be something else."

"What?"

"I don't know. That's why I'm here." Brian again looked at the ground. "You know, for what it's worth, Eric really liked you."

"Well, sometimes things just don't work out." Sandra marked her book and began gathering the remains of her lunch. "I've got to get back to work now."

"Okay," Brian said. He stepped backward a few paces while Sandra stood and walked toward the building. At about the halfway point, she stopped and looked back.

Brian was seated on the bench. His posture—elbows propped on his knees, face cradled in his palms—failed to hide his whipped, hangdog expression.

Sandra reversed direction and walked back to him. She removed her cell phone from her bag and said, "What's your number in case he calls or something?" After keying in the data, she looked back at him and couldn't help but notice the glimmer of hope in his eyes.

\* \* \*

Brian knew he was jumping the proverbial gun.

He was defying Jessie's advice, but he couldn't help himself.

Outfitted in his customary hand-me-down outfit—an oversized flannel shirt and baggy jeans that bunched at his shoe tops—he pushed through the door of Chubb's Tavern, waited for his eyes to adjust to the dimly lit interior, then surveyed the sparse crowd. When he failed to spot Dennis Vivion, he sat at a table near the door.

A waitress approached. "What can I getcha?"

"Coke."

She retreated behind the bar, scooped ice into a tumbler, filled it from the soda dispenser, and delivered it. "Two bucks," she said.

As Brian took the bills from his wallet, he said, "I'm looking for a fellow named Dennis Vivion. Do you know him?"

"Do I ever—known him since grade school. I'm Rhonda, by the way."

"Does he come around here?"

"Every night. You can set your watch by him."

"What time does he come?"

Rhonda glanced at the wall clock. "You're in luck. He'll either be here in five minutes, or hell's gonna freeze over."

"Thanks."

"If you don't mind me asking, how do you know Dennis?"

"I don't."

"Sooooo," she said, elongating the monosyllable. "What do you want to see him about?"

Brian eyed her quizzically.

"I'm his girlfriend," Rhonda said, as if in explanation. "We live together. Well, we live together unless I throw his ass out. I'm just saying, because if you're like a cop, or bill collector, or a pissed-off customer—"

"Nothing like that," Brian assured. "I just want to talk to him about something he saw."

Rhonda hesitated at the table momentarily, then—seemingly satisfied—said "okay" and left.

Brian sipped his Coke, applauding himself for not ordering a beer—or something stronger—to alleviate his heightened anxiety. He was about to signal Rhonda for a refill when the door opened, and Vivion entered.

Brian arose. "Dennis," he said. "Hi. I need to talk to you for a few minutes if that's okay."

Vivion's expression hovered somewhere between surprise and confusion. "Do I know you? I think I've seen you before, but—"

"I'm Brian Rakestraw. I'm Eric Rakestraw's brother. You came to some parties at our house a while back."

Vivion looked past him to the bar, where Rhonda already had set his customary order. "Sure. Let me grab my beer."

Brian remained standing until Vivion returned with his drink and asked, "What's up?"

"What do you know about my brother's disappearance?" Brian asked.

"I know the sheriff's been asking around about it. That's about all."

"When was the last time you saw Eric?"

Vivion sipped beer, seemingly contemplating the question. "The Fall Festival, I guess. He was with that girl he was seeing. Me and some friends hung around with them for a while."

"How well do you know my brother?"

"Look. You seem a nice kid, and I'm sorry your brother is missing, but I don't know shit about it."

"You know anything about a rust-colored pickup? I think it was a Ford F-150, like my brother's."

"Why?"

"Someone used it to run me off the road."

"You're barking up the wrong tree, kid. Are we done?"

"One more question. What did you say to Jessie after her uncle's funeral the other day?"

"Who?"

"Jessie Surface. I saw you come over to her car and say something to her after Chester Groner's funeral service. I'm her boyfriend. I was there."

"Then ask her."

"I did."

"What'd she say?"

"She told me you said you saw her car in the alley outside Chester's store the night he got hurt."

"That's right. So what about it?"

"I want to know what you're up to."

Vivion gulped the last of his beer and slapped the empty glass on the table.

"I'm up for another beer."

"I'll get it," Brian said. He bypassed Vivion, walked to the bar, and ordered the refill. When he returned to the table, Vivion was seated.

Brian set the glass in front of Vivion and sat opposite him. "So, what are you planning to do?"

"Who said I was planning to do anything?"

"If you're not planning anything, why did you tell Jessie?"

Vivion's facial expression morphed into a challenging stare. Brian attempted to match it, prompting an impasse until the front door opened, and Brian glanced at the scrawny man who entered.

"Hey, Hunk," Vivion greeted, satisfied he had prevailed.

"Hey," Hunk replied.

"Want to shoot a game?" Vivion asked.

"I don't want to interrupt," Hunk said.

Vivion looked across the table at Brian. "We're done."

"I'll shoot some pool," Brian volunteered.

"Private game." Vivion stood. "C'mon Hunk."

\* \* \*

"What can you tell me about Brian Rakestraw?" Sandra asked the sheriff.

"What do you want to know?"

"Can I trust him?"

"Why do you ask?"

"You're answering my questions with questions, Francis," Sandra said, mildly scolding. "I'm asking because he paid me a surprise visit while I was sitting outside the crime lab during my lunch break."

"I don't know him very well," Hood replied. Respecting the confidentiality of the recovery program, he intentionally withheld mentioning his role as Brian's sponsor. "What did he want with you?"

"I think he believes I can help find his brother. I told him I couldn't share my analysis of evidence, but he seems to think—because I dated Eric—I can help somehow."

Hood was disconcerted. He recalled Brian wondering if Sandra was a "psycho bitch." Was Brian attempting to assess Sandra's character and draw his own conclusion? Hood understood he was walking a fine line separating his personal desire to sponsor Brian and his duty to find his missing brother. He didn't want Sandra to face a similar predicament between helping Brian and maintaining professional confidentiality. He was disappointed Sandra hadn't rejected Brian's overture outright, but he also feared her rejection might spur Brian to take matters into his own hands. Finally, he had to admit the department's investigation into Eric's disappearance had produced nothing substantial. "What are you going to do?" he asked.

"I'm inclined to help him, if only to commiserate with him. He's distraught, but it's not only for his sake, it's for my own. Let's face it, Francis, Eric's ring and fingernail make me a suspect—maybe your prime suspect. My peace of mind is shattered. I can't focus on my job, and my OCD has ramped up so much I can barely function."

Sandra's willingness to get involved was not what Hood was hoping to hear. He knew, however, it wasn't his place to try to change her thinking. He focused on a possible upside. Brian was becoming more frustrated and more likely to take matters into his own hands. Sandra's level-headed influence might be just the thing to hold him in check.

# Chapter Twenty

Hood sat at his desk and stared at the document, but his mind was elsewhere— preoccupied by second-guessing what Brian, and Sandra, might be formulating. He wondered what rankled him more—the notion that they might impede his efforts or that they might succeed.

Focus, he scolded himself, as he began—for the third time—to study the requisition order for food to prepare meals for the jail inmates. He wondered how many of these forms he had approved during his decade-long tenure as sheriff. He determined it was at least one a week for more than five hundred weeks. Why hadn't he delegated the task to his chief jailer? Or perhaps the cook, even? Hood knew the answer to his own question. Food was a perishable commodity, and the number of inmates fluctuated. The order was not a fixed number; it was an estimate. Poor estimates could result in wasted tax dollars, so the decision was his responsibility as the elected sheriff.

He completed the order, stood, and plucked his hat and jacket from the coat rack. He stopped at Maggie's desk, handed her the form, donned his outerwear, and said, "I'm going out."

Maggie glanced at the wall clock, which indicated the time was 3:35 p.m. "Gone for the day?" she asked.

"Probably," he said.

From the moment he started his cruiser and headed to Schweinshaupten, he began to relax. He would be there in about a half-hour, which would give him plenty of daylight to search for the elusive pickup truck used to run

Brian Rakestraw off the road.

Hood didn't expect to find it. Keeping expectations low was a fundamental part of his recovery program. The theory was high expectations often result in disappointments and frustrations, which could fuel resentments and raise the possibility of relapse. In this case, however, the truck hadn't been sighted since the incident, which suggested the offending driver wasn't stupid enough to park it in plain sight.

He began scanning the scattered homes and farms along Route D even before the roadside sign welcomed him to Schweinshaupten. He slowed as he motored along the two blocks that served as the community's downtown, then cruised the outskirts of town and surveyed residential areas featuring older neighborhoods—interspersed with rundown, abandoned homes—and newer subdivisions. He saw plenty of pickups parked on streets and in driveways, but none matched the description of the suspect vehicle.

Returning to Main Street, he turned left onto Werner, crossed the abandoned MKT railroad tracks, then turned onto Pitchfork Road and surveyed the farms along the way. Although some of the derelict farms had been converted into thriving crop or livestock producers, others survived only as ghostly vestiges of Schweinshaupten's heyday. With visibility fleeting in the October dusk, Hood decided to return downtown. He steered onto a dusty drive of a long-abandoned farm identified only by a broken sign with word fragments:

Central Miss

Hog Prod

Beyond the sign, two elongated, single-story barns with sun-bleached white sides and gently sloping roofs squatted in a gravel parking area bordered by fenced acreage. He executed a K-turn, lingered to assess the dilapidated buildings that once served as symbols of prosperity, then left the gloomy image behind.

Back downtown, the streetlight outside Chubb's Tavern illuminated cars and pickups parked out front, signaling the end of another workday and the onset of what, for many residents, would be an evening of conviviality. Hood steered to the gravel lot in the back and entered through the rear door.

He bypassed restrooms and Chubb's office on either side of the hallway and joined the bar patrons inside.

"Hey, Sheriff," Rhonda greeted from behind the bar. "The usual?"

"Is it fresh?"

"So fresh it'll sass you back."

"Sure."

While Rhonda filled a white ceramic mug with coffee, Hood scanned the patrons and saw Vivion's crony, Hunk, in the pool room practicing his game. He was alone.

"Chubb here?" Hood asked Rhonda.

"Not yet."

"When do you expect him?"

"Check that calendar over there. I think he wrote seven p.m."

Hood approached the end of the bar, where a calendar was pinned to the wall. Rhonda's guess was correct.

"Thanks." Hood picked up his coffee and carried it to the pool room. He stood with his back to the wall while Hunk pretended not to notice him. The sheriff waited while the man made one shot and missed another. As he lined up a third shot, Hood said, "Hey, Hunk."

"Sheriff." Hunk remained hunched over, his sightline aiming along the cue stick.

"You ignoring me, or just concentrating?"

"I'm not supposed to talk to you."

"Who said that?"

"Doesn't matter."

"Sounds like something Vivion might say," Hood said.

Hunk stroked the shot, missed, and looked up at the sheriff as if he was to blame.

"See, I don't get that," Hood said.

"Don't get what?"

"Why you let other people tell you what to do." Hood held up an index finger as if illustrating a point. "I mean, you're a smart guy. Why do you let other people tell you what you can and can't do?"

"I don't," Hunk said. He moved around the table, contemplating his next shot.

"Just Vivion?"

"What?"

"Is it just Dennis Vivion you let tell you what to do?"

"He doesn't tell me what to do."

"Then there's nothing preventing you from talking to me," Hood said.

"That's right. I can do whatever I want."

"Then let's talk."

Hunk stroked his shot; the six ball kissed the cushion near a corner pocket but failed to drop. "Maybe I got nothing to say to you."

"Then I'll ask a question. Have you seen any unusual activity—people, vehicles—around *One Man's Trash*...?"

Hunk straightened. "Why're you asking me?"

"I'm asking everyone. You just happen to be the person I'm talking to now."

"So what if I did?"

"Might help me find out who assaulted Chet." Hood shrugged. "I mean, what's the harm in telling me? Unless you were a part of it."

"I had nothin' to do with what happened to that old man."

"What about Vivion?"

"No. Not that I know of."

"So, what is it you know?"

"I saw a car."

"Whose car?"

"Don't know. It was a red Mustang—real nice."

Hood recalled the red Mustang parked at the horse stable where he talked with Jessie.

"Do you know who owns it?"

"No. I mean, I didn't know anything until I saw it again at the old man's funeral. Some girl was driving it. I told Vivion and he went over and talked to her."

Hood recalled witnessing the encounter. "Do you know who she is?"

Hunk shook his head. "No. I'm guessing she's some family member?"

"What did Vivion say to her?"

"He told her he saw her car the night Chet was assaulted, which he didn't. I'm the one that saw it. I'm the one who told Vivion, and he went and told her he'd seen it, which was bullshit because he didn't. I did."

"Tell me exactly what you saw."

"When I saw the car, it looked like someone was in the front passenger seat, but it was in the shadows. Then I saw three people come out of the store. I couldn't see their faces because it was dark, but a girl got behind the wheel, and the other two got in the back seat."

Hood started to probe for details, but Hunk abruptly stopped talking as the color drained from his face. Hood turned and saw Vivion approaching.

"What's going on?" Vivion asked.

"N-N-Nothing," Hunk stammered.

"Hunk and I were having a conversation," Hood said.

"What about?" Vivion asked.

"I'm looking for a pickup truck, maybe a Ford F-150—" Hood stopped himself as he assessed Vivion's paint-splotched work uniform. "The vehicle we're looking for originally was white, but it may recently have been painted with rust-colored primer."

"You, too, huh?"

The question puzzled Hood, but he tried not to let it show. "Who else asked about the truck?"

"Eric's kid brother came to see me. He asked me about the truck, too. Said somebody ran him off the road with it. Is that why you're looking for it?"

Hood evaded the question by posing one of his own. "Anything like that come through your body shop?"

"Nope," Vivion answered.

"Either of you see a rust-colored pickup around town?" Hood asked.

"Nope," Vivion repeated. Hood looked at Hunk, who shook his head.

"Call me if you do," Hood said, knowing his obligatory plea was useless. "You know where to find me."

\* \* \*

Hood rapped on the door to the apartment. He had made his choice.

His conversation with Hunk suggested Jessie had driven her friends to *One Man's Trash...* the evening Chester Groner was assaulted. The question he faced was which student to confront first with the information.

Hood theorized Jessie, niece of the store owner, had instigated the trip, but why? He wanted to pose the question directly to her. He also considered talking first to Brian, if only because he sensed Brian was carrying something heavy, something in addition to Eric's disappearance. Although Brian might welcome the opportunity to unburden himself, the sheriff wondered if he would be abusing his relationship as Brian's sponsor.

He was about to knock again when Jessie peered through the glass pane, then unlocked and opened the door.

"Sheriff," she said, obviously surprised.

"Hello, Jessie. I've received some new information regarding the attack on your uncle. I'd like to ask you a few questions."

"Now?"

"Please."

"All right."

"May I come in?"

She hesitated a beat, long enough for Hood to realize his visit was unwelcome. "Sure."

Hood entered. Jessie guided him to the living area, where she sat on the sofa, and he chose a chair facing her. His eyes were drawn to a large wall hanging created by knots and braids of rope and twine in a variety of earth-tone shades and thicknesses. Hood knew he could make no remark that didn't reveal he considered it hideous, so he said, "Your red Mustang was seen in the alley outside *One Man's Trash ...* on or about the time your uncle was assaulted."

"Who said that?"

"A witness."

"Who?"

Hood gauged her response. She was a cornered, frightened creature. He adopted a quiet, deliberate tone and said, "The assault is now a homicide investigation, and I intend to get to the bottom of it. Lying won't help you and could make things worse."

Jessie surveyed the room, as if hoping some escape hatch would magically appear, then said, "We went to my uncle's store, but we found him like that. We didn't do anything."

"By we, you mean you and Brian, David and Michelle?"

"Yes, but we didn't all go inside."

"Who did?"

"Me, David, and Michelle. Brian was too drunk, so he stayed in the car."

"Why did you go there?"

"I wanted my friends to see the store. We were at my parents' house, and I started telling my friends about all the weird and wacky stuff my uncle sells, and we decided to make a road trip. My uncle was supposed to be with my folks at the lake, so I snatched the extra keys from our kitchen. But when we got there, the front door wasn't locked, so—"

"Wait," Hood said. "Did you say the door wasn't locked?"

"I don't think so. I mean, the door was closed, but when I put the key in, it didn't make a clicking sound like it was being unlocked."

"Didn't it seem strange that your uncle would leave the door unlocked since he was supposed to be at the lake?"

"It does now, but, like I said, we'd been drinking, and I guess I thought maybe I just didn't hear the click."

"Then what?" Hood prompted.

"We went in, and Uncle Chet was on the floor. He was bleeding and unconscious, but he was alive." Jessie focused on the floor, almost as if recalling the image. "David called 9-1-1 on the store phone, and we got the hell out of there."

Hood looked at her. He said nothing.

"Look," Jessie continued. "I'm not proud of what we did, all right? But there was nothing we could do to help him. We called for an ambulance. What else could we do? We'd been drinking. We were probably over the limit. I panicked. I guess we all did."

Hood allowed silence to reign.

"If we hadn't called," Jessie said, her voice cracking, "he might have bled to death on the floor. At least they got him to the hospital. At least he had a chance."

After several more beats of silence, she looked up at Hood and pleaded, "Say something."

"I have nothing to say," Hood replied.

"Am I under arrest?" Jessie asked.

Hood contemplated the question. Based on her admission, the only crime she had committed was entering a building after hours without the owner's permission. He considered the extenuating circumstances. According to her account, she entered without criminal intent, and her presence hastened medical attention for the assault victim. Hood also believed her admission was truthful and her remorse sincere.

"No." Hood watched Jessie's expression transform from concern to relief. "One thing, though," he added. "When I first met you and your parents at the hospital after the incident, you were wearing a blue coat."

Jessie nodded.

"May I borrow it? Hood asked.

"Why?"

"We found some blue threads at the scene. I want to see if they came from your coat." Hood had decided to have Sandra analyze the coat.

Confusion clouded Jessie's features. "I already told you I was there."

"I know," Hood said, "but if the fibers didn't come from your coat, they came from someone else's."

# Chapter Twenty-One

Hood and Brian faced each other. Although they sat in adult-sized folding chairs they had brought into the enclosed nursery in the basement of St. Cecilia Catholic Church. Hood could not shake his discomfort. He wondered if the feeling stemmed from being surrounded by children's furnishings or what he was about to say.

"Brian," he began. "I know you were at the scene—"

"I know," Brian interrupted. "Jessie told me."

"I think it's time for me to step aside as your sponsor, at least until these investigations are resolved."

"I didn't even go in the store. Did Jessie tell you that?"

"She did. I also know you approached Sandra Brondel about your brother's disappearance and that you drove to Chubb's Tavern and had a conversation with Dennis Vivion. I need—" Hood stopped, interrupted by the ringtone of his cell phone. He looked at the display screen; the caller was his rookie deputy, Young John Bunch.

"You need to take that?" Brian asked.

"I'll call him back. As I was saying, I need to caution you about taking—" Again, he stopped, alerted by the chime signaling a text message. He glanced at the message, which read: *Sighted truck matching vehicle in hit-and-run.* "Excuse me," Hood said. He left the nursery, walked to the stairwell, called Young John, and said, "This is Francis. Talk to me."

"I'm following a pickup that matches the description of the vehicle that ran Brian off Twenty-One Curves."

"Where are you?"

"Southbound on Route M. We just passed the intersection with Stoney Ridge."

"You run the plates?"

"There's no plate on the back."

"Okay," Hood said. "Pull that truck over, but be careful. Make it look routine, but detain the driver until I get there."

"Will do," Young John said.

Hood disconnected, poked his head inside the nursery room, and said to Brian, "Got to go. We'll talk later.

\* \* \*

Hood was about halfway to his destination when Young John came back on the line. Hood activated his hands-free connection and listened as his deputy reported, "I'm looking at the guy's driver's license. Name's Alan Heislen, age thirty-eight, lives in an apartment on the main drag in Schweinshaupten. License is valid, but he couldn't produce a vehicle registration or proof of insurance."

Although Heislen was a common Central Missouri surname, Hood didn't know an Alan. "Any warrants, criminal history?"

"I'm running it now. Hold on."

Hood pressed the accelerator as he awaited additional information.

"He's got a sheet," Young John's disembodied voice said. "Mostly misdemeanors—one drunk and disorderly, one burglary and stealing."

"Okay. Stall him for a few more minutes. I'm almost there."

When Hood arrived at the scene, he noted Young John had followed his instructions. Furthermore, his deputy and the driver—who was unfamiliar—were chatting like fast friends.

Hood stopped in front of the pickup, pinning it between the two cruisers, and joined the twosome. "Mr. Heislen, I'm your sheriff, Francis Hood."

"Nice to know you."

"Do you go by Alan or Al?" Hood purposely maintained a conversational, non-threatening tone as he studied the truck, a primer-colored Ford F-150.

"Al's fine."

The sheriff walked around the vehicle, noting both front and rear license plates were missing. The truck was equipped with a tailgate, contrary to Brian's description, but the rear bumper was dented and scratched, evidence it had made contact with something.

"This your truck, Al?" Hood asked.

"No." Al looked at his shoes. "I was tellin' your deputy—I shoulda known this was too good to be true."

"Knew what was too good to be true?"

"I found it parked outside my apartment as I was walkin' to get some breakfast. Sign taped to the windshield said: *Free*. The doors were unlocked, and the key was in the ignition."

"So you're saying this isn't your truck?"

"I should've known. Is it, like, stolen or somethin'?"

Hood and Young John exchanged looks of shared skepticism. "Where's the sign?" Hood asked.

"What sign?"

"The *Free* sign."

"On the seat."

Hood peered through the driver's side window and spotted a sheet of paper with *Free* written in block letters. He turned to Al. "Unless you can produce a title or bill of sale, we're going to have to impound this truck."

The man kicked a clod of dirt and muttered, "What an ass I am."

"Al, I'm going to ask you to wait with my deputy in his cruiser while I check on some things. Is that all right?"

"I guess."

While Young John escorted Al to his cruiser, Hood retrieved his notepad and flipped pages until he found Brian's description of his brother's truck and the VIN number he had acquired from the Division of Motor Vehicles. The numbers matched. He called Howard at the crime lab, informed him Eric Rakestraw's truck had been located, and arranged to have it towed to the lab.

Finally, he walked to Young John's cruiser and explained the need to get

Al's fingerprints.

"Am I under arrest?" he asked.

"No," Hood said. He addressed his deputy. "Print Mr. Heislen and take him wherever he wants to go. I'll wait for the wrecker. I don't want any additional contamination of the truck until the lab gets a look at it."

\* \* \*

Brian arrived at the coffee shop ten minutes prior to his scheduled meeting with Sandra. He selected a table but decided to wait for her arrival before ordering from the counter. Although he had been surprised by her call the previous evening, he was not surprised she had suggested a public location. She arrived punctually, and he stood to greet her. "I'm buying," he said. "What can I get you?"

Sandra requested a small, medium-roast coffee she had no intention of drinking.

When Brian returned with the drinks and they were settled in their seats, he said, "I've got to tell you, I didn't expect you to call."

"I don't know how I can help but doing nothing seemed wrong somehow." Sandra inhaled a long breath, hyper-conscious of her respiration. "I need to be honest with you, Brian. I talked to the sheriff before I called you."

"What'd he say?"

"I don't want to speak for him. Suffice it to say I decided to call you."

"The sheriff's a good guy, but I think I may have pissed him off. This thing with my brother has got me all knotted up."

"He is a good guy," Sandra agreed, "but when I spoke to him, I got the impression he didn't want us to get involved in the case. I understand that. You may as well know I have no intention of being part of some rogue investigation. Not only is it wrong, but it could cost me my job."

"I would never do that. All I'm doing is trying to make some sense of what's going on with my brother. You two spent time together before he disappeared. Did he give you any clue about what was going on with him or what he planned to do after the Patrol Academy thing didn't work out?"

"Not really. We mostly kept it light—music, movies, that sort of thing. We didn't talk about plans or goals."

Brian looked at her coffee cup. "You may want to pry that lid off, or it'll never cool down," he advised.

She removed the plastic lid and laid it on a napkin.

"Do you know a guy named Dennis Vivion?"

"I met him when Eric took me to Schweinshaupten's Fall Festival." She didn't volunteer that he had approached her as she sat with the sheriff at Chubb's Tavern. "Why? What about him?"

"I think he might be involved somehow. I talked to him the other night."

"You talked to him?"

"Yeah. He hangs out at that bar in Schweinshaupten, so I went there and asked him what he knew about my brother going missing."

"I don't think we're supposed to be doing things like that. I don't think the sheriff would—"

"I know," Brian said, his voice contrite. "It's just nobody seems to be getting anywhere."

"What did Vivion say?"

"Nothing useful."

"When we met," Sandra said, "you said your brother could be a jerk sometimes. What did you mean by that?"

"He was a take-charge kind of guy. I thought it was because he was my big brother, and he was looking out for me, especially after our parents died." Brian sipped coffee. "But he was like that with everything. He liked giving orders and having things his way. I guess that's why he hasn't been able to keep a job. I guess that's why he doesn't have many friends." He focused on Sandra. "I guess that's why I wasn't surprised when you broke up with him."

"Sometimes," Sandra said, choosing her words carefully, "people with dominant personalities make enemies. Can you think of anyone who might—"

"That's the thing. Eric didn't have any real friends, but I don't think he had any enemies, either. He mostly kept to himself, and people mostly left him alone."

"So," Sandra said, drawing out the monosyllable. "I don't feel like we've gotten anywhere. What do we do now?"

After a protracted silence, Brian said, "I don't know. My brother's the only family I've got. I can't just do nothing."

Sandra was tempted to remind him about interfering with the investigation but didn't. Instead, she said, "I'm going to take off." She stood and departed, leaving her small cup of coffee uncapped, but otherwise untouched.

# Chapter Twenty-Two

Hood couldn't help but notice the self-satisfied smile on the fingerprint analyst's face as he opened the garage bay door at the crime lab and stood beside the pickup truck. Howard had requested the meeting, which seemed unusual; he routinely reported his findings by a phone call or email.

"So what'd you find?" Hood asked.

Howard seemed almost to inflate as he explained, "Apparently, somebody went to great lengths to clean the cab's interior. Glove box was emptied, ashtray was dumped, seats and floors were vacuumed, steering wheel and other surfaces wiped. We found Eric Rakestraw's prints on some exterior surfaces. Initially, the only prints we found in the interior matched Alan Heislen, the driver you detained. We were stymied, about to wrap it up, until—"

Howard indulged in a dramatic pause, prompting Hood to ask, "Until what?"

"Look at the driver's sun visor."

Hood peeked inside the cab at the visor, which had been pulled down. The visor was outfitted with a small mirror.

"Until I found a distinct thumbprint on that mirror. The print's not in the database," Howard said, as if in answer to a question, "but a trace of lipstick suggests it came from a woman."

Hood pondered the information, which raised as many questions as it answered. "Good work," he said, knowing an attaboy was expected and, in this case, deserved.

"Thanks," Howard said. Basking in the compliment, he was expounding about the power of forensic science to reveal secrets when Brian steered a red Mustang into the lot.

"What's he doing here?" Howard asked.

"I need him to identify if this is the truck that ran him off the road," Hood explained. As Brian approached, Hood asked, "Is that Jessie's car you're driving?"

"Yeah. I'm still trying to decide whether to have mine fixed or just total it out." Brian studied the pickup. "Is that Eric's pickup?"

"We'll get to that," Hood said. "First, I need to know if this is the truck that ran you off the road. Have a look, but don't touch anything."

Brian walked slowly around the vehicle, inspecting it from various angles. When he finished, he said, "Yeah, that's the truck that rammed me, except it has a tailgate now. Is it my brother's?"

"Yes," Hood said. "The VIN numbers match. It's been cleaned out and primed, probably in an attempt to disguise it. Do you know an Alan Heislen?"

"Don't think so."

Hood explained the traffic stop and the driver's explanation.

"Do you believe the guy?" Brian asked.

"I have no evidence not to."

"So you're no closer to finding out who ran me off the road?"

Although Hood was rankled by Brian's comment, he reminded himself not to take it personally. "What I do know—" he began, interrupted by his cell phone's ring tone. The display indicated the caller was Wally. "I need to take this." He exited the garage bay and answered. "What's up?"

"Your wife and daughter were in an accident," Wally said, urgency in his tone. "They're on their way to the ER."

"What kind of accident?"

"Two-car collision. That's all I know."

"On my way," Hood said.

* * *

136

Questions and assumptions collided and ricocheted in Hood's mind as he sped toward Huhman County Hospital.

How bad could it be? Linda had told him she and Elizabeth planned to do some shopping after school. They were probably in town, not on a highway. The speed limit would be thirty, thirty-five max. Probably just a fender bender. Probably just shaken up. The trip to the ER was only because the EMTs were being overly cautious, particularly if they knew it was the sheriff's wife and daughter. It shouldn't be that way. Every accident victim should be treated the same. But he understood, was grateful. Get them thoroughly checked out before sending them home. Tonight's dinner conversation would be them talking about how lucky they were.

His ruminations and suppositions continued to run rampant as he rushed into the ER, where Rachel, a longtime nurse and friend of Linda's, met him in the lobby.

"They're here, Francis," Rachel said. "Linda's going to be fine. She has a broken wrist, and she suffered some contusions, but no serious injuries."

"Can I see her?"

"Of course. She's in the ER."

Hood's relief was momentary. "Elizabeth?"

"She's—"

In the instant Rachel paused, terror exploded like a grenade in Hood's gut, and he began shaking visibly.

"She's being evaluated," Rachel added.

"Evaluated?" he repeated, a question.

"From what the EMTs reported, your wife's car was crossing an intersection and was broadsided on the passenger door. Elizabeth took the brunt of it. She suffered a cracked rib, but she also sustained an apparent head injury, which the doctors are continuing to evaluate."

"How soon will they know?"

"We've already performed some of the scans necessary to establish priorities about what to address first. I wish I could be more specific, but some head injuries require us to wait and see how patients respond when they regain consciousness."

"Are you saying she could have brain damage?"

"Francis," Rachel said, her tone soothing. "All I'm saying is we don't know. We mustn't jump to any conclusions. We simply must wait."

* * *

Hood often imagined his alcoholism as an insidious symbiont.

It would always be part of him. He would never be separated from it. And it was patient, content to remain dormant until some vulnerability reawakened its devious, obsessive-compulsive power.

He was sitting beside his wife's hospital bed, watching Linda sleep, when a faint but familiar voice in his mind suggested a drink.

*Have a drink.*

He recoiled.

*Have a drink.*

The voice had strengthened. Hood reminded himself alcohol no longer was his default solution to his troubles.

*Have a drink.*

The imperative was insistent. He felt drained. Although he was the sheriff, a problem-solver dedicated to putting things right, he had no power to heal the people he loved. Some fifteen months ago, he had faced powerlessness when he admitted he needed help to stop drinking. In retrospect, surrender was the most difficult thing he'd ever done—and the most valuable.

He stood, returned to the waiting area, and called Matthew. After briefly explaining the circumstances to his recovery sponsor, Matthew said, "I'm on my way."

Hood felt immediately relieved. Having taken action, his thoughts of drinking eased, and conjecture about the accident wormed its way into his mind. He considered Linda to be a good driver, but she had a tendency to get distracted, particularly if she was involved in a conversation—or argument, as sometimes happened with Elizabeth. He stopped himself. He realized he was making assumptions—worse, he was trying to assign blame in the absence of facts or evidence.

He was about to return to the ER room when Wally and Maggie hastily entered the waiting area and joined him.

"How are they?" they asked, almost simultaneously.

The trio adjourned to a vacant corner, and Hood related what he knew about their respective conditions. He reported his wife was allowed limited visitors but was asleep when he left her ER room. In response to Hood's inquiry, Maggie informed him the collision had occurred within the St. Gotthard city limits, and she had requested a copy of the accident report as soon as it was available.

The conversation devolved into silence until Wally announced he needed to pick up one of his sons. As Wally left, he nearly collided with Matthew. An exchange of greetings and goodbyes ensued before Maggie—who seemed to possess an astute intuition—volunteered to sit at Linda's beside so Hood and Matthew could converse privately.

The two men went to the cafeteria and sat at a small table, each with a cup of coffee. "Thanks for coming," Hood said. "Did I sound desperate?"

"We have a slogan in recovery—imagine that, another slogan—*the gift of desperation*. It means when someone becomes desperate enough to ask for help. You've grown a lot in recovery, Francis, but I've noticed you're still reluctant to reach out."

"I don't want to bother people."

"I often feel the same way. It helps me justify my tendency toward self-reliance. It's my grown-up version of me pounding my fists on the table while yelling, 'I can do it myself.'"

Hood realized he was somewhat offended by the rebuke, but also amused by the image of adolescent Matthew. "I did call you this time," Hood reminded him, as if testifying in his own defense.

"You did, and I appreciate it. This is a heavy load, but you don't have to carry it alone."

"I'm worried."

"Tell me what you know to be true."

As Hood recited what he had been told, he realized much remained unknown, particularly regarding Elizabeth's diagnosis. He concluded by saying, "I guess what I'm feeling is fear."

"I understand."

"And I feel helpless."

"But you're not. If I can't fix a situation, I must accept it and seek guidance on how I can be useful. Elizabeth's recovery is in the hands of a higher power working through skilled medical professionals. You are neither. But your daughter also needs hope, love, and prayer, and you can provide those in abundance."

Hood rested his elbows on his knees and placed his head in his palms. "I don't even know how the accident happened, and I already found myself trying to blame Linda." He looked up at Matthew, as if preparing to be scolded.

"We're human," Matthew said. "Recovery encourages me to strive to be better, but I'm a long way from eliminating my character flaws. I have a hard time giving up blame because if I blame someone else, I don't have to change. The important thing is to be honest with yourself."

"If I'm being honest, right now, I just feel lost."

# Chapter Twenty-Three

Hood rubbed shaving cream on his cheeks, chin, and neck. Going through the motions of life was the only way he knew to avoid paralyzing fear. Tension gripped and twisted his back and shoulder muscles. Chills, coming in waves, coursed through his upper body. His stomach roiled. He wanted some form of relief, some fetal incoherence that would last until he was awakened and assured his daughter was okay.

He had been sent home from the hospital in the early morning hours by Linda, who had been discharged, but insisted on maintaining a vigil at their daughter's bedside. Although Hood attempted to mirror his wife's professional, stoic demeanor, he failed miserably. He was jittery, uncomfortable, and exuded a palpable tension. He was unable to sleep in the hospital recliner, and he repeatedly asked about Elizabeth's condition despite being told his inquiries were premature. Finally, Linda convinced him to go home. Hood sensed that her reasoning was two-fold—he needed rest, and he was getting on her nerves. He knew she was right because he was getting on his own nerves.

Upon returning home, he had surprised himself when he lay on the bed and slept for several hours, awakening in mid-morning. He immediately called Linda, who had received no update about their daughter's head injuries. His wife also said she had showered and eaten breakfast at the hospital before resuming her bedside vigil, and Hood promised he'd join her as soon as he got cleaned up.

As he prepared to begin shaving, he adjusted the mirror to improve the lighting, then stopped abruptly and stared at the wet thumbprint in the corner. The print triggered a memory, then a revelation.

Howard, he recalled, had surmised the presence of lipstick suggested a woman left the thumbprint on the truck's visor mirror. Hood immediately had suspected the print belonged to Sandra and was a remnant of when she dated Eric. Now, a new possibility emerged. Could it belong to Rhonda, Vivion's sometimes girlfriend?

Although Hood was trying to overcome his character flaws, which included being judgmental, he considered Rhonda to be a diva who devoted much time and effort to her appearance.

He retrieved his phone from the nightstand and noticed he had missed an earlier call from Sandra. Noting the time of the call coincided with his shower, he returned it.

Their conversation began with him apologizing for missing her call and her inquiring about his wife and daughter. He provided an update, then asked the reason for her initial call.

"Jessie's coat is not a match for the fibers found at the scene. Her coat is one hundred percent wool. The others are a blend of natural and synthetic threads."

Hood was disappointed; another dead end.

* * *

*Accept the things I cannot change.*

Hood mentally repeated that phrase from the Serenity Prayer as he sat beside his wife at their daughter's hospital bedside.

Elizabeth slept, Linda prayed, and Hood struggled to allay the fears relentlessly crowding him. Although acceptance was a fundamental of recovery, his repetition of the Serenity Prayer wasn't helping. He fidgeted, stood, paced, and sat again on the faux leather loveseat. Amid his anxiety, he had realized she might not be able to dance at her recital. The notion that he might dodge the father-daughter dance had crept in like a cat burglar, and— although he chastised himself for entertaining such a despicable, selfish idea—he knew what he was feeling was relief.

He needed to distract himself, to get out of his own head. He removed his cell phone, opened an email, and said to Linda, "Tell me again how the accident happened?"

"What are you looking at?" Linda asked.

"It's a copy of the accident report. Maggie got it from the St. Gotthard Police and sent it to me."

"What's it say?"

Hood didn't reference the report, which absolved his wife and faulted an elderly driver who had suffered a medical event, careened through a stop sign, and broadsided Linda's vehicle. Instead, he said, "Tell me what happened."

"Again."

"Yes."

"Okay," she said, her exasperation apparent. "I was on Crest, and I stopped at the four-way stop at the intersection of Crest and High—"

"A complete stop?"

"Yes," Linda said. "Another car was already stopped at the intersection on High, so I yielded. When that car cleared the intersection, I was next, so I went, and that's when I got broadsided. The third car never even stopped. That's it."

Her narrative, again, was consistent with the report. "Did you see the other car?"

"I saw it approaching, but it's a four-way stop. I expected the driver to stop."

Although he said nothing, Linda deduced from his expression that he was not satisfied. "Sometimes things just happen, Francis. Sometimes, there's no one to blame. It was an accident."

"Of course," he agreed, but his tone lacked commitment.

\* \* \*

*An accident.*

Linda's words echoed in Hood's mind as he drove toward Chubb's Tavern.

An accident implied no one was to blame, a proposition Hood found difficult to accept. And if Linda was blameless, who or what was responsible?

As a youth in the Catholic Church, Hood had been introduced in his Sunday School catechism to the Holy Trinity—Father, Son, and Holy Spirit. However, he was skeptical of the dogma and—during his active alcoholism—had stopped going to church. After reuniting with his family, he resumed attending Sunday Mass, not because he found solace there, but in support of his wife and daughter. Whatever spirituality Hood embraced, he found in the rooms of recovery, where he not only was allowed, but encouraged, to find a higher power.

He realized, at this juncture, he understood little. But the process seemed more a gradual unfolding than a singular revelation. He appreciated his recovery program's emphasis on prayer, meditation, and self-analysis. He considered himself in the infancy of recovery, with much to learn. But one thing he did know—he could not believe the same higher power who rescued him was responsible for his daughter's plight.

What he didn't know was whether he could accept that an accident—a random circumstance without rhyme or reason—could severely alter his daughter's existence and his family's future.

He parked in the gravel lot behind the tavern and entered through the back door. Consistent with the plan he and Wally had devised, Hood spotted his chief deputy sitting alone at a table. As Rhonda approached Wally's table, Hood fell in step behind her and claimed the chair opposite Wally.

"Look at you two," Rhonda said, "out of uniform and out on the town. What can I getcha?"

"Coffee. Black," replied Wally.

"The same," Hood added.

"Coffee's not my idea of a night on the town," she said, "but to each his own."

Rhonda retreated behind the bar, where she and Chubb engaged in what seemed a well-choreographed maneuver as he continued to tend bar, while she poured coffee.

The lawmen turned their attention to a big screen television mounted high on a wall in the corner. Game analysts were engaged in spirited halftime chatter, including highlights from the first half of the PAC-12 matchup being broadcast.

Rhonda returned and delivered their drinks. Before she left, Hood lifted a partially filled ashtray from the table, "Could you dump this for us? Kind of stinks."

"Sure thing." She left with the ashtray.

Hood and Wally returned their attention to the game while they sipped coffee. After a time, Rhonda returned with a half-full coffee pot. "Refill?" she asked.

"Sure," Hood answered. Wally pushed his mug toward her.

"So," Rhonda quipped as she poured. "Date night?"

"Don't tell our wives," Hood replied, playing along. "I'm in enough trouble as it is."

"Well, your secret's safe with me."

As she turned toward the bar, Hood asked, "Where's the ashtray?"

"Left it on the bar. Do you want it? I didn't know you smoked."

"Sometimes," Hood lied, "but let's keep that secret safe, as well."

After she brought the clean ashtray and departed, Hood leaned across the table and whispered, "Show time."

Both officers knew fingerprints obtained without permission were admissible as evidence in court. As Wally adjourned to the rear hallway, where the restrooms and Chubb's office were located, Hood pretended to be preoccupied watching the game while anxiously awaiting Wally's return. Fearful Rhonda might be prompt about refills and notice the missing ashtray, Hood was relieved when his deputy returned to the table and replaced the ashtray.

"Get it?" Hood asked.

Wally nodded.

When Rhonda reappeared with a coffee pot and asked about refills, Hood asked, "Is Vivion around?"

"It's a little early for him." She glanced at a wall clock that doubled as a beer advertisement. "Should be here soon."

"Thought I'd give him an update. We identified the owner of that stolen truck I was asking him about the other night."

"Is that right?"

Hood couldn't decide if her seeming indifference was genuine.

"It belongs to Eric Rakestraw, the fellow who's been missing. Somebody gave his truck a primer paint job. Your boyfriend still works at that auto body shop, right?"

"Uh-huh. So?"

"So I wonder if he primed it?"

"You'll have to ask him."

As if on cue, the door opened, Vivion entered, and Rhonda said, "Speak of the devil."

Vivion approached the table and stood beside Rhonda. "This a private conversation?"

"Not at all," Hood said. "I was just telling Rhonda we recovered Eric Rakestraw's truck. Somebody sprayed it with a coat of primer. Was that you?"

"What kind of truck?" He listened as Hood provided details, then said, "Didn't come through our shop. How'd you find it?"

"Somebody was driving it, and one of my deputies pulled him over. Driver claimed it had a *Free* sign in the windshield and the keys in the ignition. Know anything about that?"

"Who's the driver?"

"I'm not naming names."

"A *Free* sign? Sounds like a lame-ass excuse to me. Have you considered the driver is your guy? Maybe you need to lean on him a little."

"Maybe," Hood said. "What do you think, Rhonda?"

"About what?" she said.

"The stolen truck. Eric's disappearance. You hear a lot of things—"

"I think that's enough, Sheriff," Vivion interrupted. "I come in here to relax and have a beer, and here you are giving me the third degree and harassing my girlfriend, who's got a job to do."

"Chubb seems okay with it," Hood remarked as he looked to the owner, who efficiently tended the bar.

"Well, I'm not okay with it."

The suddenness with which the conversation had become confrontational caught Hood off guard. He was reminded of a question repeated by a friend in recovery, who would ask himself, *Is this the hill I want to die on today?* Hood decided to retreat, not engage. "All I'm trying to do is gather information on Eric Rakestraw's disappearance. The truck may be key. Since you two were friends, I—"

"Who said we were friends? We hung out sometimes, but I wouldn't exactly call us friends. Besides, Eric's a grown-up. He can do whatever he wants, be wherever he wants." He turned to Rhonda. "How about you do your job and get me a beer?"

As Rhonda stalked away, the sheriff stood, prompting Wally to do the same. Hood decided having the last word was unnecessary, so he bypassed Vivion and headed for the door.

# Chapter Twenty-Four

Hood hated waiting. After a time, he experienced a numbness of mind and body, something akin to the semi-conscious haze that preceded sleep. He and Linda sat in their daughter's hospital room, the only sound coming from machines rhythmically recording Elizabeth's vital signs.

Their vigil had morphed into silent inactivity. Neither of them watched TV, read a book or newspaper, or worked a crossword puzzle. They simply stared at nothing. They spoke infrequently, usually an announcement followed by a question, such as, "I'm getting more coffee. Want some?" or "I'm going to the cafeteria. Can I bring you something?" Hood was under the impression it would be unthinkable for both parents to leave the room simultaneously, even for a brief time.

Linda had maintained a nearly constant presence, eating meals and sleeping in the bedside recliner. She returned home once each day—and only when her husband substituted for her at the hospital—to shower, change clothes, and reapply her makeup.

Hood attempted some semblance of balance by putting in some hours on the job and sleeping in his own bed, but unease followed him. He was distracted at work and slept fitfully. He felt powerless, lacking the skills to heal his daughter's injuries or the rift he had created with his wife. He stood, yielding to the compulsion to leave the hospital room, which had become more oppressive and claustrophobic. "I think I'll go—"

Her eyelids fluttered!" Linda shouted as she jumped to her feet and scrambled to Elizabeth's bedside.

Hood joined her. He stared at his daughter's face, which remained impassive. "Are you sure?"

Linda reached to her daughter's face and gently lifted an eyelid. "I can't tell. I need my penlight." She stepped back. "I'm—" Doubt crept into her expression. She squinted, squeezing her own reddened and watery lids. "I couldn't have imagined it, could I?"

They continued to stare. Elizabeth remained immobile. The rhythm of the monitor droned without interruption.

"I'm calling the nurse," Linda said.

Although Hood was poised to discourage her, he didn't. Linda activated the bedside call button, and within moments, Rachel entered.

"I think I saw her eyelids flutter," Linda said.

Rachel removed a penlight from her uniform pocket, lifted Elizabeth's left eyelid, and examined her pupil. "Let me get Dr. Norris," she said.

When Rachel left, Hood turned to his wife. "That's a good sign, right?"

"I'm pretty sure."

Hood heard equivocation in her voice. "I mean, she's getting the neurologist."

Before Linda could reply, the door opened. Rachel entered and said, "Dr. Norris is on her way."

"That's—?" Hood stopped himself. He was seeking assurance. He was making the situation about him, his feelings, his fears. His recovery program encouraged self-analysis, but he asked himself, why does self-analysis have to complicate everything?

"Good afternoon," Dr. Deanna Norris greeted as she stepped into the room. She skipped any further pleasantries with the parents, consulted the monitor readings and Elizabeth's chart, then stooped over the patient and whispered, "Elizabeth."

They waited. When Elizabeth failed to respond, Dr. Norris straightened to her full height. "Let's—"

"She did it again," Linda shouted.

Everyone focused on Elizabeth as her lashes fluttered and her eyes opened. Dr. Norris stooped into her field of vision. "Elizabeth?"

"Yes." Her voice was weak, scratchy.

"I'm Dr. Norris. You're in Huhman County Hospital. Your parents are here. You were in a car accident. Do you remember?"

"Not really."

"Can you tell me your name?"

"Elizabeth Hood."

Dr. Norris made a "V" sign with her fingers. "How many fingers am I holding up?"

"Two."

The doctor posed a series of questions and, when her inquiry ended, Elizabeth said she was hungry, and lunch was ordered. "I'm going to speak with your parents for a moment," Dr. Norris told her patient, "But they'll be right back. Okay?"

Elizabeth nodded, and the doctor motioned for the parents to join her in the hallway. Outside the room, Dr. Norris said, "Her sensory and motor skills are encouraging. I'm going to order some additional tests. In the meantime, if she says or does anything unusual, have Rachel page me. I'll be here all afternoon."

"So she's going to be all right?" Hood asked, his tone expectant.

"The early indicators are positive. Additional testing and time will give us more answers."

As Dr. Norris excused herself, Hood already was comparing his daughter's condition to his own affliction; healing would be a process, not an automatic or immediate restoration.

\* \* \*

"The thumbprint you lifted from the ashtray at Chubb's Tavern," Howard said as he sat across from the sheriff's desk, "matches the print from the mirror on the truck visor."

*Rhonda*, Hood thought. He leaned back in his desk chair, unable to restrain a self-satisfied smile. Although the picture remained incomplete, some puzzle pieces seemed to be falling into place. In addition, although his daughter remained hospitalized, her condition was improving, restoring Hood's sense of stability. What puzzled him was Howard's request for a face-to-face meeting, as well as the man's fidgety behavior. "Thanks," Hood said. "But you could have called. You didn't need to come by."

Howard repositioned himself in the visitor's chair, clearly uncomfortable. "As a friend, I thought you should know there's been some talk."

"About?" Hood prompted.

"You and Sandra."

Hood cocked his head, disturbed by the implication. When Howard failed to continue, Hood asked, "What kind of talk?"

"That your relationship is more than strictly professional."

"That's absurd," Hood protested. "We've worked on some cases together, and we're friends, but that's the extent of it. I've been married for twenty-two years. Sandra's like"—he groped to do the mental math—"fifteen years younger than me. She could almost be my daughter, for heaven's sake."

"Francis, you know as well as I do that's the stereotype—a middle-aged married guy and an attractive younger woman."

Hood did know. If he was being honest with himself, his righteous indignation rang false, even to himself. When he examined his part in the scenario, he was not blameless. At age 47, he wondered if he had been trying to seek reassurance that he remained desirable. Although he conceded he may have been guilty of flirting, his end game was hardly an extra-marital affair. He had made a lifelong promise of fidelity to Linda and had no intention of violating his vow. "You're right," he said. "I can see how people may have—well, let's just say it's not true."

"I didn't mean to upset you," Howard said. "I thought you should know what people are saying."

"It's fine." But it wasn't fine. The disclosure lingered in Hood's mind long after Howard had gone.

* * *

Hood stared at the ceramic dog wearing a top hat and lifting a leg against a tree in Rhonda's front yard. He had never seen such a—how would he characterize it? —conversation-starting lawn ornament.

He pressed the doorbell. As he waited, he involuntarily practiced his jazz squares—hands on hips, right foot forward, crossing over left, left foot back.

"Dennis isn't here." The voice halted him in mid-step. He glanced at Rhonda, who had appeared from around the side of the house. Although he attempted to cover his movements, her baffled expression revealed his failure. "Just practicing—. Never mind. I wanted to talk to you, anyway."

"Come around back," she invited.

He followed her into the back yard and onto a concrete patio. Colorful leaves from surrounding trees fell sporadically as rising temperatures promised another unseasonably warm October day. "Just finishing my coffee. Want some?"

"No thanks."

"Suit yourself." She gestured for Hood to sit in an Adirondack chair, painted bright red, while she sat on a cushioned lounge and stretched her legs, but kept the back upright so she could sip from the coffee perched on a wooden table beside her. "More questions?" she asked, suggesting boredom.

"We found your thumbprint on the driver's side visor mirror in Eric Rakestraw's truck. How do you explain that?"

"What makes you think I need to explain that?"

"Because Eric is missing, and his truck was taken."

Rhonda shrugged as she lifted her cup and sipped. "So? Dennis and I hung out with Eric sometimes. We've ridden in his truck. I guess I checked out my hair and makeup in the visor mirror. What's the big deal?"

"The big deal is forensics found no other prints. The interior was wiped clean, which suggests the print left on the mirror was an oversight by whoever wiped down the cab."

"So, ask whoever that was. It wasn't me. I got enough to do vacuuming shit at home and wiping counters at work, not to mention cleaning up after sloppy drunks spilling their beers or vomiting on the floor." She stood. "Speaking of which, I've got to get ready for my shift."

Hood tried to prevent disappointment from clouding his expression. He wasn't certain what he expected to learn from Rhonda, but he had hoped to learn something. She went indoors, and he returned to his cruiser, where he punched the heel of his hand against the steering wheel in a vain effort to relieve frustration. Tonight's recovery meeting couldn't come too soon.

* * *

Hood lingered in the church basement after the meeting, which Brian had failed to attend. The sheriff helped fold and stack chairs, wipe tables, and dust mop the floor. Eventually, he and Matthew were the only two remaining.

"Anything else?" Hood asked as his sponsor dumped coffee grounds in the trash and rinsed the pot.

"You can tell me what's on your mind."

"I'm feeling helpless and depressed. I'm short-tempered, my gut's churning, and I can't sleep. I know drinking isn't going to solve anything, but numbing my mind for a few hours is starting to sound pretty good."

"Let's talk about it," Matthew said. They returned to the basement gym, unfolded two chairs, and sat. "My daughter's condition is improving, so that's a load off my mind, but some of my old behaviors have resurfaced."

"For example?"

"I still feel guilty about jumping to conclusions and blaming Linda for the accident. On top of that, I've got a couple investigations I'm not making any progress on."

"Whenever I'm unsettled," Matthew said, "it's either because I'm not getting what I want or I'm getting what I don't want."

"I want answers," Hood said.

"Precisely," Matthew agreed. "You want assurance your daughter will be fine, and your wife doesn't resent your behavior. And you want evidence that will close your investigations. But what I've learned is life doesn't always give me what I want, wrapped up neatly with a perfect bow and no loose ends. When that happens to me, I've got to look at what's really disturbing me."

"I'm just angry."

"I used to think that, too. But someone once told me anger is a secondary emotion, and it wasn't until then that I realized my anger was based on fear."

Hood's expression betrayed confusion.

"I was afraid," Matthew continued, "because I wasn't in control. What I've learned in recovery is control is largely an illusion, and my fears are largely false."

"I hear what you're saying, but nothing seems to be going right these days."

"Nothing?" Matthew asked, an obvious challenge in his tone.

Hood hesitated a beat, then said, "All right. Not nothing."

"You're sober, and you're dealing with life on life's terms. That's something, a big something."

Hood contemplated his previous alcoholic lifestyle—his self-imposed distance from family and co-workers, his impaired thinking, his debilitating hangovers.

"Francis, you're not unique, and you're not special. I'm not telling you anything you don't already know. You are, however, a good husband, father, and sheriff. You're kind and compassionate. But if you take a drink, you're going right back to selfishness and self-delusion."

"You're right," Hood said. "Thank you for talking me off the ledge."

"Any time. I've been talked off a few ledges myself. I know it's a scary place for an alcoholic."

* * *

Hood waited in his cruiser parked in the lot at Millie's Diner until Sandra arrived in her SUV.

Although the after-dinner crowd was sparse, he escorted Sandra to a booth in a far corner.

Nadine approached, armed with menus, pad, and pen. "Coffee, Francis?" she asked. When he nodded, Nadine turned to Sandra. "And you?"

An awkward silence prevailed until Sandra said, "Sure."

"Would you like menus?"

"Just coffee," Hood said. After the waitress left, he said to Sandra, "You don't

154

have to order something." As he spoke the words, he realized he sounded like a grownup instructing a child.

"I know," Sandra said, "but it seems rude. She's just trying to make a living."

"Has it—you know, the swallowing thing—gotten any better?"

"You can call it what it is. It's somatic OCD. And no, it hasn't gotten better." Hood heard pique in her tone. "I guess I'm just not comfortable—"

"It's a condition, Francis. It may not be as prevalent as cancer, or heart disease, or even alcoholism, for that matter, but that doesn't mean we should be uncomfortable talking about it."

They stopped speaking when Nadine returned. The waitress seemed to sense she was intruding because she silently placed full mugs before both and left a carafe on the table before departing.

"You're right," Hood said. "I'm sorry."

"No. It's my fault. You'd think I'd be used to it by now, but once in a while, I need to throw my own pity party because I don't like being different."

"I'm the same way. When I first realized I had a drinking problem, I tried to deny it because I didn't want to be different. Now, I think everybody is different, and—in a bizarre way—that makes us all the same."

"I like that," Sandra said. "Similarly unique."

"Or uniquely similar." Hood sipped coffee. Sandra's remained untouched.

"You said we needed to talk about something," Sandra prompted.

Hood leaned against the upholstered back of the booth. "Have you heard any office gossip regarding our relationship?"

"What do you mean 'our relationship?'"

"That it's more than strictly professional."

"That's crazy."

"That's exactly what I said."

"Who told you this?"

"I probably shouldn't say."

"It was Howard, wasn't it?"

As Hood reached for his cup, Sandra added, "Why am I not surprised?"

"I'm sorry," Hood said.

"Don't apologize. It's not your fault."

"You and I have been spending a lot of time together recently. We—"

"Professionally," Sandra interjected.

"We had coffee at Chubb's after the assault. I've been to your office, your house."

"Professionally," she repeated. "Honestly, Francis. I don't understand why people can't mind their own business without having to make up stuff about other people."

"We all suffer from the human condition."

"Uniquely similar." Sandra stood. "Excuse me," she said as she headed toward the restroom.

Hood noticed her coffee cup remained untouched.

# Chapter Twenty-Five

Hood buttoned his uniform shirt and tucked it neatly into his trousers. He looked in the full-length mirror and smoothed the few creases that remained.

*Appearances.*

The concept tugged at his thoughts. Working closely with Sandra on the investigation had created an appearance of inappropriate behavior in the minds of some observers. Hood knew the gossip was false. He recalled a recovery group member saying, "Don't believe everything you think." He appreciated that axiom—a thought is not a fact.

If he was being honest, however—and his program encouraged honesty—his relationship with Sandra was more than co-workers, as well as more than friends. Unsure how to define it, he resolved to analyze it more closely.

As he straightened his shirt a final time, he realized he had been lingering in front of the mirror. How, he wondered, was he progressing with his jazz squares? He placed his hands on his hips, extended his right foot crossing it over his left, left foot back. His movements were wooden. He was performing the step, but without fluidity or grace. He repeated the sequence until he was interrupted by Linda's voice coming from downstairs, "I'm going to fix a breakfast sandwich, Francis. Want one?"

"That would be great." he hollered back.

Downstairs, he poured his first cup of coffee, sat at the dinette table, and watched Linda maneuver throughout the kitchen. Her movements—selecting pans and plates, toasting English muffins, frying eggs and bacon—struck him as more graceful and rhythmic than his jazz squares, sashays, and kick ball changes.

"I am so looking forward to having Elizabeth home," Linda said, referencing their daughter's hospital discharge, planned for later in morning.

"Me, too, but I can't help worrying about what Dr. Norris said."

"All she said was we need to keep an eye on her for a few days."

"And report any unusual behavior," Hood reminded. "That means she's not out of the woods yet."

Linda flipped the eggs, topping each with salt, pepper, and a slice of cheese.

"Speaking of behavior," he continued, "I owe you an apology for some of the things I said at the hospital."

"This has been a trying time for everyone." Linda assembled the bacon, egg, and cheese sandwiches and delivered them to the table.

"That's no excuse for me acting like a child. I've been selfish, angry—you name it."

"I haven't been at my best, either." She sat across from him.

Silence dominated the room as they began eating. Hood attempted to relax and appreciate the shared moment. He failed. His compulsion to speak prevailed. "Just so you know—in case you hear anything—there's some gossip being spread about Sandra and me."

Linda lifted her head. "What's being said?"

"That our relationship is more than professional."

"An affair?"

"I guess, but I want to assure you there's nothing going on."

Linda placed her partially eaten sandwich on her plate. "So what prompted these rumors?"

Hood heard the transition in her tone from conversational to interrogatory. "I don't know."

"Something must have caused them," she pressed.

"Well, I mean, we've been spending more time together on this investigation. I should say investigations. She's doing the forensics on the assault, but she's also the ex-girlfriend of the guy who's missing."

"How much more time?"

"What?"

158

"You said *more* time. How much more time?

"We had a drink—I mean, she had water but didn't drink it. I had coffee—at that tavern in Schweinshaupten the night of the assault. I told you about that. And I've been to her lab and to her house—"

"Her house?" Linda repeated.

"With Wally." Hood realized he sounded defensive. He recalled the advice his campaign manager had given him when he ran for re-election— *"When you're defending, you're losing."* He was definitely losing. His explanation sounded false, even to him. How could he expect Linda to believe it? "Well," he added, "One time with Wally. Another time, I was alone."

"With Sandra?"

"Yes."

"Just the two of you? At her house?"

"Yes."

"Linda pushed her plate away. "It's no wonder people are gossiping." She shook her head. "I want to trust you, Francis. I do. And I believe you when you say you're not having an affair with her. But you need to sort out what it is that's going on. I know there's some connection between you and Sandra. I've known it since you introduced her to me. You two—you with your alcoholism, her with her OCD—share some kind of bond. Maybe you both realize you're works in progress, and you're trying to help each other become better versions of yourselves. I don't know. What I do know is you need to figure it out."

\* \* \*

Hood sat in Eric Rakestraw's pickup truck, parked across the street from Beautiful Body and Paint, which featured two garage bays for auto body repairs and a third outfitted as a paint booth. The sheriff watched through one of the open garage doors as Dennis Vivion sanded the front fender of a late-model vehicle.

Hood made no attempt to conceal his presence. Although he suspected Vivion was involved in some wrongdoing—the assault on Chester Groner,

Eric Rakestraw's disappearance, or the thefts from construction sites—he had no proof. In addition, he had no plan to obtain proof. His only strategy was overt surveillance, which translated into pestering, annoying, and, hopefully, causing Vivion to become careless.

From what the sheriff could glean, Vivion was the lone employee today. Hood speculated why the owner—or other workers, if there were any—weren't on the job. Perhaps they started later, were absent due to vacation or illness, or weren't needed because of a lack of work. Ultimately, the reasons didn't matter; what mattered was Vivion had noticed the sheriff's surveillance and appeared flustered.

When Vivion switched off the sander, Hood exited the truck and walked to the open garage door.

"Is this how the sheriff's department spends my tax dollars?" asked Vivion, who held the sander at his side.

"Today it is. And probably for the foreseeable future."

"You got a problem with me, Sheriff?"

"You recognize that truck over there?"

"Nope."

"It's Eric Rakestraw's truck. Somebody primed it. Was that you?"

"Nope. Already told you that. Besides, it's a shitty paint job. I can see that from here."

"What do you mean?"

"Stoop down, and you can see the sliver of white where the hood meets the fenders. Whoever painted it didn't even lift the hood. And look at the overspray on the chrome headlight trim. I couldn't do a primer coat that bad if I tried."

"Do you mind if I look in the paint booth?"

"What for?"

"Evidence of primer."

"Of course, there's primer. We use it all the time."

"Same brand? Same color?"

"How should I know?"

"We can have it tested at the lab."

160

# CHAPTER TWENTY-FIVE

"What for?"

"To see if Eric's truck was primed in that paint booth."

"You got a warrant?"

"No."

"Then you need to ask the owner."

"Who's that?"

"Chubb."

Hood was dumbfounded. "Chubb?" he repeated, a question.

"He bought the place when it came up for sale a while back. I'm the only person on the payroll. Chubb doesn't do shit, but I guess he's making some profit, or he would have closed it by now."

Hood pulled his cell phone from his pocket. "What's Chubb's number?"

Vivion recited the phone number from memory, and Hood keyed it in. "That's the bar number," Vivion explained. "Chubb doesn't want me calling his cell."

Hood called the number, but, as expected, the call went unanswered.

"I'd better get my ass back to work."

As Hood pocketed his phone, he looked through the open door connecting the garage bay to the office, which contained a cot, with pillow and blankets, and an open suitcase stuffed with clothes, some folded and others scattered about. "Home away from home?" he asked.

"Rhonda threw my ass out again," Vivion said. "Smoking weed mellows me out, but she's right. I need to grow up, take some responsibility."

"There're recovery programs for that, for drugs and alcohol. They don't cost anything and—"

"Yeah. I tried that for a while. It didn't work. Are we done?"

Hood was tempted to say recovery didn't work for him either until he committed to it, but what he said was, "We're done, for now."

* * *

"It's time," Jessie said to Brian.

"For what?"

161

"Remember when I said I need to go back to Uncle Chet's store? It's time."

"It's a crime scene," Brian argued.

"It's been cleared and released to my parents. They've already hired a lawyer to walk them through the legalities of inheriting my uncle's estate. I heard them talking already about what to do with the store, whether to sell the building, auction the contents, that kind of stuff."

"What's the rush? If your parents are going to inherit the store, you'll be able to go back—"

"You're not hearing me, Brian. I've been waiting, and I can't wait any longer. I need to act before something happens."

Brian had known this was coming. Jessie was too persistent to let go of the idea, and Brian knew he was incapable of refusing her. "Okay," he agreed.

"Good. We'll go tonight."

* * *

The sheriff parked in the lot behind Chubb's Tavern and entered through the rear door. As he had hoped, the mid-afternoon hour translated into only a few customers, including the elderly man who rested his head on the bar and the middle-aged woman with the garish makeup who sat alone in a booth.

Hood sat at the bar, as far as possible from the sleeping barfly.

"Coffee, Sheriff?" Rhonda asked.

Hood nodded. "Where's Chubb?"

"Took the afternoon off." She filled a ceramic mug and set it on the bar. "He'll be here tonight, after five."

Hood tested the coffee, which was surprisingly good. "He left you in charge, huh?"

"Nothing I can't handle." Rhonda glanced briefly at her seemingly inanimate customers. "It's not like the joint is jumping."

"Where'd he go?"

"Damned if I know. Something I can help you with?"

"I just found out he owns the body shop where your boyfriend works."

"Yeah. I guess because Dennis and me work at different places, I never thought about us having the same boss."

"I guess I should have called to see if he was here." Hood spoke as if thinking aloud. "I assumed he was a permanent fixture. He's always here whenever I come in."

"Used to be that way. Chubb opened the place and stayed 'til closing, just like Sleepy Cliff and Margie over there," she added, gesturing to her customers. "Not anymore."

"Did he get a girlfriend, start a hobby?"

"Damned if I know. All I know is I'm getting more hours. He writes when he plans to be gone on the calendar over there," Rhonda said, pointing to a calendar tacked to the back wall. As she spoke, the man she identified as Sleepy Cliff lifted his head and croaked, "Rhonda."

"Duty calls," she said.

Hood slid from the stool, retrieved his notebook, and noted the times and dates when Chubb was not on duty.

* * *

Sandra placed her reading pillow against the headboard, stretched her legs, and opened her book—another cozy mystery.

She was fastidious about her bedtime habits, which included being in bed by 9 p.m. and reading two or three chapters, depending on length, before switching off her light.

Sandra heard the tinkle of the tiny bell she had attached to the cat door, signaling Lady Jane, also a creature of habit, had come in for the night.

She continued reading as she heard the feline jump on the bed. Typically, Lady Jane snuggled at her side, but tonight, the cat was unsettled, gyrating, straining, and biting at some annoyance.

Sandra closed her book and stared at the twisted contortion of legs and paws. "What's the matter, girl?" She reached to perform the always appreciated chin rub and felt something, some unknown object, attached to her collar.

Sandra sat up. "What did you get into this time?" She pulled Lady Jane closer and examined her.

Attached to her collar was a small plastic evidence bag. Sandra gasped at the contents, scrambled out of bed, and called the sheriff.

* * *

Hood and Linda were watching a classic movie—*After the Thin Man*, the second in the Nick and Nora Charles series—when his cell phone rang.

Seated in his recliner, Hood looked at the caller ID. "I'd better take this," he said.

Linda lifted the remote from the sofa arm and paused the DVD.

"Hello," Hood answered. To Linda, he silently mouthed the words, "It's Sandra."

"Francis, can you come over?"

Hood heard alarm in her tone. "Now?" he asked as he looked at his wife.

"Please. Something's happened. I don't know what to do."

"Well, I'm—right now, I'm actually—"

"Go," Linda said.

He covered the mouthpiece. "Are you sure?" he asked his wife, because he wasn't.

"Just go," she said.

"I'm on my way," he told Sandra.

* * *

Within minutes, he arrived at Sandra's house. She apparently had been awaiting his arrival. Before he could knock, she opened the door and embraced him. He stiffened but did not immediately pull away. She seemed fragile, breakable, as he held her gently. "What's going on?" he whispered.

"Come see." She led him to her bedroom.

He hesitated at the door, uncertain if she expected him to follow.

"There," she said, pointing to an object on the rumpled covers.

164

Hood stepped nearer and stared at the clear plastic bag, identical to the countless evidence bags he had used over the years. Inside was the tip of a finger, severed at the top knuckle. The fingernail was missing. "Where did this come from?"

"It was attached to Lady Jane's collar. She has a cat door so she can come and go as she pleases. I was in here reading when she came in and jumped on the bed. She wouldn't settle. When she got my attention, I saw this."

"Did you touch it?"

"I unfastened the bag from her collar. She was trying to get it off, and I was afraid she might go back outside. My fingerprints are on the bag."

Hood breathed deeply. "I'll need to take this."

"Of course. You think it's Eric's?"

"I'd rather not speculate."

"How could it not be?" Her voice was shaky, bordering on hysterical. "What is happening?"

He had no answer.

# Chapter Twenty-Six

Wally and Lester were seated in the conference room when Hood entered. "Sorry I'm late," he told his deputies. "I had a delivery to make." He didn't explain the cause of his tardiness; he had taken the severed fingertip to Howard, who had promised to expedite identification.

The deputies were seated in chairs facing a whiteboard labeled *Construction Site Thefts.* Hood took his notebook from his pocket and asked, "Do we have a list of when the thefts occurred?"

"They're on the board," Wally said.

Hood approached the board, opened his notebook, and compared the dates. "I'll be damned. They match."

"What matches?" Lester asked.

Hood explained how the dates of the thefts corresponded with Chubb's absences from his workplace.

"You think he's involved?" Wally asked.

"He's involved in something. We've been operating on the theory that a theft ring is responsible. You two have been working the cases. How many people would be needed to pull off these thefts?"

"Minimum of two," Wally said. "Could be more, but at least two guys would be needed to load some of that heavy stuff."

"Plus," Lester added, "you'd need someplace to store the stuff."

Synapses fired in Hood's brain. "Like an abandoned hog farm?"

"That would work," Lester agreed.

"As I recall, Vivion's parents operated one of those farms before they shut it down."

"Central Missouri Hog Producers," Wally said.

"You'd also need some way to make money from the stolen goods," Lester chimed in. "Contractors in Central Missouri all know each other. I don't see any way to unload hot merchandise around here."

"I agree," Hood said. "You'd need a fence—somebody who has contacts with buyers outside Central Missouri."

"Like Chester Groner?" Wally wondered aloud. "He'd know buyers and sellers, including the shady ones."

"Possibility," Hood affirmed.

"Could help explain a motive," Wally speculated. "Start with some thieves, add a fence, stir in some greed, and you've got a recipe for conflict."

"And assault," Lester added.

Hood cocked his head slightly as he reviewed the scenario. "The thing is, I've never thought the assault on Chester was premeditated. If you plan to hurt or intimidate someone, you bring a weapon. The assailant chose a weapon of convenience. Whoever it was snatched a guitar off the wall and whacked him."

"Maybe what started as a conversation turned into an argument," Wally surmised.

"Maybe," Hood agreed, "but a conversation with who?"

"My money's on Vivion," Wally answered. "Let's face it—he's a fuck-up. Plus, don't forget he's got a record."

"His record's mostly small stuff, misdemeanors," Hood reminded.

"Maybe he's graduated to felonies," Lester suggested.

"And if Vivion's involved," Wally added, "his flunky, Hunk, probably is, too."

"Let me toss out another possibility," Hood said. "Have either of you ever met Eric Rakestraw?"

"Our missing man?"

Hood nodded. "His kid brother, who reported him missing, said Eric hung out with Vivion and some of his Schweinshaupten cronies."

"You think he was involved with the theft ring?" Wally asked.

"I don't know," Hood said. "It's always bothered me that he disappeared around the time the thefts were occurring. What's the phrase? Too much of a coincidence."

The three men lapsed into silence, as if contemplating possible scenarios, until Lester finally asked, "So what's the next step?"

\* \* \*

Jessie parked her Mustang in Brian's driveway, texted him, and consciously slowed her breathing. She was in tune with her body's signs of tension—the shallow breaths, the quickened heart rate, the churning gut.

Her anxiety morphed into anger as she observed Brian stagger down his front steps, followed by the unmistakable aroma of alcohol as he slid into the passenger seat.

"Really, Brian? This is important to me."

"What?"

"What?" Jessie repeated. "You've been drinking. Tonight, of all nights."

"I'm, I'm," he stammered, uncertain whether to defend his actions or apologize for them. "I've been a basket case all day, ever since we talked about this. I just needed to take the edge off. I couldn't—"

"Why do you keep that stuff around if you're trying to quit?"

"I don't know."

"I think you do," Jessie said. "I think you know, deep down, you're not ready to quit. You don't want to quit."

The rebuke stung Brian. He made no reply.

"Am I right?" Jessie said, her tone insistent.

"I guess."

"It's like being on an emotional roller coaster with you. I don't know—"

"Can we just go? I don't want to fight right now."

"You're not going to throw up or pass out on me, or anything like that?"

"No. I'm not that drunk. I only had a couple. Can we go?"

"Fine." Jessie shifted into reverse, backed onto Route D, and headed toward Schweinshaupten, where she parked in the darkened alley beside the store.

She used her parents' key to unlock the side door and walked swiftly to the front room and behind the counter, where an oak, roll-top desk was positioned against the side wall. She pulled out the bottom right drawer, reached inside, and triggered some mechanism on the underside, opening a hidden compartment containing stacks of cash, secured by rubber bands.

"Holy shit," Brian said. "How much is it?"

"No idea." Jessie began stuffing the cash into an oversized bag. "We'll count it later." She shut the compartment and closed the bag. "Let's go."

"What's on the other side?"

"What other side?"

"It looks like there's another compartment on the left."

Jessie opened the left drawer, located a lever, and pulled, revealing a second compartment. She reached in and removed a leather-bound volume.

"What is it? Brian asked.

"Some kind of book, I guess."

"Let's take a look."

"We can do that later." Her tone had become more assertive. She placed the book in her bag. "We need to go."

# Chapter Twenty-Seven

Hood parked at Millie's Diner and studied his reflection in the rearview mirror.

The person he saw was a drunk. He had not taken a drink, but his face revealed imperfections, including dishonesty, selfishness, and anxiety.

He looked forward to the breakfast meeting he had arranged with Matthew. A virtue of his recovery sponsor's retirement was his availability.

Fear was at the top of Hood's list of discussion topics. He had faced armed felons in dark alleys but dreaded performing a few simple dance steps on a stage illuminated by footlights. His fear seemed foolish, particularly in comparison to what Sandra and Brian dealt with on a regular basis. Sandra couldn't swallow; Brian suffered acute social anxiety. Their fears were paralyzing. Their fears altered their choices and affected their lives.

Was the source of his anxiety as simple as fear of public humiliation? He recalled his conversation with Sandra and his reference to the human condition. Humans have the capacity to strive for excellence, but cannot attain perfection. Was he afraid to reveal his imperfections?

As he opened his car door, his ringtone sounded. The caller was Howard, who confirmed what he suspected—the severed finger belonged to Eric Rakestraw.

Hood crossed the parking lot and entered the diner. Matthew was seated in a booth, where a coffee carafe and two white ceramic mugs already were on the table.

"How's Elizabeth?" Matthew asked as Hood slid onto the bench seat opposite his sponsor.

"She gets to come home today. Linda's picking her up."

"Great. By the way, thanks for inviting me to breakfast. I usually skip it."

Further conversation was suspended when Nadine appeared tableside. After placing their orders, Hood said, "I have an ulterior motive. I've got something on my mind I wanted to run by you."

"I'm listening."

"Elizabeth's recital is coming up, and the instructor has the fathers and daughters rehearsing a dance to perform."

"Wonderful," Matthew injected.

"You'd think so, but, truthfully, I'm dreading it."

"Because?"

"That's what I've been trying to figure out. I guess I'm afraid of making a fool of myself in front of a bunch of people."

Matthew leaned back. "I'm reminded of what I've heard Mac say at several meetings. It's a quote. I think he attributes it to Mark Twain, something like *'I've faced many fears in my life, some of which turned out to be real.'*"

"I know," Hood said. "Elizabeth's doctor needs to clear her to dance, which may not even happen before the recital."

"Who knows?" Matthew shrugged. "I might also remind you those parents are there to watch their children. They don't give a damn about what you're doing. But those aren't the real issues. The question is, why are you experiencing this anxiety, and what can be done about it."

"I wish I knew."

"I think you do know," Matthew said. "Tell me about your relationship with your higher power."

Nadine's reappearance forestalled Hood's response. She placed their breakfast plates before them before asking if she could get them anything else. When she left, Hood answered. "As you know, I've always had trouble with that. You might say I believe in a higher power by default. My obsession to drink has gone away, my family has reunited, and I've experienced grace. I know I was unable to do those things on my own, so I have to attribute them to a higher power."

Matthew leaned forward and propped his elbows on the table. "But do you trust your higher power?"

"I don't understand my higher power. I don't even have an image of who or what it is. How can I trust something I don't understand?"

"I'm sure you're familiar with the slogan, *Let go and let God.*"

"I am, but I'm not there yet. I'm the sheriff. I'm expected to solve problems. When someone comes to me and says, 'I was beaten and robbed,' I can't say, 'Let's let God solve this one.' It's up to me to investigate."

Matthew chewed and swallowed. "Are you investigating?"

Hood sipped coffee, momentarily distracted by the thought that he and Matthew were casually doing what Sandra couldn't do. "I'm not sure I follow you."

"I know I must continue to investigate my relationship with my higher power. There are things I probably will never know, at least not in this life. But as long as I'm investigating, I'm making progress."

"I think I am." Hood's tone revealed more doubt than certainty. "I mean, that's kind of what I'm doing right now."

In the silence that ensued, Hood contemplated whether to bring up the recent discord with Linda. He decided against it. Matthew had said previously that although he was willing to share his experience as a recovering alcoholic, he was not a licensed therapist or marriage counselor.

When they finished eating, Matthew said, "Willingness." He laid his utensils on his plate, lifted his napkin, and wiped his lips. "For me, the key is a willingness to explore and examine new ideas. As long as you're doing that, there's really nothing to fear."

* * *

Jessie opened the logbook in her lap as she sat beside Brian on the sofa in his living room. She flipped pages as they silently stared at three columns under the headings: Date, Lot Number, Amount.

"What is this?" Brian asked.

"No idea."

"Could it be a record of sales from his shop?"

"Maybe, but I don't see any listing of merchandise."

"The lot numbers might mean merchandise," he suggested.

As she flipped pages, the hand-written columns ended on the date six days before the assault on her uncle. "There's no key to what the lot numbers mean, at least not in here."

"Could it be in another book he hid somewhere else?"

"Why would my uncle be so secretive about the junk he sold?"

"Maybe this has something to do with why he was assaulted?"

Jessie shrugged.

"You think we should show this to the sheriff?"

"I don't know," Jessie said. "We'd have to explain why we went back to my uncle's store."

"So? It's no longer a crime scene. You said it was released to your family. Just say your uncle told you he left something for you, and you wanted to see what it was."

"What if he asked what it was? Would I have to tell him about the money?"

"That's up to you."

"I really don't want to get the sheriff involved."

"He's already involved," Brian said. "He's investigating the assault. Something's going on, and I'm getting the feeling it's all tied together somehow. Don't you want to get to the bottom of who killed your uncle?"

Jessie sat silently for what seemed a long time before closing the book. "All right. But I'm going to say my uncle left me only $500 in case the sheriff needs to take the cash for evidence or something. I'm keeping the rest. Uncle Chet saved that for me."

"That's fine."

"Okay," Jessie said. "When do you want to call him?"

"Right now."

\* \* \*

Hood's phone rang as he pulled from the lot at Millie's Diner. "Hello, Brian," he answered, activating the hands-free feature in his cruiser.

"Sheriff, can you come to my house?"

"When?"

"Right now."

"Yes. What's going on?"

"Jessie and I found something we think you should have a look at."

"Can you tell me more?"

"I will when you get here."

"I'm on my way."

When he arrived at Brian's house, the trio congregated in the living room, and Jessie explained her uncle, before his death, had confided in her that he intended to leave her money. He also showed her how to access a secret compartment in a desk, where he planned to conceal the cash. She said she and Brian visited the store earlier and found $500 in the compartment. They then discovered—in a similar, but previously unknown, hidey hole—a mysterious logbook. She pointed to a worn, leather-bound volume resting on an oval coffee table.

Hood pulled on gloves and carefully leafed through the pages. "What am I looking at?" he asked.

"We don't know," Jessie answered.

"We thought it might be a record of sales," Brian added, "but the merchandise is listed only by lot number, so your guess is as good as ours."

"Who else has seen this?"

"As far as we know, just us and, I guess, Uncle Chet."

Hood focused on Jessie. "What about your parents?"

"No. We brought it straight here, opened it, and decided to call you."

"I'll need to ask your parents about it," Hood said. "And I'll want the crime lab to take a look, so I'll need your fingerprints for comparison."

Both nodded, nearly in unison. "What about the money?" Jessie asked.

"I'll need to have that analyzed, too, but if it's not stolen, you'll get it back. I'll give you a receipt." Hood paged through the book. "Do you know if your uncle had other hidden drawers, secret panels, that kind of thing?"

Jessie shook her head.

"What about other books like this? Maybe a companion volume that would explain these numbers?"

"None that I know of."

Hood flipped to a series of blank pages, then returned to the pages with writing. He noticed characters on the final two written pages appeared different from the writing on the earlier pages. He scratched the back of his neck. "I'm going to have the crime lab take a look at this." He slid the book into an evidence bag, stood, and faced Brian. "Would you walk me to the door, Brian?" the sheriff asked, indicating he wanted a word in private.

After they were on the porch with the front door closed, Hood said, "We've obtained a portion of a finger, severed at the top knuckle. It belongs to your brother, Eric."

"Fuck," Brian shouted, a staccato outburst. "What the fuck is going on, Sheriff?"

"We're starting to get some things sorted out. I know it may not look like we're making progress—"

"That's just not good enough anymore. My brother's in danger. I know it. I need answers."

\* \* \*

Hood deliberately made an appointment with Howard when he knew Sandra would be away from the lab on her lunch break.

"What did you bring this time?" the fingerprint analyst asked as he studied the leather-bound logbook on the stainless-steel table.

"I need to know if there are any identifiable prints on this," the sheriff answered.

"Where'd it come from?"

"Chester Groner's store. It was found by his niece, Jessie Surface, and her boyfriend, Brian Rakestraw. Their prints are on the book, so I brought samples for comparison."

"Good."

"I also brought some cash—five hundred dollars. The numbers aren't sequential, and the denominations vary. I don't think it's stolen, but I thought you should have a look."

"I'll pass those on to Sandra. She—"

"If it's all the same to you, I'd rather keep Sandra out of this."

Howard, who was using a gloved finger to turn pages in the logbook, offered a quizzical expression.

"I know," Hood said in answer to the unspoken question. "She's worked the initial crime in the Chester Groner case, but I've learned, since then, that somebody who was at the store has been bending her ear. Plus, there's the whole thing with the ring and finger of a missing person. It's all very complicated."

"That's probably more than I need to know," Howard said without looking up from the pages. "By the way, did you notice the writing on the last two pages is different from—"

"I did," Hood said.

"What's going on?"

Hood and Howard turned at the sound of Sandra's familiar voice.

"I thought you were at lunch," Howard remarked.

"I was. I finished my lunch and my book, and I've got a lot to do, so here I am."

Both men simply stared at her, long enough for Sandra to add, "Or can't you tell me?"

"I brought this logbook for Howard to determine if there are any identifiable prints," Hood said. "We both noticed the handwriting is different on the last two pages."

"You may not know this, Sheriff," Howard said, hesitancy in his tone, "but Sandra studied handwriting analysis before she decided to specialize in trace evidence."

"I wasn't aware of that." Hood realized he had opened a door he might be unable to close.

"Let me see." She pulled on a glove, squeezed between the two men, and examined the pages. "Keep in mind that there's some difference of opinion concerning the admissibility of handwriting analysis in judicial proceedings.

Defense attorneys invariably challenge the evidence. Plus, I don't know if I would even qualify as an expert witness if it comes to testifying in court."

"Maybe it's better if you don't spend a lot of time and energy on something that's not going to hold up in court," Hood said.

"But this writing," Sandra said, as she paged back and forth, "is distinctly different from what's on the earlier pages. Notice the tiny hook atop the number one and the line bisecting the stem of the seven." She looked at the sheriff. "Do you have samples of Mr. Groner's writing that can be positively identified?"

"There were papers scattered on the desk in his shop. I'm sure his family—"

"Good. Once we identify what pages he wrote, we can focus on who wrote the other pages."

# Chapter Twenty-Eight

"Why did you agree to this?" Brian asked Sandra.

"I honestly don't know." She maintained the speed limit as she drove her SUV northbound on Route D toward Schweinshaupten. "Because you asked, I guess."

"Is it because you pity me?"

She hesitated a beat before saying, "I don't know if pity is the right word. I know you're hurting, and you're upset. But I've got a stake in this, too. Since your brother went missing, his ring was found in my truck, and his fingernail and severed finger were delivered to my house. Right now, I'm probably at the top of the sheriff's suspect list."

"I find that hard to believe. You don't strike me as the type who could harm someone. You're kind. My brother thought so, too. He thought you had some idiosyncrasies, but he really liked you."

"Idiosyncrasies?" Sandra repeated the word as a question, obviously seeking specifics.

"He thought maybe you were sad, like you had some regrets, but I don't know if I agree."

"What do you think?"

"I probably shouldn't say. I don't know you very well. It's just a feeling I get."

"Tell me," she insisted. "Now you've got my curiosity going."

"I guess 'preoccupied' is the best way I can describe it. It's like you're here, but not completely here. It's like you're constantly distracted by something."

Sandra was struck by the accuracy of his observation. She had come to realize that her OCD, specifically her somatic OCD, was always on her mind. In every situation, every conversation, thoughts of swallowing—fear of swallowing—intruded. "What else did your brother say about me?"

"I think he felt like he didn't deserve you."

"Why?"

"You're smart. You have a college education. Eric never went to college. Maybe he didn't want to, but I think he felt obligated to help raise me after our parents died. Sometimes, I wonder why I'm even in college. Maybe I believe if I graduate, somehow, I can repay my brother for what he sacrificed."

Sandra glanced at Brian, who seemed engaged in a stream-of-consciousness introspection. "I mean, my grades aren't good, and I'm not feeling any better about myself. Maybe the Rakestraw brothers share a sense of inferiority. I have a girlfriend, but I don't feel I deserve her." Brian shook his head. "Sometimes I feel like I'm hanging on for dear life in our relationship. I'm afraid every moment I'm with her. I'm afraid she's going to see me for who I really am and dump me."

Sandra was stung by the relationship comparison. She felt guilty as charged; she had seen the real Eric and dumped him. She searched for comforting words to offer Brian, but none materialized.

"I've got pretty severe social anxiety," Brian continued. "I've had it for as long as I can remember. It's hard to live with. It affects everything I do. No, actually, it prevents me from doing things, which is worse. You can't begin to know how tense I am right now. That's probably why I'm blathering on. Going to talk to Vivion a couple nights ago was hard for me. I had to keep reminding myself it wasn't about me. It was about Eric. And I didn't want to come here today, but the sheriff's family was in that accident and—you know about that, right?"

Sandra nodded.

"So I knew he wouldn't be working the case for a while and, anyway, I wouldn't be doing this if you hadn't agreed to come."

"What exactly are we going to do?"

"We're just going to nose around a little."

"So we're clear, I don't want to do anything behind the sheriff's back. He and I work together, not independently of each other."

"I understand, but I can't help but think Vivion is involved in something or knows something."

"What?"

"I don't know. It's a vibe. I asked around and did some checking on him. According to the county recorder's office, he inherited a hog farm, Central Missouri Hog Producers, that's been in his family for generations. It's on Pitchfork Road, so I'm guessing it's one of those abandoned properties. He works at an auto body shop in Schweinshaupten. He doesn't own his own house or rent an apartment. He lives with his girlfriend, Rhonda Snellen, who lives at 403 Melody Lane. I thought we'd check that out before we go to the old farm."

\* \* \*

"That's it," Brian said, "the blue house on the left."

"You sure?" Sandra said.

"It says 403 on the mailbox."

"Looks kind of girly," Sandra observed as she steered her SUV onto the packed dirt that formed the right shoulder of the asphalt street. She placed the vehicle in park but left the engine running as they both stared across the street.

The Melody Lane house was an unpretentious, single-story rancher—slate blue with white trim—with an attached one-car garage. The surroundings, however, could only be characterized as ostentatious. Multi-colored pinwheels lined the sidewalk, a large wreath of twisted twigs and pinecones adorned the front door, and an antique milk can stood sentry on the front stoop. Colorful garden gnomes posed among the foundation plantings, and statues of two deer, an alert buck, and grazing doe populated the lawn. Dream catchers and light-refracting prisms hung from a head-high wooden cross in the front yard, shaded by a lone maple tree where a ceramic dog in a top hat lifted its leg.

"Not what I expected," Sandra remarked.

"Me, either," Brian said.

As they watched, a woman appeared from around a corner of the house. She carried a flag or pennant that was impossible to identify because it was rolled up.

"I know her," Sandra said. "She works at Chubb's Tavern."

"Her name's Rhonda. She's Dennis Vivion's girlfriend."

Rhonda inserted the flag into a holder attached to a porch support and unfurled it, revealing a colorful fall cornucopia. She turned, stopped abruptly, and looked directly at them as they watched her from the front seat of the SUV.

"Shit," Brian muttered. He shielded his face with an open palm, like a defendant leaving a courthouse. Sandra shifted the SUV into drive and pulled away.

After she turned a corner, Brian asked, "You think she knew who we were?"

"I don't know if it matters."

"What if she recognized us and tells Vivion we were watching the house?"

"So?" Sandra shrugged slightly.

"So, remember I tracked down Vivion a few nights ago to ask him about my brother's disappearance. If he puts two and two together, that could—"

Sandra waited to see if he would continue. When he didn't, she said, "Maybe we should skip going to the farm?"

"Why? We've come this far. Besides, it's abandoned."

"Okay," Sandra said, her reluctance apparent.

Brian provided directions as she drove the few blocks to Pitchfork Road, lined on either side with farms. Two had been modernized and transformed from livestock to crop production, although the fallow fields awaited spring planting. The remaining farms were dingy and deserted. They traveled about a mile before Brian said, "See that broken sign ahead on the right? Turn there."

Sandra steered onto the dusty lane, and they approached a parking area adjacent to a group of derelict barns, with peeling paint and sun-bleached exteriors.

They exited the car and stood beside each other.

"Sure looks vacant," Sandra said.

"Let me see if that door's unlocked," Brian said.

He had taken only two steps when a tall, thin figure they both recognized as Hunk emerged from the side of the barn and asked, "What're you doing here?"

Brian and Sandra hesitated a beat before she said, "We got turned around somehow. We were trying to find Route D, and we ended up on that road out there."

"Why'd you get out of your car?" Hunk asked.

"I was curious about what these old pig barns look like," Brian said. "Thought as long as we were here, I'd take a peek."

"This is private land."

"We're sorry," Sandra said. "We were just turning around. We didn't mean to trespass."

"You're Sandra, Eric's girlfriend, right?" Hunk asked.

Sandra nodded.

Hunk turned to Brian. "And you're his brother?"

"Yes," Brian said.

Hunk squinted, as if puzzled by a difficult equation.

"We'd better get going," Sandra said.

"You know anything about my brother's disappearance?" Brian asked.

"Why would I know anything about that?" Hunk's question bordered on threatening.

"I didn't say you did," Brian replied. "I was just asking."

Hunk stared, his features impassive.

Sandra, who had sidled beside Brian, tugged at his sleeve and said, "We'll just be on our way." She pulled his sleeve and was relieved when Brian moved toward the car. She felt her heart racing as she started the ignition and reversed course.

When they were back on Pitchfork Road, she and Brian exchanged a look of shared confusion. "What the hell was that all about?" she asked.

"No idea."

"We need to tell the sheriff."

"Tell him what? That some guy caught us trespassing on private property and ran us off?"

"That Hunk guy knows Eric," Sandra said. "And what was he guarding if those are just vacant barns?"

"But what if the sheriff responds and the barns are empty? He'll come down hard on us for messing with his investigation."

"All I'm saying is we saw suspicious activity, and we should report it."

"What if we verify it first?"

"Verify how?" Sandra asked.

"We could come back tonight."

"Absolutely not. If Hunk or anybody is guarding the place and has a gun, they could shoot us for trespassing."

"I see your point," Brian conceded. "But before we say anything to the sheriff, give me some time to think about it."

"You're not going to do anything foolish, are you?"

"Of course not. I just want to think it over."

Sandra didn't know him well enough to know what to believe. Reluctantly, she said, "Okay, but you'll tell him tomorrow. Right?"

"Right."

# Chapter Twenty-Nine

Hood stood with Sandra in the waning sunlight and rang the front doorbell at the Surface house. She carried a cloth bag that contained the logbook and items she would need to collect handwriting samples. With the exception of the last two pages, the writing had been identified as Chester's.

Despite Sandra's equivocation about whether she was qualified to testify as an expert witness on handwriting analysis, Hood was undeterred in his quest to obtain additional samples. His priority was identifying and questioning the writer of the mystery pages. He would address any courtroom challenges if and when they arose.

"Has Brian called you today?" Sandra asked.

"No," Hood answered. "Why?"

Further conversation was interrupted when Adam Surface opened the door. Although the sheriff had called ahead to arrange the visit, he had not revealed the reason for it or that he would be accompanied by a forensic analyst. Seeing the surprise registered on Adam's face, Hood introduced Sandra.

Adam led his guests to the family room, where Irene sat in a recliner, adroitly manipulating knitting needles. Introductions were repeated, pleasantries exchanged, and drinks offered and declined. Hood and Sandra sat in separate chairs, and Sandra set her cloth bag between them. Facing them were Adam and Irene, who were side-by-side on a large sofa.

"So," Adam said, "how can we help you?"

"I'd like each of you to submit a writing sample," Sandra said. She reached into the bag and produced two yellow legal pads and two ballpoint pens.

"Why?" Adam asked.

Hood fielded the question. "We've obtained written materials, and we're trying to identify the handwriting."

"What materials?" Adam asked.

"Suffice it to say," Hood replied, "identifying the writing may help our investigation of the assault on Chester Groner."

"If it'll help catch whoever killed my brother, I'm fine with it," Irene said. She reached and accepted a pad and pen. "What do you want me to write?"

Sandra retrieved a typewritten page and handed it to Irene, who laid the pad in her lap and began copying the words and numbers.

Adam sighed audibly, then said, "I don't know what this is about, but why not?" He followed his wife's lead.

When they finished and handed in their work, like students completing tests in a classroom, Sandra produced a page shielded by clear plastic. "Are either of you familiar with this?"

"What is it?" Adam asked as he accepted the document.

"It's a copy of a page from a book we obtained," Hood said. He didn't identify it as the logbook's final page containing the unfamiliar writing.

"No," Adam said as he passed it to his wife.

Irene studied it, then shook her head.

"What about this one?" Sandra produced a second page.

Although Adam failed to identify it, Irene said, "I don't know where it came from, but this is my brother's writing."

"Yes," Hood said. "A comparison with other documents signed by Mr. Groner established he is the writer."

"So why did you need our samples?" Adam asked.

"Something doesn't fit," Hood answered, hoping his officious—intentionally vague—answers would be acceptable.

"Such as?" Adam persisted.

Hood knew it was time to stop dodging. "Do either of you have reason to believe Chester might have been involved in clandestine activities?"

"What do you mean by—?" Irene began.

"He means a crime," Adam interjected. He focused on Hood. "What, exactly, are you getting at, Sheriff? What is this book you're talking about, and how did you get it?"

So much for the delicate approach, Hood thought. "I'm afraid—"

"My brother was not a thief," Irene interrupted, her tone adamant.

"Do you have any proof?" Adam added as his wife began to cry, quietly at first but intensifying.

"As of right now," Hood said, "the investigation is ongoing."

Adam stood. "Now you've upset my wife. Perhaps it's time for you to be going."

Hood exchanged a knowing look with Sandra, and they stood.

"I'm sorry. I didn't mean—" Hood aborted his attempt to explain and allowed Adam to escort them out.

Back in the cruiser, Sandra said, "You don't need to be an expert to see their samples don't match that last page in the logbook."

"Another dead end," Hood said. "The only thing I'm succeeding at is annoying people."

"We're just getting started. Who's next?"

"Dennis Vivion."

"Let's go," Sandra said.

As they drove, Sandra parried with her conscience. Although it was only mid-afternoon, Brian had not yet kept his promise to inform the sheriff about yesterday's trip to the barn and the encounter with Hunk. Was it her responsibility to tell the sheriff? She was reluctant to do so, but why? Was she deferring to Brian? Was she fearful that Hood would disapprove of their actions? Would he perceive it as a rogue investigation? Was she engaging in deceit by omission? "I don't know if this is helpful," she said, "but I understand Vivion's family used to own and operate Central Missouri Hog Producers."

"Good memory," Hood said. After his discussion with Wally and Lester about the construction thefts, Hood made inquiries about the property. "Vivion put it on the market some years ago, but received no offers. I find it ironic."

"What's ironic?"

"That he's a modern land baron with worthless acreage."

"You don't think much of him, do you?"

"I'm interested to see how he responds to our request for a handwriting sample."

They lapsed into silence as Hood turned onto Route D. He considered broaching his wife's concerns—*"you need to sort out what it is that's going on with you and Sandra"*—but the timing seemed wrong.

Twilight had gathered, and evening dampness had settled by the time they parked in the lot at Beautiful Body and Paint. The garage bays were darkened, and the doors lowered, but Vivion was visible in the illuminated office, where he sat reading a magazine, his feet propped on a desk.

Hood and Sandra exited the cruiser. The sheriff tapped on the glass.

Vivion looked up, recognized his visitors, and scowled. He placed the open magazine upside down on the desk to mark his place. He twisted the deadbolt and opened the door. "Now what?"

"We'd like you to provide a handwriting sample," Hood said, hoping to be invited inside the bright, heated office.

"Why?" Vivion focused on Sandra, his gaze moving from her face to her body, to the cloth bag she held.

"We want to compare it with some other documents," the sheriff answered.

"No chance," Vivion said.

"It might help eliminate you as a suspect," Hood reasoned.

"Knowing you guys, you'd find some way to use it against me."

"I'm a forensic evidence technician," Sandra interjected. "I'm not trying to trap anybody. I'm only interested in facts."

"Well, it's a fact that I'm not taking your test, so go peddle your papers someplace else."

"We're trying to make this easy," Hood said. "Getting a court order and forcing you to comply is messy and time-consuming." He shrugged. "Why not just give us the sample?"

"Because you're a pain in the ass, and I don't trust you. You don't believe me when I tell you I didn't do anything, so why should I make things easier for you?"

Before Hood could think of what to say, Vivion stepped back inside, closed the door, and turned the deadbolt.

\* \* \*

Dusk had yielded to full dark by the time Hood and Sandra entered Chubb's Tavern. The sheriff was not surprised that Sandra selected the same table they had occupied previously or that she immediately began repositioning the ashtray and napkin holder.

Hood was still pulling an arm from a coat sleeve when Rhonda appeared. "Let me guess. A water and a coffee?"

Hood nodded.

"I think I'll have a beer," Sandra said.

Hood winced, as if he'd been slapped, while Rhonda listed draught and bottle options and Sandra made her choice. When Rhonda left, he stared quizzically at Sandra.

"Surprised?" Sandra asked.

"Absolutely."

"It's an experiment. I thought, as long as I'm out at a bar, why not see what happens?"

"Why not?" Hood echoed his tone supportive.

"So, are you going to get a court order for Vivion's handwriting?"

"I haven't decided yet."

"What about—?" Sandra began, aborting her question when the ever-efficient Rhonda returned.

"Bear with me tonight," the barmaid said. "I'm on my own, and the joint is jumping. I'll do my best, but if you get impatient, you may want to come to the bar to order."

"Chubb gone again?" Hood asked.

"Yeah, and I'm getting sick of it."

She left, and Hood turned his attention back to Sandra. "You were saying?"

"I was wondering if you were going to ask Rhonda or Chubb for a writing sample, but it looks like it's not going to work out."

"Not tonight."

"Well, let's see how this works out. Wish me luck." She lifted the beer glass to her lips and took in a mouthful.

Hood watched as she held the liquid in her mouth, swished it like mouthwash, then raised an index finger. He deduced the success of the experiment was in doubt as she arose from her chair and walked quickly to the rear hallway where the restrooms were located.

Hood returned his attention to sipping coffee while televised sportscasters debated a pass interference call. In the periphery of his vision, he saw Sandra approaching, her gait was unusually quick and her movements a shade jerky. In that instant, he knew something was amiss. "One failed experiment," he consoled, "is nothing—"

"No," she interrupted, her tone adamant. "I saw a blue coat and muddy boots."

Confusion prevailed in the moment before Hood realized the significance of her revelation. "Evidence from the assault case?"

"I don't know. I won't until I analyze them."

"Where did you see them?"

"In Chubb's office. The ladies' room was occupied, so I was standing in the hallway when Rhonda walked past me, opened the door to Chubb's office, and went inside. While the door was open, I saw a coat—a navy blue peacoat—hanging on the back of the desk chair. I also saw a pair of muddy boots on the floor."

"Okay. Hold on." Hood's thoughts careened chaotically in his mind. He needed to think. He had been willing to downplay the admissibility of the handwriting analysis because identifying the writer was paramount. The coat and boots were another matter. He resolved to go by the book and build a solid case. Defense attorneys, and the courts, were sticklers for procedure. He doubted he had probable cause to seize the coat and boots without a search warrant. Even Sandra's glimpse of the items might be challenged in court. "We need to get a warrant."

"But what if Chubb hides the evidence, or destroys it?"

"He's not here right now. If the evidence is what you think it is, I'm not willing to risk having it suppressed on a technicality. Let me call Wally, tell him what we found, and ask him to get a warrant. Then we sit here, act like nothing's happened, and make sure nobody goes in that office until Wally gets here."

# Chapter Thirty

While Wally was arranging for a warrant, Brian was creeping along a hedgerow that paralleled Pitchfork Road, where he had parked Jessie's Mustang.

To fortify himself for the task, he had taken several swigs of vodka, which had rendered him wobbly. The alcohol, however, had done little to reduce his anxiety. His heartbeat seemed to hammer more loudly than his footfalls. His fears bordered on combustible as he struggled through tangled brambles. He believed if he stopped moving, his churning guts would spew vomit in the same moment his bowels released. He held his cell phone, ready to shine its flashlight app if needed, but the illumination reflected from a half-moon provided enough light for him to see the outline of the hog barn ahead.

When the concealment afforded by the hedgerow ended, he crouched silently and watched the empty parking lot for signs of activity. He saw no sign that Hunk remained on the premises and, as time passed, his discomfort slithered from his stomach to his brain. He considered abandoning his plan, but he recalled a line from Shakespeare's *Macbeth* where the title character says, *"Stepped in so far that, should I wade no more/Returning were as tedious as go o'er."*

Motivated by having come this far, he sprinted across the parking area and flattened his back against the side of the barn.

No motion-sensitive lights illuminated the darkness, and no alarms sounded. He crept along the side of the building, punctuated with white-washed windows designed to repel heat. The coating also rendered them translucent. He found a window where the glass pane was broken, but the interior was too dark to discern anything. Still uncertain whether the building was occupied, he decided not to shine his phone light into the interior.

He came to a side door, but a twist of the knob indicated it was locked. Brian removed his student ID from his wallet, jimmied the lock, and pushed the door open. He listened for a response—any response, the sound of footsteps, the pump of a shotgun, the muffled voice of his missing brother. Nothing.

He stepped inside. The interior afforded only a dim, gauzy view, so he reached and felt rough wood that he assumed was the waist-high enclosure of a hog pen. He ran his hand along the wood until he located a gap, indicating a door. He groped for a latch and lifted. As he eased the door open, the rusted hinges screeched like a wounded banshee.

Immediately, a powerful flashlight was switched on. In that instant, Brian crouched behind the wall of the pigpen.

"Who's there?" a voice shouted. The beam swept to and fro as someone approached along the center aisle.

Although the voice sounded familiar, Brian couldn't place it. He peered through the slats of the pen and saw the silhouette of a man holding a gun— either a rifle or shotgun. The glare of the flashlight rendered the man's face indistinguishable. Brian looked around the enclosure, ostensibly for a weapon, although he wasn't sure what he would do if he found one.

"Aha," the voice said.

Brian knew he'd been caught. He felt simultaneous panic and relief. He tried desperately to think of some lie to explain his presence as he looked through the slats and saw the beam of light illuminating a fat raccoon in the center aisle. The critter posed momentarily before skittering into darkness.

"Shoulda shot you in the ass," the man said. He turned and walked away, the illumination dimming as his footsteps receded.

Brian reached for his cell phone.

\* \* \*

Rhonda, who had been presented with the search warrant, watched helplessly from the hallway. Sandra bagged the peacoat and handed it to Wally while Hood, who had obtained Chubb's cell number from Rhonda, waited impatiently for his call to be answered.

While collecting the muddy boots, Sandra's phone sounded, signaling an incoming message. She activated the display and read it. She tapped Hood on the shoulder, but he ignored her while his own phone transferred him to Chubb's voicemail. At the beep, he said, "Chubb, this is your sheriff. Call me back at this number. It's urgent." He disconnected and faced Sandra. "What?"

She showed him Brian's message, which read: *Trapped at hog farm. Send help.*

"Where? Which farm?"

"Must be the one he and I visited earlier today."

Although questions swirled in Hood's mind, he focused on the immediate concern. "Can you get us there?"

"Yes."

"You've got the coat and boots?"

She lifted the bag containing the boots while gesturing to Wally, who held the coat.

"Let's go. Wally, follow us."

As they rushed past Rhonda to their cruisers, the recovery slogan—*First things first*—echoed in his mind.

* * *

"It's the abandoned Vivion farm on Pitchfork Road. The one Dennis inherited," Sandra said as Hood steered from the curb and activated the lights and siren. Wally, following in his separate cruiser, did likewise.

"I know it," Hood said, not trying to hide that he was rankled. "What I don't know is why you and Brian were there?" He turned from Main Street onto Werner Road.

"Can we do this later? We're almost there."

Hood glared at her as he turned onto Pitchfork Road.

"I'll explain everything. I promise."

Hood said nothing as he, then Wally, stopped in the gravel lot, the lights from their cruisers creating a red and blue strobe-like effect on the barn walls.

"Stay in the cruiser," Hood instructed Sandra as he and Wally exited and fanned out in front of the barn. Hood hammered on the door and shouted, "This is your sheriff. Open up."

No answer.

"Open the door," Hood repeated, "or we're coming in."

A lone light pole in the parking lot suddenly illuminated the officers, followed by glows from the windows, signaling the interior lights had been switched on. Within moments, the door opened slightly, and Chubb peered at the officers. "What?"

"We're coming in," Hood said.

"You got a warrant?"

Hood smiled at the irony. "I've got probable cause to believe a crime has been committed."

"What crime?"

"Trespassing." Hood pushed through the door, causing Chubb to stagger backward, nearly falling.

"I'm not trespassing," Chubb protested. I got permission—"

"Not you. Him." Hood pointed at Brian, who emerged from a hog pen and approached along the center aisle. Hood noticed a slight stagger in his steps.

"What the—" Chubb began, clearly stunned by the appearance of the intruder.

"Wait outside by the cruiser," Hood told Brian. To Wally, he said, "Don't let Chubb out of your sight. I'm going to look around.

Hood's inventory revealed a treasure trove of tools, equipment, and building materials carefully sorted and stored in the numbered hog pens. Walking the center aisle, Hood noted an array of lumber, wallboard, oak floor planks, kitchen sinks, toilets, vanities, power and hand tools, and more.

When he made his way back to Chubb, Hood asked, "What's going on here?

"I'm not saying nothing."

"You said you had permission to be here. From who?"

Chubb remained silent.

"This is quite the inventory you've got here. Where'd it come from?"

"I think I want to talk to a lawyer."

"Fine," Hood said. "You're under arrest for possession of stolen property." He turned to Wally. "Read him his rights and bring him in for processing."

The sheriff left the barn and confronted Brian, who was speaking with Sandra through the open passenger window. "Care to tell me what the hell is going on here?" he asked.

"I found out," Brian replied, attempting to avoid slurring his words, "Dennis Vivion inherited this farm. I talked Sandra into coming with me to check it out. I thought this place was abandoned, but Hunk was here, and he ran us off, so I got suspicious. I borrowed Jessie's car tonight and drove back here. I needed to know if they were holding my brother prisoner."

"No one was inside except you and Chubb. This place is now a crime scene, so we're going to seal it and inspect every inch of it. If there's any evidence your brother was being held here, we'll find it."

"Okay. Can I go?"

"No, you can't go." Hood's tone was emphatic. "You trespassed on private property. You interfered with a police investigation, and I'm pretty sure you've been drinking."

"I had a couple, but only after I parked. Jessie's car is up the road."

"I should keep you in jail overnight," Hood said, as if debating aloud with his own conscience. "I'm also going to need a full statement from you, but we're not going to do that now. Be in my office at 8 a.m. tomorrow. Sharp."

"Okay."

"And you're not driving. I'll take you home, and Sandra will follow in Jessie's car. You okay with that?"

Brian nodded.

"Okay," Hood said. "Let's do it."

# Chapter Thirty-One

The next morning, before seven a.m., Brian parked Jessie's car in the lot at her apartment. He pulled down the sun visor and looked at himself in the mirror. He didn't like what he saw. His eyes were reddened and bleary, his hair disheveled, and his head throbbed.

As he approached Jessie's apartment, her door opened, and she stepped outside.

"I came to return your car." He extended the keys.

She snatched them. "You look hung over."

"A little."

"Did you drive drunk?"

"No. The sheriff drove me home. That's why I didn't bring it back last night."

"Where were you? And why did the sheriff need to drive you home?"

"It's a long story. Last night was like a night from hell."

"I don't have time for long stories, Brian. I have a class at eight, then a riding lesson. And, quite frankly, I don't want to hear about your night from hell."

"I was hoping for some understanding."

"What I understand is you always have an excuse for drinking. You were anxious, you had a bad day, you had a rough night, nobody understands you." As she spoke, she became more impassioned. "What I understand is, I'm not helping you, I'm enabling you."

Brian looked at his shoes. "What are you saying?"

"Maybe we need to take a break for a while. Maybe I need some time to

196

figure out some things."

"What things?"

"I don't know. I just know this isn't working."

"Is it David?"

"What?" She was incredulous.

"Is it because you want to go out with David?"

"You are so off base. Why would I want to go out with David?" She spat the question.

"Because he's everything I'm not—Mr. All-American Athlete. Mr. Cool." Brian exhaled a plosive sound. "I'm not blind. I know he's been making a play for you."

"Unbelievable. I have no interest in David. If he's willing to dump Michelle to pursue his next new conquest, why would I want to become the next to be dumped?"

"So you're dumping me instead?"

"I'm not dumping you. I love you. But I don't love you when you drink. I don't even like you. I need some time, that's all. And I think you need some time to look closely at where your life is going."

They faced each other in silence—Jessie on the threshold with her hand on the open door, Brian on the stoop.

Finally, Brian said, "I'm supposed to be at the sheriff's department at eight. Can you give me a ride?"

Jessie shook her head in disbelief and closed the door in his face.

* * *

"He's in your office," Maggie said to her boss when he came through the door.

Hood didn't need to ask who "he" was. He poured his morning coffee, then topped off Maggie's cup. "Chubb still in jail or did he post bond?"

"He's still here. He wasn't able to get in touch with his lawyer until this morning. Ray Mosley's supposed to be here around nine."

"Mosley. Great." Hood's tone was unmistakably facetious. "Oh, I asked

Sandra last night if she would come by this morning to get a writing sample from Chubb. Send her to my office when she gets here. Okay?"

"Will do. And, so you know, Wally called. He spent most of the night at the barn comparing the stockpile of goods to recent theft reports. How did he put it—'Tell Francis I'm up to my elbows in stolen property.'"

"Looks like it's going to be a busy morning." Hood carried his coffee to his office, where Brian was seated in a visitor's chair. He wore the clothes he had been wearing last night and looked like he hadn't slept. He also appeared harried, a result of arriving only minutes before the deadline after calling Michelle for a ride.

Hood's anger had softened since last night. Although Brian had taken matters into his own hands, he obviously was troubled by his brother's disappearance. Hood also considered an aspect of his recovery program that encouraged him to ask himself, *What is my part in it?* When he did so, he acknowledged his investigation had stalled, and he had been preoccupied with his daughter's injuries and convalescence.

He silently stared at Brian, whose facial expression reminded him of a penitent puppy preparing to be punished. "Relax," Hood said. "I'm not going to ask the prosecutor to charge you."

"You're not?" Brian's surprise was apparent.

"No. I can see in your face you know what you did was wrong. I admit I was pretty pissed off last night, but I've had some time to calm down since then." Hood had other motives, which he left unspoken. One was that a criminal charge could be a heavy burden for someone trying to finish his education and start a career. Another was that Brian's crime had uncovered a cache of stolen goods. "What I'd like," he added, "is your word that this kind of thing won't happen again."

"Fine by me. I was scared shitless when I saw the silhouette of that guy with the gun. I thought it was Hunk. I had no idea it was the bartender until you guys showed up."

"What I need to know, Brian, is whether you saw or heard anything that could be helpful."

"Like what?"

"Was anyone else with Chubb while you were in the barn? Did you hear him talking on the phone?"

"No. Nothing like that."

"This is no time to be holding out on me," Hood warned. "If you know something and you think you can go it on your own, I'm—"

"I'm not."

The two men sat quietly, Hood's gaze fixed on Brian, who looked away. "You've missed the last couple of recovery meetings," Hood said.

"I know. I'm going to get back on track."

"Good. Now get out of here."

Brian stood. "You think the bartender had anything to do with my brother?"

"That's one of the things I intend to find out."

When Brian left, Hood rose and walked to the aisle between his desk and the visitors' chairs, the most open area in his office. He practiced his jazz squares, hands on hips, right foot forward, crossing over left, left foot back.

"Francis?" The puzzled voice belonged to Sandra.

"Sorry." He retreated behind his desk so she could enter. "My daughter's dance recital is tonight."

"Still practicing the father-daughter number, I see." Sandra remained standing just inside the door frame. She held her evidence kit in one hand and the cloth bag in the other.

"I'm a basket case. I know I'm going to screw it up."

"You'll do fine. Did you already meet with Brian?"

"He left a few minutes ago. Hold on." He dialed Maggie and asked her to let him know when Chubb's attorney arrived.

"Well, I hope you weren't too hard on Brian."

"I'm glad I waited until this morning. I was pretty steamed last night, but—the more I thought about it—he may have helped solve a series of thefts."

"I take it the items in the barn were stolen?"

"We're working on it even as we speak, but, so far, Wally said the stuff we recovered matches items reported stolen."

"Are you going to pursue charges against Chubb?"

"That depends. You're going to get a handwriting sample, so we'll see if that tells us anything. I also forwarded Chubb's prints to Howard to compare them to the upside-down prints he found on the guitar. And then there're the coat and the boots. Have you had time to look at those?"

"Not yet. I still try to get a decent night's sleep now and—" She stopped in mid-sentence and stared at the floor. "What's that?"

"Hood followed her gaze to the loose soil. "That's where Brian was sitting. It must have come from his shoes."

"Those white granules look like the soil we found at the crime scene. I'm going to grab a sample. As she opened her evidence kit and stooped to collect the sample," she said, "I'll also want a sample from the barn."

"We can arrange that with Wally," Hood said. "He's out there cataloguing the evidence." As he spoke, his synapses fired with the realization of what Sandra had implied. "Wait! Are you thinking soil from Chester's store came from the barn?"

"I'm thinking anything's possible. I won't know until we collect and analyze all the samples."

Hood was encouraged that an evidence trail was taking shape, but a coherent picture continued to elude him. His mind was exploring permutations and combinations when Maggie notified him that Chubb's attorney had arrived.

"They're ready for us," Hood said to Sandra, "but, before we go, I still have one question."

"What's that?"

"When we were at Chubb's Tavern yesterday, what happened to that swig of beer you took?"

Sandra pondered a moment. "I completely forgot about it."

"Did you spit it out?"

"No. I never got in the restroom. I was in the hall, Rhonda came and opened the office, I looked in, then everything started happening at once."

"But it was gone when you told me what you'd seen."

"You're right," she said. "I guess, somewhere along the line, I swallowed."

\* \* \*

Young John was posted outside the door to the interrogation room. "Need me to stay?" he asked his boss.

"Please. This shouldn't take long."

Hood and Sandra entered and greeted Chubb and his counselor, "Only" Ray Mosley. The attorney had served for decades as a public defender before opening a solo practice to pursue his not-so-lucrative passion to champion the accused, who he believed were society's real victims. He had acquired his nickname based on his propensity to diminish a client's culpability, as in "he's only a kid" or "he didn't hijack the car. He only swiped the radio."

"Are you ready to release my client?" Mosley asked, before Hood had a chance to speak.

"Not yet." Hood unfolded the court order and placed it on the table. "First, Sandra from the crime lab is here at my request to obtain a handwriting sample from Chubb."

Mosley studied the document for what seemed—in Hood's estimation—longer than necessary. "Okay," the attorney said, his reluctance unmistakable.

Silence prevailed as Sandra obtained the sample, then was excused by Hood, who sat at the table opposite Chubb and Mosley.

"So, Chubb," Hood began, "tell me why you were in a vacant hog barn on Dennis Vivion's property late at night armed with a loaded shotgun and guarding a bunch of stolen merchandise."

"Has the merchandise been confirmed as stolen?" Mosley asked.

"The process is ongoing," Hood answered. "But so far, it's coming up hot."

"My client was unaware—"

"Save it, Ray," Hood interrupted. "I have no interest in sparring with you. Either let Chubb answer my questions or don't."

Mosley conferred briefly with Chubb, who replied, "Somebody asked me to guard some stuff."

"Who?"

"I never met the guy."

"How did he 'ask you?'"

"He called me."

"On your cell?"

"No, at the tavern."

"What did he say?"

"He said he'd pay me to babysit some stuff he had stored in a barn. He said he'd put the directions and a key in the tavern mailbox and leave the money on a table in the barn."

"How much money?"

"Couple hundred bucks."

"So, who babysits this stuff when you're not there? I know you're not doing it twenty-four/seven."

"No idea."

Hood leaned backward and released an audible sigh. "I have more questions, but I can't listen to any more of this nonsense." He turned to Mosley and added, "And, Ray, you should be ashamed of yourself for letting your client pitch such horseshit."

"I object to your characterization," Mosley said, eliciting a whimsical smile from the sheriff, who was humored by the objection and tempted to point out the interrogation room was not a courtroom. "My client assumed whoever owned the materials was aware of the recent thefts—which, need I remind you, remain unsolved. Perhaps the owner was motivated to increase security as a result of law enforcement's failure to protect property."

"And you expect me to believe Chubb agreed to this for a 'couple hundred bucks?'"

"I honestly don't care what you believe. My initial question stands. Are you ready to release my client?"

"And my initial response stands. Not yet. I can hold him until tonight. In the meantime, I'll be seeking charges of possession of stolen property."

Chubb released a guttural moan. Mosley said, "You're not serious."

"I'm entirely serious. If you've got a problem, take it up with the prosecutor and the judge." Hood rose. "Take as much time as you need. A deputy is outside the door. Knock when you're finished, and he'll escort Chubb back to his cell."

Hood left the room and was passing the dispatcher's desk when Maggie, who was speaking into her headset, flagged him down. "Hold on," she told the caller. "He's right here." She focused on her boss. "It's Wally. He found what he thinks could be a shallow grave."

"In the barn?" Hood's question was nearly a shout.

"In one of the stalls."

"Call Loeffelman," Hood instructed Maggie, referring to the medical examiner, and tell Wally I'm on my way."

# Chapter Thirty-Two

Hood and Wally stood together in the barn's center aisle and watched as Loeffelman and an assistant carefully removed soil to reveal the vague outline of a body in one of the stalls.

"What tipped you off?" Hood asked his chief deputy.

Wally shrugged. "I got tired of cataloguing evidence, so I got up to stretch. Rather than stand around, I decided to take another look in the stalls listed as empty—in case we overlooked something. The straw scattered in there looked new, so I went in and kicked it around a little. That's when I noticed the soil was mounded. I dug around a little and uncovered denim and part of a belt, so I called it in."

"Good job," Hood said.

They lapsed into silence as they watched Loeffelman and his assistant work efficiently and methodically. Hood wondered if their proficiency resulted from experience, well-practiced rehearsals, or both. He found himself mesmerized by their delicate choreography as they alternately removed small amounts of soil, then brushed the surface of the excavation as they inspected their progress.

Hood was yanked from his trance-like hypnosis when the medical examiner turned to him and said, "Francis, would you like to take a look before we lift him out of here?"

"Have you got him uncovered?"

"Yes."

"Is he missing the tip of his right ring finger?"

"How'd you know?" Loeffelman asked.

*\*\**

Although Hood was grateful to serve as sheriff, he detested some duties.

Opposing thoughts battled for dominance as he rapped on Brian's front door. Part of him hoped no one would answer, providing a temporary reprieve; another part wanted this to be over.

Although this was his top priority, he was acutely aware he could only hold Chubb for a few more hours, and he had not yet conferred with Sandra about her analysis or with the county prosecutor about criminal charges. And—lurking in his mind like some unwelcome symbiont—was the father-daughter dance.

He placed his hands on hips and lifted his right foot to cross over, halting in mid-step when the door was opened by Brian.

"Sheriff."

The word, more observation than greeting, seemed loaded. Hood heard elements of puzzlement, alarm, dread, curiosity, and more. He removed his hat. "May I come in?"

"Sure. Can I get you anything?"

"No." Hood remained standing in the entry. "There's no easy way to say this. I'm sorry to report your brother, Eric, is dead. We recovered his body earlier today. He's been identified by description and fingerprints, but, as next of kin, I'd like you to come with me and provide a positive ID."

Brian staggered as if he had been shot in the gut. He stepped backward, went down on one knee, and buried his face in his palms.

Hood waited. He turned his hat in a circular motion by walking his fingers along the brim.

"How'd he die?" Brian croaked, barely audible.

"That hasn't been determined yet. There are no visible wounds, so there's no apparent cause of death."

"Who did it?"

"We don't know. The investigation—"

"Where'd you find him?"

"In the barn where you were the other night. While we were processing the contents, a deputy noticed a mound of soil in one of the empty stalls. We contacted the medical examiner." Hood resumed fidgeting with his hat as Brian continued to kneel in silence. Based on experience, the sheriff had come to expect varying reactions to grief. He no longer attempted to console or intercede. Instead, he waited.

After a while, Brian asked, "Are you sure it's Eric?"

"As I said, the photograph you provided, his description, and the finger-prints match. Even the missing fingertip. Of course, as next of kin, if you could—"

"Yes." Brian stood. "Take me to him."

A somber silence dominated the drive to the courthouse annex, where the medical examiner's office was located.

As Brian's recovery sponsor, Hood had intended to emphasize the joy he experienced as he emerged from alcoholic isolation and began rebuilding relationships. Brian, however, no longer had any family relationships to rebuild. How could he not feel alone? Hood suspected Brian's feelings of isolation—perhaps even abandonment—were going to be obstacles to his recovery. The sheriff had decided he would listen, but not advise or interfere, if Brian brought up his relationship with Jessie. Hood had to remind himself that his role was recovery sponsor, not parent, counselor, or relationship advisor.

When they arrived at the annex, Hood asked Brian to wait in the corridor while he determined if the medical examiner was ready for them.

Brian slumped on a cushioned bench while Hood pushed through the door. He looked first at the white sheet covering the contours of a body on a stainless-steel gurney, then at Loeffelman, who was at his desk writing in a file.

Loeffelman turned to the sheriff. "Did you bring the brother?"

"He's in the hall, but before I bring him in, I wanted to ask if you've had a chance to determine cause of death?"

"Not yet."

"Any guesses?"

"You know me, Francis. I don't guess. But I have ordered a tox screen, if that tells you anything."

It did. Shooting, stabbing, strangulation, and blunt force trauma obviously had been ruled out. A drug overdose, however, was the prime candidate. "Do me a favor," Hood said. "Don't tell the brother."

"My job is to tell you. Who you tell is your business."

"Okay. Let me get him." Hood opened the door and asked Brian to join them in the morgue. Silence reigned as Brian stood beside the gurney, and Loeffelman lifted the sheet to expose the face of the dead man. Brian nodded affirmatively in the moment before his body convulsed with retching and sobbing. His knees collapsed, but Hood caught him before he hit the floor.

\* \* \*

Hood waited impatiently as Huhman County Prosecuting Attorney Leonardo Pancrazio read the sheriff's report.

"In a hurry, Francis?" Pancrazio asked.

"My daughter's dance recital is tonight," Hood said. He didn't elaborate, knowing any additional explanation would be counterproductive. Nothing about Pancrazio—from his appearance to his approach to prosecution—was hasty or haphazard. Although his suit coat hung on the back of his office door, Pancrazio wore the matching pin stripped vest and trousers. His long-sleeved shirt was a powder-blue Oxford and his silk tie featured primary colors shouting a bold pattern. His jet-black hair was styled to defy imperfection.

The prosecutor was not a Huhman County native, a rarity among elected officeholders. He was one of three sons of a patriarch who had built a successful family-owned business distributing spirits—liquor, wine, and beer—in Kansas City and its environs. Although his place in the company was assured, he had opted instead to pursue a career in criminal justice— much to the dismay of his father and brothers.

Hood liked Pancrazio. The prosecutor's priority was justice, not bolstering his win-loss record to increase his chances of re-election. In addition, he routinely consulted victims, their families, and law enforcement before accepting or offering plea bargains.

After what seemed an exorbitant amount of time, Pancrazio laid the report on his desktop. "You're seeking one charge—possession of stolen property—against this—," he glanced at the document, "Ernest Maasen?"

"He goes by Chubb, and, yes, that's all I'm asking for right now. There's a lot more going on, but I'm going to need—"

"I'd say there's more going on. Your report says you found a body in the same barn where the stolen merchandise was recovered."

"I'm waiting for more evidence on the death, but, in the meantime, the clock has almost run out on the stolen property arrest. A criminal charge and bond would at least give us something—"

"Consider it done," Pancrazio said.

* * *

*Hands on hips, jazz square, right foot forward, crossing over left, left foot back.*

Hood stood in the wings, in a line with other fathers and daughters, mentally rehearsing the routine in an attempt to ease his discomfort. He had asked Wally to arrange for Chubb's arraignment on the charge and to oversee his release on bond. And, although his chief deputy had reported successful completion, Hood's mind was not at ease.

He was terrified. Nausea roiled his stomach, perspiration dampened his underarms, and paralysis threatened his coordination. He wasn't sure he could walk, let alone dance. He recalled the recovery slogan that the only way to walk through fear is fearfully.

"We're on," Miss Heather announced.

Hood robotically walked onstage, stopped, and stared, mouth agape, into the darkness surrounding the theater audience.

The music began, cuing his movements. Hands on hips, jazz square, hands on hips, jazz square, arms out, sashay left, arms out, sashay right, arms up, ball change, arms up, ball change. He glanced at Elizabeth. They were in step. He smiled, amazed at their synchronicity. And, in the moment he began to feel joy, the music ended, the curtain closed, and he and Elizabeth were hurried offstage amid continuing applause.

When he stopped to catch his breath, his daughter encircled him in her arms and said, "You were great, Dad. You were the best one out there."

Hood inflated. He felt buoyant and powerful. He wanted to continue.

Elizabeth released him from the embrace, stepped back, and added, "Thanks for doing this. I know this was hard for you."

Were his misgivings, particularly early on, that obvious? He thought he had hidden his concerns pretty well, but apparently, he had only fooled himself. Linda had sensed he was afraid, Miss Heather had advised him to have fun, Elizabeth had tutored him and encouraged his progress. Did they all know he had made this all about him—his fears, his selfishness, his ego?

When the curtain call came, the performers returned to the stage to take their bows. Then, the house lights illuminated the auditorium amid mingling, conversations, and congratulations. When Linda found them backstage, she kissed Elizabeth and handed her a bouquet. Then she embraced her husband, kissed his cheek, and handed him a single rose. "For you," she said. "Thank you."

He accepted the flower, pricking a finger with a lone thorn that had been overlooked. As he squeezed blood from his fingertip, he sensed his reward was appropriate. In spite of his inclination to be a self-absorbed jackass, he had managed to do the right thing.

# Chapter Thirty-Three

"Fentanyl," Loeffelman said.

Hood was familiar with the potent synthetic opioid that drug dealers were combining—more and more frequently—with other illegal drugs, including cocaine, methamphetamines, and marijuana. "So Eric overdosed?"

"That's what I wrote on the line marked *Cause of Death*."

Hood was baffled. "I've never heard anything about Eric being a drug user. Did he snort it, shoot up—"

"There's nothing to indicate he was a habitual drug user—no track marks, no damage to the mucus membrane in the nostrils. The science tells me the fentanyl was ingested orally."

"He took a pill?"

Loeffelman spread his palms helplessly, indicating he had no alternative explanations.

"Okay," Hood said. "Thanks."

He crossed from the annex to the courthouse and was headed to his office when he bypassed Wally's door and was surprised to see his chief deputy at his desk.

Hood stopped in the doorway. "I thought you'd still be out at the barn, cataloguing the merchandise."

"We got most of that done," Wally said. "We moved what remains to the evidence room, so we wouldn't run up the department's budget posting a deputy at the barn twenty-four/seven."

"Good."

"Do we have enough evidence to charge Chubb with anything more than possessing stolen property?" Wally asked.

"I have reason to believe he was involved in the assault on Chester Groner, but I'm waiting to hear what Sandra found out about the coat and boots?"

"Anything to connect him with Eric Rakestraw's death?"

"No, but I'm glad you're here. I was planning to drive out to the hog farm to talk with you."

"What about?"

"You've got your finger on the pulse of the drug scene in the county. I just came from Loeffelman's office. He said Eric Rakestraw died from a fentanyl overdose."

"Fentanyl." Wally pronounced the word as if weighing its gravity. "It's becoming a real problem in St. Gotthard—city police are seeing more of it—but this is the first I've heard of a case out in the county."

"Well, now it's shown up in Schweinshaupten."

"Schweinshaupten has been mostly drunks, potheads and meth makers. I remember when Hunk used to deal marijuana out there, but when the state lawmakers legalized recreational use, they pretty much put him out of business. The town still has its share of unabashed pot smokers—Hunk and Vivion top the list—but now they're law-abiding citizens paying their share of taxes for the privilege."

"What about the meth cookers? Could they be branching out into fentanyl?"

"It's possible, but they're a different breed of cat. The ones on our radar like to keep to their paranoid selves. They tend to be pretty mobile and largely invisible, except when they blow up a kitchen or set something on fire."

Hood shook his head. "I don't get it. What's the attraction of putting some unknown something in your body, knowing it might kill you?"

"Dealers like fentanyl because it's cheap. Users like it because it's potent. Nothing about these drugs is sensible. Remember, we're not dealing with rational thinking; we're dealing with addiction. Let me nose around a bit. See what I can find out."

"I appreciate it." Hood finished his coffee and stood. As he headed for a refill, he considered Wally's words. Why, he wondered, did Eric take the drug? Did he do so willingly? Was he tricked, perhaps forced?

"There you are," Maggie said as the sheriff poured coffee. "Sandra called. She said to tell you she has the results, but she's headed for lunch, and she doesn't bring her phone. She said she'll try you again when she gets back to the office."

Hood headed toward the door, abandoning his coffee cup on the counter. "I'm joining her for lunch," he told his dispatcher as he left.

* * *

The sheriff hurried along the asphalt path that snaked through the shaded grove separating the Highway Patrol headquarters from the crime lab.

Sandra was seated on a bench, a container of chicken salad on her lap, a fork in one hand and an open book in the other. She looked up.

"I got your message," he said, explaining his presence.

"My message was I would call back after lunch."

"I couldn't wait."

Sandra closed the book, placed the lid on the container, and stored both in a bag at her feet. "Sit," she said, sliding to create space for him.

"So you know, Chubb has been charged with possession of stolen property. He's already been released on bond." He sat. "Your message said you had the results."

"I can link Chubb's coat and boots to the scene of Chester Groner's assault. The fiber from the coat matches the one I found in *One Man's Trash*.... The soil from his boots is consistent with the soil on the floor of the store and soil from the barn. All the samples contain traces of corn starch, corn meal, and other chemical compounds commonly found in pig feed. And Howard asked me to tell you Chubb's fingerprints match a set of upside-down prints on the guitar neck."

As Hood contemplated the information, Sandra added, "Most important, however, is the partial footwear print in the blood. Each person walks differently, so the wear and tear on their footwear is definitive, similar to a fingerprint."

"Okay," Hood said, his inquisitive tone indicating he was thinking aloud. "The evidence puts Chubb's coat and boots in the store, but not necessarily Chubb himself? What if he claims somebody else stole or borrowed them to frame him? Can we rule out that possibility?"

Sandra steepled her fingers in front of her lips. "The only DNA inside the shoes belongs to Chubb. If someone else pilfered the boots and had the presence of mind to wear some plastic baggies or some prophylactic over their feet—even if they didn't sweat through their socks—their DNA might not be present. To answer your question, no evidence supports or refutes the purloined-boots theory."

"I'm not sure there's enough forensic evidence to charge Chubb with attacking Chester Groner."

"That's your call," Sandra said.

Hood stared vacantly at the twisting path that seemed to disappear within the copse of trees. He knew he would need to ponder the evidence, confer with Wally, and perhaps with the prosecutor.

Amid the protracted silence, Sandra said, "Is there something else?"

"You read my mind," Hood answered. "I don't know how to say this, so I'll just say it. My wife thinks I need to sort out what's going on with us. I mean, what's going on with me, in relation to us, that is."

Sandra quietly considered his statement. "What do you mean, 'sort out?'"

"I've been thinking about it." Hood deliberately avoided eye contact as he spoke. "Linda's not wrong. I like being around you." He plucked a ballpoint pen from his breast pocket and began twisting and twirling it with his fingers. "I mean, it's not what the gossip's about. An affair is the last thing—"

"Good," Sandra interrupted, "because I have no intention of being the other woman. I couldn't do that to Linda, to you, or to me."

"And I've already driven Linda away with my drinking. I don't intend to mess things up again."

"I know that, Francis."

"So why does our relationship—whatever it is—create so many problems?"

"Some people would call it an affair of the heart—emotionally connected if not physically intimate."

"Do you think that's what it is?" Hood asked.

"What do you think?"

Hood returned the pen to his pocket. He was conscious that she, like his recovery sponsor, had answered his question with one of her own. "When I'm around you, I feel—what's the word? —free. It's one of the few times I can just be me. With other people, I'm either husband, father, sheriff, provider, or some role that requires me to be in control, to set the agenda, to show strength. But with you—and, sometimes, in recovery meetings—I can be vulnerable. I can reveal my fears and flaws, and not feel judged."

"That's the way it is for me, too. You accept me as Sandra, with all her quirks and doubts and weird behavior."

"So why can't that be okay? Why do I feel guilty?"

"Because you care about what other people think. And Linda deserves that."

Hood knew she was right. He also knew that during his drinking days, he didn't give a damn about what other people thought.

* * *

Brian sat behind the wheel of Michelle's car, which he'd borrowed and parked in the lot behind Chubb's Tavern. He lifted the handgun from his lap. The weapon conformed to his palm and fingers as he wrapped them around the grip. The gun felt natural despite his unfamiliarity with guns.

His brother liked guns. Eric owned a variety of firearms—some he inherited from their father, some he purchased for himself. Brian wondered which one he had taken from Eric's collection. Was it his service weapon from when he was a cop?

Brian watched through the tinted car windows as customers exited the back door, got into their vehicles, and left the lot. Although he was confident he could not be seen he crouched lower in his seat in an attempt to further disguise his presence. Then he laid the gun in his lap and waited. He waited as the cars and trucks thinned out, leaving only one other vehicle in the lot. A single light pole illuminated the lot in the otherwise dark night. In his side-view mirror, he detected movement and knew it would be Chubb. He grabbed the gun and, in that instant, he became paralyzed. He couldn't exit the vehicle; he couldn't confront the bar owner.

He closed his eyes, silently berating himself for planning, driving, and patiently waiting for this moment, only to freeze. "You're a chicken," he scolded himself. "You've always been a chicken."

As if on cue, he flinched at the sound of someone tapping on the window. Brian looked through the glass at Chubb, who motioned for him to roll down the window. He opened the window about an inch, revealing his eyes but keeping the remainder of his face obscured.

"You okay?" Chubb asked.

"Yeah."

"Because sometimes, after hours like this, I find someone passed out behind the wheel."

"I'm fine," Brian said. He intended to sound reassuring, but knew his presence was puzzling. "I was visiting a friend. Sorry I parked in your lot."

Chubb continued to stare, and Brian feared the tavern owner was struggling with his recall. His fears were allayed, however, when Chubb said, "Well, if you're okay."

As the tavern owner turned and walked away, Brian got out of the car. He concealed the gun behind his back and called. "Just a minute."

Chubb stopped and faced him.

"I'm Brian Rakestraw," he said as he approached.

"I know you. You were the trespasser at the barn the other night."

"And I'm the brother of Eric Rakestraw, who was found dead in that barn."

"I don't know anything about that, son."

"Bullshit," Brian spat. "And don't call me 'son.' Let's go back inside before someone sees us."

Chubb dutifully unlocked the rear door and was marched inside, where stools and chairs had been upended on the bar and tables to facilitate cleaning.

"Now," Brian said, "you're going to tell me what happened to my brother, or I'm going to start shooting, starting with your kneecaps."

Chubb stared at the wavering gun barrel in Brian's trembling hand, more afraid he would die from an accidental rather than an intentional gunshot.

# Chapter Thirty-Four

With the siren screaming and the light bar atop his cruiser flashing, Hood sped as fast as he dared along Route D's treacherous curves. He glanced at the dashboard's digital clock, which read 2:08 a.m.; fewer than fifteen minutes had elapsed since he was awakened by the call from Chubb.

The call had been a baffling tirade of hysteria and panic—including, "He had a gun," "I told him what he wanted," "He tied my hands," "Get here now," and "Backdoor's open"—before Hood heard the clattering of the cell phone falling to the floor. The call disconnected.

Hood's repeated callbacks went unanswered, forcing him to speculate about what he might be rushing toward. Who had held Chubb at gunpoint? What had Chubb revealed? Was the call a trap?

The cruiser skidded to a stop in the rear lot. Hood drew his weapon and hastily, but cautiously, entered through the rear door and saw Chubb. His hands had been zip-tied behind his back, and his cell phone rested on the floor near his feet.

"Finally," Chubb said.

Hood approached and removed his pocketknife. "What happened, Chubb?" He sawed the zip tie with the blade.

"That Brian Rakestraw kid stopped me in the parking lot after closing." Chubb's tone was frenzied. "He stuck a gun in my face."

"Okay," Hood said. "Take it easy. What did he want?"

The severed zip tie fell, and Chubb rubbed his wrists with his hands. "He wanted to know about his brother."

"What about his brother?" Hood prompted.

Chubb hesitated. "Maybe I should talk to my lawyer before I say anything else."

"Chubb, you said Brian's got a gun. What did you tell him?"

"I, I—" Chubb stammered. "I told him about Rhonda."

"What about Rhonda?"

"He made me call her." Chubb's tone was simultaneously defensive and apologetic. "I had no choice. He said he'd shoot me. He was desperate."

"What did you tell him?" Hood repeated, emphasizing each word.

"He made me call her and tell her to meet me at the barn."

"Meet when?"

"Right away."

Hood glanced at the phone on the floor. "Is that yours?."

"Yeah. After I made the call, I put my phone on the bar before Brian tied me up. That's how I called you, but then I knocked it on the floor."

Hood picked up the phone, scrolled to recent calls, and pressed Rhonda's number.

"None of this was supposed to happen," Chubb lamented. "Everything was going so good, and it all just turned to shit." He faced the sheriff. "You need to find Rhonda."

As Hood waited for his call to be answered, he glanced at a chalkboard on the back wall where a series of numbers—9, 14, 17, 22, 35, 37, PB 4—had been written. He was dumbfounded. The hooks on top of the ones and the slash through the seven mirrored the unidentified handwriting in Chester Groner's logbook.

"What are those numbers?" Hood asked Chubb.

"What numbers?"

As the ringing continued, Hood pointed to the chalkboard. "The ones posted on the board back there."

Chubb's expression revealed his confusion. "The winning lottery numbers. Why?"

"Who wrote them?"

"Normally, I do," Chubb said, "but those were announced when I was in your jail, so Rhonda probably wrote them."

Hood's call went to voicemail. He didn't leave a message. He tossed Chubb's phone on the bar and rushed to his cruiser.

\* \* \*

Hood approached the hog farm without strobe or siren. The outdoor light illuminated two vehicles, both unfamiliar to him, parked in the gravel lot. Exiting his cruiser, he entered the barn, where the door was unlocked, and the indoor lights were on.

He paused at the faint sound of voices, which became more audible as he crept along the center aisle, stopping at the final stall—the one where Eric's body was recovered.

Brian sat in the dirt, his back against a wall, pointing a handgun at Rhonda, who sat against the opposite wall. "Brian," Hood said, as calmly and confidently as he could, "please put down the gun." The sheriff held his weapon in what he hoped was a non-threatening manner, although he was poised to fire if necessary.

Brian remained silent and immobile for a long moment before he said, "She killed my brother, Sheriff."

"It was an accident." Rhonda's voice quivered. "I didn't know. You have to believe me."

"Shut up," Brian shouted, slowly enunciating each word.

Hood assessed the situation. Although Brian had not shot anyone—yet—he remained unpredictably volatile. "We can sort this out, Brian. Tell me what you know."

"She," Brian said, waving the gun barrel at Rhonda, "lured my brother here. She doesn't deny it."

"It was Chubb's idea," Rhonda blurted.

Brian brandished the handgun. "Shut the fuck up, I said."

"Let me hear from Brian," Hood said, hoping Rhonda would remain quiet.

"My brother figured out Chubb and Rhonda were up to something. I guess he started snooping around, so Rhonda lured him out here and drugged him to try to find out what he knew."

"He wasn't supposed to OD." Rhonda's pitiful cry preceded a series of wracking heaves.

"Not another word," Brian extended his arm and pointed the handgun at Rhonda's face.

"Brian," Hood said, "this is all very tragic, but let's not make it worse. Put down—"

"What could be worse?" Brian's question was an anguished shriek. "My brother died in a pig pen. He was buried here," he added, pounding the ground with his free hand, "in a fucking pig pen."

Hood heard a detached hopelessness in Brian's voice. Although his experience typically indicated how things would go, he realized he was in unfamiliar territory. He was clueless and fearful—for Rhonda, for Brian, and for himself. "I need you to put down the gun." Hood attempted a commanding tone, but a tremor in his voice betrayed his apprehension.

"I don't know if I can live with this," Brian said.

"You can. Not for me, or for you, but for Eric's sake. Put down the gun. Please."

Hood felt the shiver in his spine as Brian looked from him to Rhonda and back at him. Realizing the situation was beyond his control, Hood braced himself for whatever would be.

In a moment, it was over. Brian slowly laid his handgun in the dirt.

# Chapter Thirty-Five

In addition to Chubb and Rhonda, Hood arrested Brian.

Brian admitted his guilt and accepted the consequences: probation for two counts of exhibiting a weapon in a threatening manner.

Chubb and Rhonda initially pleaded not guilty, but, contrary to the axiom about honor among thieves, they eventually sold each other out. Rhonda implicated her boss in the attack on Chester Groner, and Chubb fingered Rhonda for Eric's fatal overdose. Eventually, both confessed and agreed to plead guilty in exchange for reduced punishment.

Hood was grateful for Sandra's role in bringing the case to a just conclusion. He invited her to coffee and, as they sat across from each other in a booth at Millie's Diner, he said, "As it turns out, we were on the right track. Chubb, Rhonda, and Chester were operating a theft ring, with Chester serving as the fence."

Sandra sat with her hands folded on the tabletop. Hood noticed she hadn't repositioned any objects on the table.

"I appreciate all your hard work," he continued, "but since neither case will go to trial, you won't need to testify, and we won't be relying on the forensic evidence."

"Okay."

Hood detected a hint of disappointment in her tone. "I want you to know the forensics helped us narrow our focus. We would have needed it at trial if Chubb and Rhonda hadn't decided to throw each other under the bus, cut their losses, and plead to manslaughter charges."

Sandra reached for the napkin holder, then refolded her hands.

"Manslaughter?" she repeated, questioning.

"That was probably the best we were going to do, anyway. Neither of them meant to kill someone. I believe that. According to Rhonda's statement, Chester told her and Chubb he wanted out, leaving them with a barn full of stolen goods and no fence. Rhonda said she was with Chubb when he announced he was going to see if he could change Chester's mind. She watched him cross the street from the tavern to *One Man's Trash*.... When he returned, Rhonda saw blood spatter on Chubb's pants as he hurried to his office to change. An hour or so later, the EMTs and Wally were at the scene."

"What about Eric's overdose?" Sandra asked.

"Chubb admitted he and Rhonda both wanted to find out what Eric knew. A drug-fueled seduction was the ruse Rhonda used to lure Eric to the barn. Chubb said he was surprised when Rhonda called him later and said something terrible had happened. The something terrible, of course, was that Eric overdosed and died. Both admitted they worked together to bury him."

"What about the finger?"

"They were both in on that, too. Their intent was to implicate you in Eric's disappearance. Rhonda planted the ring in your trunk the day you returned to Schweinshaupten to gather the soil sample. And both painted Eric's truck with a primer coat at Beautiful Body and Paint at a time when Vivion wasn't living there. Rhonda, incidentally, also confessed to being the driver who ran Brian off the road on Twenty-One Curves."

"What about Vivion? I know at one point you thought he was involved."

"Rhonda and Chubb were the brains, if you can call it that. Vivion and Hunk were paid to guard the stolen goods sometimes, but they were considered too lazy or irresponsible to be part of the theft ring."

"And Chester?"

"He was paid a percentage of what he fenced."

"What a shame." Sandra shook her head. "Two people are dead. And the two people responsible claim it was accidental or unintended."

Hood looked around the diner, which was beginning to empty as the morning coffee drinkers vacated and the staff began clearing tables and preparing for the lunch crowd. Hood wasn't quite ready to leave but had no reason to linger. "I'd better get going." He stood. "Now that this case is over, I guess we won't be seeing so much of each other."

"That may be for the best, Francis. Maybe it will put an end to the gossip."

Hood considered not only the gossip, but his wife's admonition, that he sort out his relationship with Sandra. "I know," he said, "but I'm going to miss you."

"We'll keep in touch," Sandra said, an assurance that seemed to lack conviction.

\* \* \*

Hood used his dinner napkin to wipe any stray barbecue sauce from his lips, then laid it on his plate with the cluster of bones from the ribs he had devoured.

"Are you going to group tonight?" Linda asked. They had dined alone. Elizabeth was at Claire's house, ostensibly doing homework.

"Yes. I'm hoping Brian will be there."

"How's he doing?"

"I don't know. I mean, the investigation is over, the questions answered, but everything has changed for him. Again."

"Is he staying sober?"

"I have no idea. Maybe he'll confide in me. Maybe he won't. I just want him to know I'm available."

They settled into a comfortable silence until Linda said, "Well, I'd better clear the table. These dishes aren't going to clean themselves."

"One more thing," Hood said as she began to arise.

She sat.

"I had coffee with Sandra today. I wanted you to know in case there's more gossip. I wanted to update her about the plea bargains. That should be the end of it. There's no reason for us to see each other anymore."

"I have a reason. The hospital foundation is planning a fund-raising trivia night, and I signed up to assemble a team. I was planning to ask Sandra to join us."

Hood eyed her quizzically.

"I've realized I was being selfish. I was jealous of Sandra because she provided you with something I didn't. I felt slighted. But I like Sandra and, as I said before, I trust you, Francis. I don't want you to deny your feelings. When I hear you talk about being available for Brian, and for Sandra, I realize the value of those feelings. You help them, and they help you. I know that now."

\* \* \*

Hood unfolded his chair and sat among the tiny furnishings in the nursery. The toys and blocks, all in primary colors, were throwbacks to simpler times—times of nurture, connection, innocence. Across from him sat Brian.

"How're you doing?" Hood asked.

"Okay. I've decided to take time to grieve, finish probation, and get some stability in my life. I'm not going to make any drastic changes, like deciding what to do with the house, right away."

"And your recovery?"

"Today is my third day sober."

"Good for you."

"I messed up," Brian said. "I couldn't stop drinking, and Jessie left me. I don't know how to get her back."

"Not long ago," Hood said. "I was right where you are now. I couldn't stop, and my wife and I separated. I realize now that she didn't leave me. I drove her away. I wasn't there for her—or my daughter—and she got to where she couldn't live with me. My first reaction was fear. I feared being unloved, and, more than that, I feared I was unlovable. I felt abandoned."

"I feel that, too. My parents, my brother, Jessie. It's like everyone's leaving me."

"It's scary," Hood agreed. "My first impulse, my alcoholic impulse, was to get my wife and daughter back. Thankfully, my sponsor intervened. He suggested I resist that impulse and work on me. He said I couldn't create a healthy relationship unless I was healthy. He told me alcoholism is a family disease, and I needed time to heal, just as my wife and daughter needed time to heal."

"Maybe I need to give Jessie some space."

"Think of it as creating an opportunity instead of an outcome."

"What do you mean?"

"When I impose my will to get what I want, I'm attempting to dictate the outcome. But when I practice patience and tolerance, I create the opportunity for grace, which I've heard defined as 'unmerited favor.' Grace has nothing to do with what a person deserves or earns. It's freely given."

"You think recovery is a path of grace?"

"I believe grace has always been available to me, but I was too selfish to recognize it and too unwilling to receive it."

Brian remained quiet for a long time. "I can't do this alone. I need help."

"That's the first step."

# Acknowledgements

Thank you, readers. Literacy needs you.

The substance of one of my fears can be found in recent surveys of readership in America. One national poll found almost half, 48.5 percent, of adults, age 18 or older, didn't read a book in 2023. Another finding revealed a mere 7 percent read 50 or more books annually.

These staggering statistics are not a result of a scarcity or the high cost of books. Thousands of fiction and non-fiction titles may be borrowed from libraries at no charge.

I remain bewildered and dismayed by the number of people who choose not to read, despite the abundance of knowledge, ideas, and imagination at our disposal.

I am blessed to be surrounded by family, friends, and other writers who promote literacy, by example and by advocacy. Among them are professionals willing to share their knowledge and expertise in law enforcement, criminal justice, medicine, and other disciplines. For this book, I sought information, guidance, and inspiration from: Anji Gandhi; Randall Haight; McKenzie Job; Madeleine Leroux; Rebecca Martin; Will Randle; and Greg White.

In addition, I deeply appreciate being invited by Verena Rose to join the wonderful team of crime writers at Level Best Books. I have enjoyed the opportunity to work with Verena, Shawn Reilly Simmons, Deb Well, and the entire LLB team.

Finally, my enduring thanks to my wife, Kristie, and my children, Heather and Jane, for their love and inspiration.

# About the Author

Richard F. McGonegal is the author of three Sheriff Francis Hood mysteries—*Sense of Grace* in 2020, *Ghoul Duty* in 2022, and *The Forget-Me-Knot* in 2023. The unpublished manuscript of *The Forget-Me-Knot* was honored as second runner-up at the 2021 Killer Nashville Claymore Awards.

In addition, 24 of his short stories have been published, including nine in *Alfred Hitchcock's Mystery Magazine*. Four of those nine have been reprinted in anthologies. He is an active member of Mystery Writers of America.

McGonegal retired in 2017 as an editor for the News Tribune Co. in Jefferson City, Mo., where he worked for more than 40 years.

He received a Bachelor of Arts degree in 1969 from Rutgers University, New Brunswick, N.J., and a Master of Arts degree in 1973 from the University of Virginia, Charlottesville. Both degrees are in English literature and language.

He and his wife, Kristie, live in Jefferson City, and are the parents of two adult daughters, Heather and Jane.

Before he joined Level Best Books, his books were published by Cave Hollow Press, Warrensburg, Mo.

SOCIAL MEDIA HANDLES:
  Facebook: Richard F. McGonegal

# Also by Richard F. McGonegal

*Sense of Grace*: Sheriff Francis Hood series, Book 1; Cave Hollow Press

*Ghoul Duty*: Sheriff Francis Hood series, Book 2; Cave Hollow Press

*The Forget-Me-Knot*: Sheriff Francis Hood series, Book 3; Cave Hollow Press